# INDIA BLACK AND THE SHADOWS OF ANARCHY

"This is a wonderful series written in first person that advances from adventure to adventure, trimmed with clever language, historical details and wonderful characters. It is an incredibly fun read." —*RT Book Reviews*

# INDIA BLACK AND THE WIDOW OF WINDSOR

"Following a strong debut . . . Carr's Victorian series just gets better. Featuring historical authenticity, sharp vocabulary and plenty of parenthetical asides, this romantic suspense romp delivers both action and guffaws." —*Library Journal* (starred review)

"Fans of historical murder mysteries should rejoice at the appearance of a second India Black adventure and the prospect of more—the madam comes highly recommended." —*Open Letters Monthly*

"Carr's second India Black novel is fast, entertaining and funny as well as an engaging mystery." —*RT Book Reviews*

# INDIA BLACK

"A breathless ride through Victorian England . . . You'll be hooked on this unique mystery from the very first line."
—Victoria Thompson, author of *Murder in Chelsea*

*continued . . .*

# INDIA BLACK AND THE GENTLEMAN THIEF

### Carol K. Carr

BERKLEY PRIME CRIME, NEW YORK

THE BERKLEY PUBLISHING GROUP
Published by the Penguin Group
Penguin Group (USA) LLC
375 Hudson Street, New York, New York 10014

USA • Canada • UK • Ireland • Australia • New Zealand • India • South Africa • China

penguin.com

A Penguin Random House Company

INDIA BLACK AND THE GENTLEMAN THIEF

Library of Congress Cataloging-in-Publication Data

Carr, Carol K.
India Black and the gentleman thief / Carol K. Carr.
pages cm.—(A madam of espionage mystery)
ISBN 978-0-425-26248-1 (pbk.)
1. Nationalists—Scotland—Fiction. 2. Spies—Great Britain—Fiction. I. Title.
PS3603.A7726I53 2014
813'.6—dc23
2013039581

PUBLISHING HISTORY
Berkley Prime Crime trade paperback edition / February 2014

PRINTED IN THE UNITED STATES OF AMERICA

10 9 8 7 6 5 4 3 2 1

Cover illustration by Alan Ayers.
Cover design by Rita Frangie.
Interior text design by Tiffany Estreicher

# ONE

At that moment, I'd have given anything to have a rapier in my hand. I'd have used it to fillet French. I believe the poncy bastard knew it too, for he was casting about the room for a means of escape.

Now I ask you, after scattering a nest of anarchist vipers and nabbing one of Tsar Alexander's best agents and finally settling down to a glass of champagne with a chap you've had your eye on for donkey's years and that same fellow has finally discovered that indeed you are a woman and a deuced fine one at that—I ask you, is it fair that all this bliss should disappear like so much fairy dust? Damned right, it's not fair. One moment I was admiring the dark, lithe figure of French and calculating how many glasses of champagne it would take before I could carry the bloke off to bed, and the next I was contemplating a missive from that maddening old trout, the Dowager Marchioness of Tullibardine, informing me that the object of my affection (French, in the event you had forgotten) was well-informed about the murky past of yours truly.

Dedicated readers of these memoirs will recall that ever since the marchioness had informed me that she had known my mother, screeching out this information at a train station in Perth as her carriage pulled away, I had been attempting to find out just what the wretched woman knew. Her correspondence had been evasive until this letter.

I quote her message here, so you'll appreciate just how much kindling the marchioness had dumped on this particular fire.

*Dear Miss Black,*

*If you want to know about your mother, ask French.*

> *Sincerely yours,*
> *Lady Margaret Aberkill*
> *Dowager Marchioness of Tullibardine*

I do not think I need to emphasize just how irritated I was to find that French knew more about my family history than I did. Hence my desire for a rapier. Lacking that weapon, I brandished the marchioness's letter at him.

"I suggest you find a means of defending yourself, as I intend to tear you limb from limb. After you've told me what you know, of course."

I do believe the fellow actually considered for a moment whether I would make good on the threat. I could see the wheels turning as he reckoned his chances. In the end, he made the right choice. He believed me. He's no coward, though. He drew himself up and put on his usual mask of polite indifference.

"I assume that note is from the marchioness and that she has informed you that I can shed some light upon your past."

"Brilliant deduction. Now, if you and the marchioness are through playing your little game, please be so good as to explain what you know about my family and how you've come by the information."

Despite what the gospel grinders would have us believe, I am convinced that the Whiskery Old Gent Upstairs plays favourites from time to time. Clearly he took pity on French, for just as the treacherous knave opened his mouth, someone hammered on the front door with such purpose that the champagne glasses trembled on the mantel.

I was disposed to ignore the caller at the door, for though I like custom as much as the next madam I was preoccupied with other matters just then.

French leapt to his feet. "I'll answer that."

"Let it go," I snarled.

"It might be a messenger from the prime minister."

"I don't care if it is. Dizzy can find some other agent to take care of his problem. We're in the middle of a discussion and I won't brook any interference."

Really, Benjamin Disraeli was becoming a bloody nuisance. You'd think that after I (with a little help from French and that odiferous street Arab, Vincent) had exposed that anarchist cell and captured a nasty Russian agent, the prime minister would slacken the reins.

The pounding on the door resumed. Bugger. If I didn't

answer the summons I'd soon have a gaggle of whores descending the stairs in their dressing gowns, standing around like a herd of cows and scratching their backsides while they gazed at French's tousled black curls and giggled behind their hands.

"Damnation!" I shook an admonitory finger at French as I scuttled past him. "Don't move, French. I'm not finished with you."

I yanked open the door and confronted the bloke on the porch. He was a wormy little runt but polite, for he swept off his hat and pushed a hand through a thatch of brown hair, combing it down with his fingers.

"Miss Black?"

"We're not open yet. Come back later."

I was already closing the door when he thrust a boot inside.

"Wait, ma'am. Please. I got somethin' here for you."

I pushed open the door warily. When you're a government agent, or, come to that, the proprietress of a thriving brothel, you've got to be on the *qui vive* at all times. One slip in concentration and you might be kidnapped or assaulted or worse.

However, I had already taken my measure of the fellow at the door and concluded that even in a fair fight, I had the advantage over the scrawny specimen in front of me. Not that I'd be fighting fair, you understand. I've always preferred the underhanded method myself, as it saves time.

Anyway, this bloke really did have something in his hand, which he thrust at me.

It was a buff envelope of good quality and light as a feather.

"Colonel Mayhew sent it," his messenger said.

I examined the envelope and handed it back. "You're mistaken. It's addressed to Colonel Mayhew."

The impertinent fellow shoved it back at me. "I know. Colonel Mayhew give it to me to bring 'ere. 'E said 'e'd be along dreckly to pick it up from you."

I expelled an exasperated breath. The colonel was a client, albeit not the best. He ambled into Lotus House from time to time and deigned to purchase a bottle once a year. The girls didn't care for him much, as he tended to pay only for services rendered and considered the giving of gratuities a mortal sin. He usually appeared in *mufti,* but his sweeping mustache, erect bearing and inability to make conversation that did not include the words "cannon" and "trumpet" revealed him as the soldier he was. In fact, he hardly spoke a word when he was on the premises, preferring to drink a single glass of brandy before selecting one of the girls and following her upstairs. I suspect the colonel did not receive many invitations to parties.

I hadn't seen the man in a month, or perhaps longer, and he'd never used my brothel as a postal box before. I found it deuced strange that he did so now and frankly, it wasn't at all to my liking. I discourage my clients from viewing Lotus House as a gentleman's club where they can have a meal or exchange messages. I might consider offering such services in the future, but only at a price.

"Did the colonel say when he'd be by to pick up the envelope?"

"No, ma'am. Just said he'd be here soon, or somethin' like that."

"And when did he give you this?"

"Last night, ma'am. Round ten o'clock it must 'ave been. I brung it 'ere, but some battle-axe tol' me she wouldn't be responsible for it and to bring it back this mornin'."

Mrs. Drinkwater, no doubt. My cook and housekeeper (I use those terms charitably) did the minimum amount of work necessary to remain in my good graces and was not likely to take on additional duties without first negotiating an increase in her wages. Frankly, it was just as well that she hadn't taken the envelope last night as very likely it would still be tucked in the pocket of her apron, where it would have remained until she was sober enough to remember its existence, if she ever did.

I was not inclined to take Colonel Mayhew's envelope but I *was* inclined to get back to my study and find out what French knew about my genealogical predecessors. Consequently, I sought to avoid a protracted discussion and consented to keep the bloody thing. The colonel's messenger looked relieved and stuck out a hand, no doubt expecting a coin for his trouble. I disabused him of the notion by shutting the door in his face.

I strode back into the study, like Boudicca about to confront the Romans.

"What's that you have there?" French asked, in a blatant attempt to divert my attention.

"It's an envelope from one of my clients, addressed to him."

"Curious," said French.

I picked up a silver dagger I keep on my desk for opening letters and slid the blade into the fold.

"What are you doing?" asked French, though it was perfectly obvious what I was doing. "You're going to open the man's personal correspondence?"

"You're a ruddy spy, French. I thought spies enjoyed intercepting messages."

"In the line of duty, of course."

"I consider it my duty to find out what's in here. There's obviously a reason Colonel Mayhew sent it to Lotus House. I don't like my business being used as an accommodation address without my permission. Next thing you know, I'll have every thief in London lined up to leave his swag with me."

"The colonel's swag is very flat indeed."

"A counterfeit bond doesn't take up much room," I retorted. I will not be mocked.

The dagger's blade made a soft ripping noise as it sliced through the envelope. I turned it upside down and shook it. A single piece of paper floated onto my desk.

French leaned over to look at it at the same time as I did and our heads knocked together gently.

"Pardon me," said French.

"So sorry," I mumbled. Deuced if we weren't as polite to each other as old married folk. That would never do. "Your reprieve only lasts until I've examined this document, French."

"I did not expect otherwise."

I rubbed my temple absently and scanned the sheet of paper. "Bill of lading dated two weeks ago, for the merchant ship *Comet*, sailing on the twentieth of this month—"

"That's tonight," French interjected.

I ignored this gratuitous comment and read on. "Ten crates of tools, various, including shovels, axes, hammers and rakes. Consigned by the Bradley Tool Company, Peter Bradley, principal, of 28 Salisbury Street, for delivery to the authorized agent of the South Indian Railway Company, at Calcutta."

"That's odd," mused French. "Why would a British army colonel care about a transaction between two private companies? And why would he send the bill of lading to you?"

"He didn't send it to me. He intended to retrieve it from Lotus House. And in answer to your first question, I haven't a clue as to why Mayhew would have this bill of lading." I shrugged. "Perhaps he's an officer in the Royal Engineers.

They're always slapping together a bridge or a road. The army could have hired this railway company to do some work. The colonel needed the bill of lading before he'd reimburse the Bradley Tool Company."

"I also find that odd. Tools such as these are easily manu-factured in India. Why would the army purchase them in England and ship them halfway around the world?"

I could see that French wanted to have a long chat about that bill of lading, probably to delay our pending discussion about the marchioness's message and any bodily injury that might result therefrom. I wasn't having that.

"Well, whatever the colonel's interest in the bill of lading, I can't see that it affects me one way or the other. I shall give it to him when he's next in and inform him that I will not be acting as his agent in future." I stuffed the sheet back in the envelope and dropped it on my desk. "Now, then. You were about to explain to me . . ."

Someone knocked at the front door. Bloody hell. Usually the clients were just leaving Lotus House at this hour of the morning; now they were clamouring to get in.

"Perhaps it's Mayhew," said French.

I marched to the door, prepared to chew off the ears of the unfortunate colonel.

But it was not Colonel Mayhew at the door. I pulled up short, taken aback at the sight of the three men gathered on my doorstep. They were rough brutes, and certainly not the type of clients who would cause me to run upstairs and roust three tarts out of their beds.

"Yes?" I asked in a brusque voice that implied I had better things to be doing, as indeed I did.

The chap closest to me tugged his battered bowler down

over his ears. Then he closed the distance between us, hooked the toe of his boot behind my knee and shoved me in the chest. I toppled over like a skittle. My head bounced off the Carrara tiles of the foyer and I lay crumpled on the floor like yesterday's washing. The bloke who'd walloped me spared me a glance as he stepped over me, his face as cold and smooth as the marble floor beneath my cheek.

Dear old French came riding to the rescue. My ears were ringing and there was a droning sound in my head that did not bode well for the future, but even so I heard his bellow of rage as he hurtled through the door from the study. My attacker was caught off guard. His hand moved to his pocket but if he had a weapon he had no time to draw it before French buried his head in the man's stomach and sent him flying across the foyer into the wall. The house shook and flakes of plaster fluttered lazily to the floor.

For a moment there wasn't a sound, save for my moans and the rasping breaths of the fellow against the wall. Then one of his companions shouted and French turned to meet the other two blokes as they rushed at him. They hit him high and low and the three of them staggered back into the study. I heard an almighty crash. The man French had felled shook his head, growled menacingly and clambered to his feet. He was a bit unsteady on his pins, but he staggered off to join the tussle in the study.

Now French is a capable fellow and knows a few tricks when it comes to wrestling with Russian agents and assassin types, and I had no doubt that on a good day he could hold his own even when the odds were stacked against him. But we'd been up all night, chasing anarchists and dodging bullets, and for good measure French had taken a dip in the

Thames while pursuing one particularly pesky Slavic foe. He'd also had a glass or two of champagne. All that is by way of telling you that I didn't think French would be in tip-top form today and might have his hands full with these three lads. Yes, he would need my help and I'd rush right in there and offer it to him just as soon as I could sit upright without being sick all over the floor.

This was proving difficult, and my first attempt was unsuccessful. Oh, dear. Mrs. Drinkwater would not be pleased. I gathered myself and made a second try and was relieved when I managed to roll up to a sitting position. My head swam and I closed my eyes against the wave of nausea that crashed over me. But I could tell from the noises emanating from the study that if I intended to be of any assistance at all, I'd best chivvy myself along and get in there. The sounds of battle were dying. I forced myself upright as I heard the sickening thump of a fist hitting flesh and a groan that could only have come from French.

I staggered through the door and took in the scene. French, as you might expect, was putting up a good fight but it was clear he was nearing the end. He'd landed a few blows, for one fellow's nose was streaming gore and the chap who'd shoved me was wiping blood from his mouth. But poor French had his back to the fireplace and our assailants were closing in on him like a pack of wolves. I caught the glint of a knife blade and the sight galvanized me into action. I forgot my throbbing head and charged into battle. No one was going to skewer French, unless it was me. I had not forgotten he owed me an explanation, you see.

I hurdled an overturned chair, snatched the champagne bottle from its silver bucket and stormed the breach like the Forlorn Hope at Badajoz. Well, there was no breach, really, but I made one by smashing the bottle over the head of the bloke nearest me. He collapsed to the floor and the other two stopped pummeling French long enough to stare at me in openmouthed surprise, which gave French just enough time to grab a candlestick from the mantel and swing it in a vicious arc that terminated on the wrist of the fellow with the knife. He howled like a banshee and dropped the weapon. French swooped to the floor, reaching for it. But the cool fellow who'd toppled me kicked away the blade and brought a fist down on French's head. French grunted once and folded faster than a piece of campaign furniture. He was out of this fight.

So was I. It was all I could do to stay on my feet and much as it pains me to admit this, I had nothing left. The bloke who'd pushed me down could see it as well. He stalked over to me, clearly upset that he'd wasted valuable time thrashing French and me.

"The envelope," he demanded.

"What envelope?" I should have known better, but then I don't take kindly to being attacked by strangers in my own house.

I received a backhanded slap across my mouth from the fellow. I staggered a step or two, then fell to my knees. My head spun. A drop of blood fell from my lip and splashed on the floor.

"On the desk," I heard myself say, in a voice I hardly recognized. I like to think it was quivering with anger, but I suspect it was fear.

I followed the sounds of my attacker's footsteps as he walked to the desk. I heard paper rustling.

Someone screamed. I turned my head and saw the gaggle of whores I'd been worried about earlier, crowding through the study door.

"Here!" shouted Clara Swansdown. "What are you lot up to?"

The ringleader barked instructions and he and his cronies made for the door. I wondered briefly whether the tarts would make a stand. God knows I wouldn't have, so I didn't blame them when they parted like the Red Sea, gaping at the thugs as they strode out of the study and through the front door. Colonel Mayhew's envelope accompanied them.

# TWO

There was no shortage of bints eager to tend to French's wounds, but I had to resort to threats to get a cold compress for my temple and another wet cloth to dab the blood from my face. That damned blackguard had left me with a throbbing head and a split lip. French was rather worse off. A goose egg was growing under his left eye and the right had swelled shut. He tweaked his nose gingerly and tentatively touched his ribs.

"Anything broken?" I enquired from the sofa, where I reclined with a pillow under my head.

"I don't believe so," said French, "although my nose hurts like the devil and I can't see out of my right eye." The girls were still fluttering about, offering to disrobe French so that they could examine his wounds, and demanding that I send for a raw beefsteak to put on his eye.

"There's no need to go to that expense," I snapped. "Mrs. Drinkwater, prepare some tea. No, on second thought, bring us each a glass of whisky and then clear the room."

It took quite an effort for Mrs. Drinkwater to pour out the spirits without diving in herself, but she exerted iron control and managed to deliver a glass to French and one to me. Then she scuttled out, no doubt to retrieve a bottle from her not-so-secret stash, and driving the whores before her. They were loath to leave, having not seen such excitement around Lotus House since Sir Theodore Fotheringill had challenged the Canon of Seagate to a duel over a greyhound bitch. The door closed behind the rabble and I drew a relieved breath.

"What the devil just happened to us?" I asked.

French winced as his fingertip probed a tender spot on his torso. "Obviously, those chaps wanted that bill of lading. I'd wager they followed the messenger here."

"I had reached the same conclusion," I said acidly.

"Perhaps your question should not have indicated that you hadn't." French could be quite cranky after taking a walloping.

"I'm not going to take this lying down, you know. No one trespasses in my home and beats me like a cart horse."

"They were jolly good at their trade." French had his own compress and now pressed it to his eyes. "They thrashed me dreadfully."

"It *was* three against one. I thought you stood up manfully to the brutes."

He gave me a wry smile. "Thank you for that, India. And may I add that I was most pleased to see you stumble into view with that bottle in your hand. Otherwise, you'd be summoning a doctor right now."

"Should I?"

He pinched his nose lightly and shuddered. "My nose may be crooked after this, but I don't think it's broken." He swallowed his whisky in one gulp.

I staggered upright and refilled both our glasses. "Forget about your nose. No one cares if a chap has a nose like a turnip. What about my lip? I've got money riding on this lip."

French scowled, as he usually does when I allude to my profession. He drained the second serving of whisky and rose unsteadily to his feet.

"Do you think you should be moving about just yet?"

French smoothed his weskit and examined his face in the mirror over the mantel. "Like you, I take exception to being beaten for no apparent reason. We're going to find out what's behind this attack. Tidy yourself. I intend to have a chat with Colonel Mayhew."

Now you may wonder why French and I did not leave well enough alone and simply be glad that we'd seen the backs of those three thugs. But as I've explained, neither of us is the type to slink away after being thoroughly skunked. We had a reputation to uphold. And while French might pretend to be above such things, I possess enough curiosity to scribble a thousand cats. I wasn't about to let the unexplained mystery of Colonel Mayhew's envelope go unsolved. I reckoned French felt the same, for all his lofty airs. What was so important about a bill of lading for tools that a gang of miscreants would lay into us without so much as a by-your-leave?

And if Colonel Mayhew had deliberately endangered me by

sending the envelope to Lotus House, well, then, it's safe to assume the chap would never make general after I was through with him.

We freshened ourselves as best we could. I offered French a bit of powder for the scrapes and bruises on his face, but he declined. Unfortunately powder did nothing to cover the bump on my forehead or my swollen lips. I'd be avoiding mirrors for a bit. Another reason, in my mind, to seek vengeance. I'm rather proud of my looks, if I do say so myself. I've sable hair that sets off my brilliant blue eyes and a creamy complexion that I've worked hard to maintain. I consoled myself with the thought that my luscious figure usually proves the main attraction anyway, and as our attackers had done nothing to damage those goods I still had more than enough firepower at my disposal.

And lest you think that French and I are rank amateurs and would likely stumble into a situation that proved too much for us, let me remind you that he and I are old hands at this sort of thing, being agents of Her Majesty's government and having had, I modestly admit, a modicum of success at the game of espionage. Why, we had even saved Her Royal Rotundity from an assassin up at that draughty heap called Balmoral. A few run-of-the-mill villains and an army colonel would hardly present a challenge.

We availed ourselves of a café on the corner of Haymarket and Charles Streets, for after the events of the previous night and this morning we required sustenance. Mrs. Drinkwater could no doubt have rustled up some comestibles, but as they would have been inedible we declined to punish ourselves further. I retain Mrs. Drinkwater as my cook not because she can cook but because she is totally oblivious to half-naked tarts and drunken clients, being, as she usually is, three sheets to the wind most of the time. I expect the nudity doesn't even register.

After a hearty repast and several cups of coffee, French hailed a cab.

"To the War Office," he instructed the driver. We lurched away from the curb and headed down Haymarket, turning right onto Pall Mall.

"We'll obtain Mayhew's address from the records office and then pay the man a visit," French explained as we rode along.

Our journey would take a few minutes and being the sort that doesn't waste an opportunity, I thought I'd gently broach the subject of the marchioness's letter.

"What the deuce do you know about my family, you treacherous bugger?"

French looked pained. "Must we speak of that now?"

"We must," I said, mimicking his poncy pronunciation. "Spill it, or there'll be the devil to pay."

He sighed and touched a welt that had risen on his cheek, glancing at me from the corner of his eye. I had thought French was past expecting sympathy from me. He must be desperate to avoid this conversation.

I poked him in the ribs, which made him jump. He swore loudly.

"Oh, very well. Two years ago the marchioness retained my services. She asked me to find you."

"I believe I know why," I said. "She's my great-aunt, isn't she? My grandfather's sister." I am good at mathematics and accounts, you see, and had added up a couple of sums to reach this conclusion. I'd spent a bit of time tracking my mother's last movements around London and found she'd spent a few years as the mistress of that dreadful scoundrel, Charles Goodwood, the Earl of Clantham. He hadn't been able to tell me much, but he did remember that my mother had told him she'd taken refuge with her aunt when her father had discovered her affair with the family's groom and banished my mother from the family home.

"Yes."

"But why did she choose you?"

He shifted uncomfortably in his seat. "She is acquainted with my family. She knew I'd served as an intelligence officer in the army and I suppose she thought I possessed the necessary skills to locate you." He leaned out the window. "Would you believe it? Here's the War Office already."

We had indeed arrived at that unprepossessing building. The government had certainly saved a bit of money by eschewing architectural style in favor of three utilitarian stories of red brick and Portland stone. A paved courtyard ringed by a waist-high iron fence separated the building from the street. Guards occupied two small stone buildings on either side of a gated entrance to the courtyard.

The cab was still moving when French wrenched open the door and jumped out. I shifted in my seat, preparatory to following him, but he stuck his head inside and gave me his most charming smile.

"I'll only be a moment."

"I'm coming with you," I said.

"I'd rather you waited here. You'll prove too much of a distraction to those poor clerks in there."

"You flatter me." I shoved him to one side, exited the hansom and trotted off to the guardhouse. I heard a stifled oath behind me and then French caught me by the elbow.

"I'll do the talking, India. This is my bailiwick."

I shook off his hand. "French, I could swear that you're ashamed of me."

"I am not." He sounded indignant. "But you have an annoying habit of putting yourself forward even when someone else is better suited to the task. No," he said, reconsidering. "That's not precisely what I mean to say. What I meant is that you have an annoying habit of considering yourself better than anyone else at just about everything."

As I am rather more capable than most, I found this comment perplexing and said so.

"Never mind." French had to concede as by now we'd reached the guardhouse. He pushed past me and addressed a uniformed figure.

"Good morning, Sergeant."

The sergeant, a big fellow, gazed placidly at us. "Morning, sir. May I be of assistance, sir?"

Soldiers are like whores; they recognize each other instantly whenever they meet. Despite French's civilian clothes, the sergeant had responded to his military bearing. His battered face did not elicit a reaction from the guard, who probably reckoned French had gotten his black eyes and bruises leading a charge against some inferior native force in some hot and dusty land far from England's verdant fields.

"We'd like to consult the rolls, Sergeant. I'm searching for an old friend."

"Of course, sir. Go right in. Up the stairs to the second floor. The second door on the right is the records office." The sergeant's eyes shifted to me for a second, lingering on my thick lip and the knot on my forehead, but his expression never changed. They train them well in the army.

French thanked the fellow and we crossed the courtyard to the entrance. Inside, the building was buzzing with activity on this day of rest. A hard life, the army. Even whores usually get a rest on Sunday. Clerks ran up and down stairs, dashing officers strode purposefully from room to room and bright young fellows who'd just received their commissions swanned around giddily. I have a fondness for uniforms and the men in them and found myself rather distracted by all the glittering medals and the broad chests upon which they were displayed. I'd been rather pleased to learn that French was a soldier himself, a major in the Forty-second Regiment of Foot. I had *not* been pleased to learn that information from a Russian spy and not from French himself. Another issue to take up with his nibs. I sent him a look as sharp as a dagger just to keep the fellow on his toes, and he loftily ignored it.

The records office was a drab room, with a row of dingy windows facing out onto the Mall and a ceiling stained the colour of mud from years of pipe and cigar smoke. There were six desks in the room, and each sported an earnest young fellow with ink-stained fingers and a myopic expression. French chose the one nearest the door and we walked briskly to his desk. The clerk had a wispy brown mustache and thick spectacles, and looked amiable, if a little vague.

French dropped his hat on the desk. "I'm Major French of the Forty-second. This is Miss Black."

The youngster wasn't nearly as well trained as the guard. He gaped at us. I'd like to think it was my beauty that struck him dumb, but perhaps it was our various bumps and abrasions. He was not alone, however, for all activity in the room had ceased while the occupants gazed at us.

After a moment the clerk recovered himself. "May I help you?" he stammered.

"Yes. I'm looking for a chap named Mayhew. We've lost touch and I'd like to have a chat with the old fellow."

"First name?"

"Francis. Colonel Francis Mayhew."

"Regiment?"

"I'm not certain. He started in the Buffs," said French smoothly, "but I believe he may have transferred since."

"Ah, the Third Regiment of Foot. Date of enlistment?"

"I'm sorry. I don't know."

The clerk sighed at the idiocy of those who hadn't the wit to keep track of friends and all relevant information pertaining thereto and went off to rummage through several filing cabinets. He opened one, then another, and then a third, muttering to himself all the while. He had no luck in the cabinets, for he closed the drawer of the last with a bang and went to the other side of the room where row upon row of clothbound journals were stored. He ran a finger over a shelf of dusty volumes, selected one, and paged through it slowly. He uttered a soft cry of discovery, and carried the heavy book over to us.

"Here he is," he announced. "Francis John Albert Mayhew. Not with the Buffs, sir. He's with the Twenty-third, sir. Royal Welch Fusiliers. Currently serving in the quartermaster general's office. That's on the next floor up. They'll know where to find him."

I thanked him prettily and got an enormous grin for my reward. I was pleased to note that the dull scratching of pens on paper had not resumed by the time we left the room. No doubt it had something to do with the view of me exiting the chamber. I often have that effect upon chaps.

We climbed another flight of stairs and repeated our enquiries to another clerk. Due to the fact that he had only to search through a few hundred names rather than tens of thousands, he found Mayhew's address after a brief search.

"Colonel Mayhew resides at 18 Milner Street, sir."

"He lives in London? Then he's stationed here, at the War Office?" asked French.

"Yes, sir."

Damn and blast. It would be just our luck for the colonel to amble through the door and find his disheveled madam and a disfigured stranger enquiring after his whereabouts.

"But he's not in today, sir."

I felt French relax at my side. I breathed a bit easier as well. I'd rather have my scene with Mayhew in the privacy of his abode.

"I trust he's well," said French.

"I wouldn't know, sir. I just know who the colonel is and that his desk is down the hall and he hasn't been there at all today."

"Surely he doesn't work on Sundays?"

"Yes, sir, he does." The clerk smiled thinly. "You know the army, sir. Someone's got to be on duty."

"I do hope he isn't ill," said French, turning to me. "Perhaps we'd better pay him a call and see if the fellow is alright."

I murmured my agreement with this plan.

In the corridor, French said, "Thank you, India."

"For what?"

"For letting me handle this."

"You are competent at some things, French."

He spared a brief smile for me.

We had descended to the ground floor and were almost to the door when I heard a shout.

"French, old boy! Is that you? Where the devil have you been hiding?"

I heard French's sharp intake of breath. He did not look at me, but pasted a frozen smile on his face and turned round. "Bunny Alcock," he said, with forced enthusiasm.

I took a look at the tanned and muscular fellow striding toward us. Bunny? I've no idea what's wrong with the British upper class. Despite their wealth and breeding, they persist in tagging each other with the most infantile nicknames: Boy, Tubby, Stinky, Bunny. It does make you wonder how we've managed to hang on to the Empire with these puerile types running the show. I was anxious to meet Bunny, however, for it was clear that French would have preferred I did not.

Bunny sported a wicked gleam in his eyes and a sabre slash across one cheekbone. Whip-thin and brown as a nut, he looked as if he'd just returned from one of the colonies.

"Good God," he said as he drew close, inspecting our faces. "What the deuce happened to you, French?"

"Carriage accident."

"You don't say. Must have been a real smash-up. You look shattered." Bunny turned his attention to me, doffing his hat. "It appears, ma'am, that you too were a victim of the accident." He said it innocently enough, but the gleam in his eye was positively wicked.

"Bunny, allow me to introduce Miss Black," said French. "My cousin."

I'd been wondering how French would handle this situation. Now I knew. He'd chosen cowardice. I gave Bunny a charming smile, the effect of which was no doubt dimmed somewhat by the ugly gash in my lip.

"The pleasure is mine, ma'am." Bunny winked roguishly at

French. "I'd no idea you had such delectable creatures in the family. I would have cultivated your friendship assiduously, in hope of an introduction."

"French is rather good at keeping secrets," I said. I do not believe that I succeeded in removing the acerbity from my tone.

"He's quite accomplished in that field," Bunny agreed. "I didn't even know he was engaged until a few weeks ago. I heard it in the mess, at dinner. My congratulations, French. When are the nuptials?"

I was rather interested in that information myself. I'd known French for several months now, but he'd omitted advising me of several interesting details about his life, such as his Christian name, his military background, and the fact that he was betrothed to Lady Daphne Kenilworth, daughter of the Duke of Allingham. To add insult to injury, a bloody Russian spy had been the one to share these details with me, and he'd done so just last night. For some reason, French seemed worried about the fiancée, as though she presented some obstacle to the relationship between him and me. French can be so drearily ethical. I had no doubt that much of his reticence on the subject of his beloved was due to his reluctance to dash my hopes of a cozy hearth scene with children about my feet and French gazing devotedly into my eyes. Dear, sweet fellow. I could have told him (and would have done so if only there'd been a minute to spare in the last twenty-four hours) that his marital arrangements were irrelevant to me. I had no wish to shackle myself to any man. I am an independent woman. I own property and I make a damned good living. I must remember to inform French of this.

French pressed my arm, shifting me toward the door. "Wonderful to see you, old boy. Sorry to dash, but we're late for an appointment."

"Tea with a maiden aunt?" Bunny asked and brayed like a donkey at his own wit. "I'll be at the club most evenings, French. Drop in some night and I'll stand you a drink." He tipped his hat to me, grinning devilishly.

Outside I shook French's hand from my arm and stalked toward the hansom. "Your assistance is unnecessary. I can manage on my own. 'Cousin,'" I added.

"It would have taken all day to explain who you were and why we look as if we'd lost a prizefight. Besides, Bunny is an incorrigible gossip and I'd rather he knew as little as possible about me or you or us. God knows, he'll fabricate something anyway, but why give him even the slightest morsel?"

French handed me into the cab and gave Colonel Mayhew's address to the driver. We snapped back into our seats as the cab jolted forward. French stared out the window and I could almost feel the poncy bastard willing me to silence. Well, it would never do to let him think that was an effective strategy with me.

"By the way, French, when is the marriage to be held?"

He cursed loudly and swung to face me. "Confound it! Why must you prick me like this? Do you not understand how I feel about you? And yet I've made a vow to another. What am I to do about that, eh?" His expression was agonized.

I opened my mouth to speak, but for once in my life thought better of it. I'm quite comfortable flirting with a chap, or tearing a strip off him, but I'd rather have a Saturday night without customers than blather on with a fellow about romance—not, mind you, that I've done much of that. I wasn't sure I'd be able to do that with French, if you must know the truth. When he looked at me and those steely grey eyes softened, my heart fluttered and my stomach quaked. I was fond of him, you see. Well, perhaps more than just fond. That's why I hated to see the poor chap in such a bind. Having very little concern for society and its conventions, it's dashed difficult for me to understand how these moral dilemmas can turn a perfectly reasonable chap into a dithering wreck, but I knew that French was in no state to discuss the matter at the moment. Nor did further probing into his knowledge of my past seem wise at this time.

I pondered for a moment, considering what a sympathetic and caring woman would do in this situation. It was a bit of a stretch for me, but in the end I think I did the right thing. I reached across the divide that separated us and rested my hand lightly on French's thigh. After a long moment, so long that I considered withdrawing my peace offering, I saw the corner of his mouth turn up ever so slightly, and his hand came down to rest on mine. Well, you have to throw the fellows a bone now and then, or they'll grow discouraged and wander off. We rode the rest of the way to Mayhew's address in silence.

# THREE

The colonel had taken rooms in one of those awful row houses that developers had been throwing up all over London for the past few years. No doubt you've seen them, those hulking structures of orange-red brick crowned with a variety of fantastical stone ornaments, with a fern in every bay window. This one was just off a leafy green square, down a quiet side street. As it was just rising eleven o'clock on Sunday morning, the pavement was deserted and not a carriage or cab could be seen.

"Quiet as a tomb," observed French after he'd paid our fare and the hansom had creaked away, wheels sounding unnaturally loud in the silence.

"I wouldn't be surprised to find that the colonel is holding down a pew somewhere. He seems to be a great one for rectitude."

"I do hope we haven't wasted a trip," said French, looking irritable at the thought that someone would venture out to observe the sacraments without consulting him.

"Perhaps we can find a café or a stall where we can have a cup of coffee. Lord knows, we have a great deal to discuss."

French looked sour at the prospect of an intimate discussion and rapped on the door of Mayhew's lodgings. I smoothed a stray lock of hair into place and trusted that my immaculate coiffure might distract attention from my swollen lip.

The door opened wide enough to permit one suspicious eye to stare out at us. The eye narrowed at the sight of our bruised countenances. "Yes? What is it? If you're selling something, go away. It's the Sabbath."

French swept off his hat. "So it is, ma'am, and I'm very sorry to disturb you on your day of rest. I am Major French of the Forty-second, and this is my cousin, Miss Black. We are acquaintances of Colonel Mayhew and would like to speak with him."

The eye swept from French's face to mine, and appeared unconvinced. "Friends of the colonel, you say?"

"Pardon our appearance, ma'am. Our carriage overturned on the way to town yesterday, and we suffered a few injuries."

"We are fortunate that we were not seriously hurt," I added, "but John, our poor driver, was most grievously injured. He'll be in hospital for some time."

My fabricated concern for our fictitious employee had the desired effect. I must learn to exhibit these normal human emotions more frequently, as it does seem to engender a bit of trust among the naïve. The door opened wider to reveal an elderly, thin-faced woman in a prim dress of dark wool. The suspicion had disappeared from her eyes, replaced by a maternal concern.

"My goodness. What a fright you must have had." She cocked her head at French. "Major, did you say?"

"Yes, ma'am. The Black Watch, ma'am. The 'Gallant Forty-twa,' as they call us in Scotland."

"Heavens! I remember your brave lads from the Battle of Alma, back in '54. You gave those Russians a proper thumping." She beamed at French, why I don't know, as he would have been a lad in short pants in those days, but that didn't stop him from basking in the old girl's approval. "I'm Mrs. Sullivan. Won't you come in?"

We followed her into a dim parlour crowded with furniture, and took a seat on a faded velvet settee. The landlady settled into a rocker and automatically picked up her knitting from the basket on the floor. She looked ready to settle in for a long palaver about the Crimean War, and I could see French squirming.

"Colonel Mayhew?" he prompted.

"Yes, of course. I'm sorry, but the colonel isn't here. He always spends Sunday at the War Office. He's got quite a responsible job there, you know."

French frowned. "That's odd. We've just come from there and the colonel was not in his office. One of the clerks told us he hadn't been in today. Have you seen him this morning?"

"No, I have not. He never takes breakfast on Sunday, as he likes to be at his desk bright and early and always has something brought in to the office. I do worry that he doesn't eat regular meals, you know. I've told him many times, I've said, 'Colonel, you must have something nourishing to eat before you leave for work.' The army's food is inadequate, as you well know, and I worry that Colonel Mayhew isn't getting a proper meal with porridge and bacon and eggs. Men like that sort of thing, you know. Builds them up. I expect you eat a proper breakfast, Major."

"I do," said French, who had politely held his tongue during this soliloquy, though I could see he was champing at the bit to ask more questions. "The clerk thought the colonel might be ill. Did you hear Colonel Mayhew depart at his usual time?"

The landlady shook her head. "I never do. I always visit my sister on Saturdays. She has a small cottage in the country and I take the train out to see her. I spend the night with her and then return to London on Sunday morning. The colonel always departs for his office before I arrive home from the station." She cocked her head. "Dear me. I've forgotten my manners. May I offer you some refreshments? A cup of tea, perhaps, and some biscuits?"

"That's very kind of you," said French. "But we can't stay. We only dropped by to have a quick word with the colonel. Would you mind seeing if he's in his room? Perhaps he is ill and he's still sleeping. That would put my mind at ease."

"Certainly, Major. I'd be delighted to be of assistance. Though, mind you, if the poor man is asleep I won't disturb him."

"Oh, best not to, I think. He'll need his rest, and we can come back at another time."

The landlady dropped her yarn and needles into the basket and bustled out of the room. We heard her tread on the stairs.

"It's odd," mused French, "that the colonel is not at his desk this morning and hasn't bothered to send word why he is not."

"Perhaps he went to Lotus House to retrieve his envelope."

"Damnation. I wish I had thought of that. One of us should have stayed behind."

I've heard a lot of screams in my time, but I shall never forget the one that echoed through the house at that instant. A thin, quavering cry brought a chill to my bones, and then the cry became the full-throated shriek of a woman who was staring evil in the face. French was out of the room in a flash and I was close on his heels. The scream was still echoing down the staircase when we cleared the last riser and looked anxiously for its source.

Mrs. Sullivan reeled out of a room at the end of the hall, wailing like a soul that's just glimpsed Hades. I've said I won't forget that scream, and I'll be remembering the landlady's face for the rest of my days. It was a mask of terror, the eyes staring and sightless, the mouth wrenched open in a rictus of fear and horror. French dashed down the hall and past Mrs. Sullivan, entering the room she'd just exited. I reckoned he thought I'd do the womanly thing and rush to the landlady's aid, shushing her cry and leading her away for a cup of tea or something stronger, but I've an unhealthy curiosity and so I darted past the tottering figure and into the room behind French.

Oh, how I wish I hadn't. The room looked like an abattoir, only no self-respecting butcher would have created this much mayhem. Blood pooled on the floor and spattered the walls. The smell was revolting. I put my forearm over my mouth to avoid breathing in the sickly sweet aroma. I had nearly crashed into French, as he'd pulled up short as soon as he'd entered the room. He turned now and grasped my arms.

"Don't look," he muttered. His face was pale and his lips tightly crimped. He looked as nauseous as I felt.

"Dear God," I muttered. "Mayhew?"

"Dead, poor fellow."

"No one could lose this much blood and still be alive," I said with some asperity. Torture always makes me snappish, and torture, I am afraid, is the only thing that could account for the amount of blood now drying on the damask wallpaper and the pine floors.

"What the devil did they do to him?"

A vein throbbed in French's temple. "They cut the man to bloody pieces."

"Do you think they were after the envelope?"

"What else could it be? Someone wanted it very badly and Mayhew thought it would be safer with you." He ushered me out the door, closing it behind him. "This would explain why those fellows showed up this morning at Lotus House. It looks as if Mayhew held out as long as he could, but he must have told them what he'd done with the envelope. Then they slit his throat and came after it."

Mrs. Sullivan had managed to wobble down the stairs and was leaning against the newel, sobbing hysterically. She glanced up as we came into view and let out a piercing howl.

"Murder!" she yelled. She looked at us frantically and scrambled for the door. She wrenched it open and stumbled down the steps to the pavement. "Help! Murder!" She staggered off in the direction of the square, shrieking.

"What should we do?"

French shrugged. "Nothing. As loudly as Mrs. Sullivan is screaming, she'll have the local constable here in a few minutes."

Mentioning the police had its usual effect upon me. "We can't stay here and wait for the peelers to show," I said, horrified. "Mrs. Sullivan may buy the carriage accident and the

friends of the colonel routine, but I don't relish being questioned by an inspector as to the depth of my acquaintance
with the deceased."

"Hmm. I see your point. That could be awkward. Why
don't you duck out the back and down the alley? I'll tell the
inspector that I've sent you home as you've suffered a terrible
shock. If he's a gentleman, he won't press the issue. If he's not,
I'll pull rank on him."

"Splendid idea," I said, and it was, but not, unfortunately, a
timely one. For at that moment Mrs. Sullivan pelted into view
with a constable on her heels.

I did not care for Inspector Allen. Nor, I believe, did the inspector care for me. He sauntered behind my chair with his hands
in his pockets, a matchstick dangling from his lips.

"So, you are a cousin to Major French?"

The parlour had become an interrogation room. French
and I were closeted there with the inspector and his sergeant,
who had taken a chair in the corner and produced a notebook
from his pocket to record my lies. In my defense (as if I need to
provide one), French had lied first. He'd taken one look at
Allen and decided that the inspector would have to find out
by himself about Lotus House, the bill of lading and the reason for our appearance at the house on Milner Street. I didn't
blame French for determining that Allen would get no assistance from us. I'd pegged the inspector at first sight as a
pompous, dim-witted, vainglorious toad. Perhaps it was the
suit. Only music hall performers should go about in checked
suits. Maybe the inspector aspired to the acting profession or
sang in a quartet on the weekends. In any event, he had a

nasty little mustache that he smoothed constantly, as if stroking a pet mouse, and a sly, knowing manner that would have played well on the stage as he delivered a double entendre and winked at the audience.

Nor was my impression of the inspector improved when he insisted on treating French and me as suspects. Allen had already put French through the mill, despite French's military rank and his relationship to the prime minister, which he had trotted out immediately. Allen affected to be unimpressed. Then he'd turned on me.

"And you say you are Mr. French's cousin." He said it blandly enough, but there was a trace of smugness all the same. I resisted the urge to paste him in the mustache.

"Yes, I am, as Mr. French has already informed you."

Allen's lips twisted around the matchstick in a smirk of outstanding proportions. "Really?"

I remained mum. I wasn't going to be provoked by the impudent fellow.

"On which side of the family?" asked Allen. What an infernal nuisance he was.

"Maternal," said French. "And that will be the last question we answer regarding family matters."

Allen shrugged. I doubt the fellow would know when he was defeated and those types of policemen are the worst. This one might prove to be a real thorn in my side.

"Had you met Colonel Mayhew?" The inspector directed the question at me, having already ascertained that French had run across Mayhew at some army doings and had promised to pay a call on him sometime.

"I had not. He was an acquaintance of my cousin."

"I see." The tone was both disbelieving and impertinent.

Allen sauntered from his position behind my chair and leaned against the wall, chewing the matchstick with grinding patience. He shot his cuffs and crossed his arms, staring at French.

"Is there any particular reason you chose to visit the colonel on a Sunday? It's an unusual day and an unusual hour for a social call."

The inspector might not be as dim-witted as I had thought.

"I've already explained this to you, Inspector. I remembered that I had promised Francis I'd drop round the next time I was in London."

"Was the colonel a religious man?"

"I don't know. I suppose it didn't occur to me that he might have gone to services. If he'd been out, I'd have left my card. I plan to return to the country this afternoon."

Allen looked at him gravely. "And no doubt you forgot that most people are off to church on Sunday as a result of that blow to the head you suffered during the carriage accident. Tell me, sir, where did your accident occur?"

I hastily revised my opinion of the chap. This Allen was shaping up as a formidable foe.

"The accident occurred on the road," said French, coldly. "Where carriage accidents usually do. And my driver will be well soon." I could see that French was regretting his invention of an accident to explain our injuries, but we could hardly divulge the truth.

"At what time of day did the incident occur?" Allen asked politely, but there was an undercurrent of skepticism that sounded ominous.

"Saturday afternoon," said French. "Will you be requiring an affidavit?"

Allen laughed heartily. "Me, sir? Doubt your word, sir? I'm just asking as a matter of course. Getting it all straight in my head, as it were. Who was where and at what time. You know, *investigating the crime*, sir. I didn't mean to cast aspersions on your statement, sir. Not at all." He simpered behind the matchstick.

"I should hope not," said French, sounding very posh and arrogant. Good for you, I thought. No need to let this little bugger put us on the back foot with his questions. When you've got the trump card of social status, you may as well lay it on the table at the beginning of the game.

French stood up, clapped his hat on his head, and proffered me his arm. "Now, if you don't mind, I shall take my cousin away from here. She's suffered a terrible shock."

I tried to look faint, which wasn't all that difficult as I recalled the horror upstairs.

"If you have any other questions, you may leave word for me at the prime minister's office," said French. "I collect my mail there most days."

Ooh, that was a palpable hit, and Allen acknowledged as much with a faint smile.

Out in the open air, the smell of Sunday roasts wafted over the street and the pavement was busy with families returning from various houses of worship. The activity at Mrs. Sullivan's drew a great deal of attention of the English sort—a surreptitious glance in the direction of the house, a whispered confab between husband and wife, and a shushing of excited questions from children. Murder may have been done, but it would be unseemly to appear excited about it in public. Mind you, these same folk would be rushing out the door for the evening papers tonight, but respectable people did not exhibit too much interest in this sort of thing. It would be socially unacceptable to be caught staring at French's bruised eye or my swollen lip.

The averted eyes and hushed voices were as unnerving as Allen's questions, and I sighed with relief when we'd turned the corner and French found a hansom.

"To the War Office," French told the driver, and we settled in for the journey.

"I think the inspector has us in the frame for the colonel's murder," I said. "If he asks around, he'll soon find that Major Lachlan French doesn't have a cousin named India Black or a driver named John, and that yours truly owns a first-class brothel on St. Alban's Street. He'll be back to ask us how we got these injuries. Count on it."

"I'm sure he'll nose around. It is his job, after all. But I'll ask the prime minister to have a word with the Home Secretary, who'll have a word with Allen, and that will be the last we see of the inspector."

"Thank God. That suit was blinding."

French laughed. "It was horrible, wasn't it?"

I shared the laugh, but not French's confidence that we'd seen the last of Inspector Allen. I had the feeling that underneath the clownish exterior was a dogged huntsman, who would be reluctant to lose two perfectly good suspects just because the British prime minister told him we were off-limits. But I set aside such thoughts and concentrated on the matter at hand, namely my personal safety. And French's, of course.

"I suppose Mayhew told those chaps that he'd sent the bill of lading to Lotus House and that's why they paid us a call."

French scowled. "Of course he did. They flayed the man alive. When I catch those buggers—"

"You mean you're going after them?"

"If you had seen what they did to the poor sod . . . " His voice trailed away.

"They must have visited the colonel while Mrs. Sullivan was at her sister's," I observed.

"No doubt," said French. "I expect the colonel made a great deal of noise. They wouldn't have dared torture him like that with the landlady in the house."

"I doubt they'd scruple at killing Mrs. Sullivan if she'd been there. These blokes are cruel." I recalled the metallic tang that had assailed my nostrils, and the pattern of blood drops across the walls. That had been enough to turn my stomach, and French had seen the worst of it.

"That bill of lading was important enough for those men to savage Mayhew. We need to find out why." French had a distinctly Old Testament air about him. I could see he was in the mood to smite someone.

"We do?" I asked. "I mean, I'm not keen on being thrashed in my own house by thugs and normally I'd chase them to the ends of the earth just to give them a good walloping, but these fellows aren't your average villains. Look what they did to Mayhew."

"All the more reason for us to find them."

I should have been pleased to be included in this vigilante party and I did feel a momentary burst of pleasure that French considered me as capable of hunting down these ruffians as he was. But the prospect of tangling with a pack of murderers with a fondness for knives was somewhat daunting. Still, the

colonel hadn't deserved to die like that and I could understand French's feelings.

"I suppose you consider it your duty to track down these
men, and we're going back to the War Office to find out more
about Mayhew."

"Yes. The bill of lading might relate to a personal matter, or
it might be connected to Mayhew's work. I don't think Mrs.
Sullivan is in a fit state to answer any questions at the moment
and even if she is, Allen is there. We'll start at the War Office
and see what we can find out about the colonel."

I like to think that I'm an intelligent woman and know
when to leave well enough alone, but the truth is I'm damned
inquisitive and congenitally stubborn and have never learned
to turn the other cheek, especially when it's bruised and
swollen.

"Very well. Let's run these fellows to earth and find out
what's so bloody important about that bill of lading."

French looked sideways at me. "I don't suppose you'd be
willing to sit this one out?"

"I should say not. Look at my lip. Those bastards will pay
for this. No one splits India Black's lip and lives to boast about
it. And don't looked so concerned, French. I have a rapier and a
revolver and I know how to use them."

"These fellows are rather skilled with blades, India. I suggest you forgo the sword and use your Webley Bulldog."

"There is a certain satisfaction in plugging a bastard with a
bullet."

"Yes, I noticed that you rather enjoyed yourself when you
shot me."

"I did derive some pleasure from that exercise." Primarily

because I'd been furious to learn of French's engagement from our mortal enemy, the Russian Ivan. I did not want French to know this, of course. Better to send him off on a false scent, so I waved a hand airily and said, "Of course I wouldn't have shot you if I'd known you were my cousin."

# FOUR

The lads at the War Office were stupefied to learn that Colonel Mayhew had joined the great heavenly choir and henceforth would not be spending the Sabbath at his desk down the hall. French spared the youngsters the details of the killing, which was just as well as I didn't have the heart to hear them myself, but the word "murder" sent them into a swoon and it was difficult prying any information from them. I had never seen French in his role as major, and I confess to feeling pleasantly stimulated by his stoic demeanour and air of command. If he'd only been wearing a uniform I might not have been able to restrain myself, but as he was still wearing his crumpled suit from the night before his virtue was safe for the moment.

While I'd been thinking about how splendid French would

appear in the No. 1 Dress Uniform of the Forty-second Regiment of Foot, he'd been informing the clerks that we would be in the colonel's office. I fear for England, I really do, for if a major in street clothes and a whore can waltz into the War Office and sift through a fellow's belongings with nary an objection, our country's secrets might as well be published in the newspapers. It must have been French's plummy vowels that paved the way for us. We took advantage of the lax security and hurried off to Mayhew's compartment to plunder his desk.

The colonel's office was fastidious. There was a pile of official documents stacked neatly on one corner, a writing pad perfectly flush with the edge of the desk and a pen lined up precisely above the center point of the pad. I wondered if we'd find a ruler in the colonel's effects.

"Hurry," said French. "It might occur to those young idiots out there that we have no business in here." He picked up the stack of papers and paged through them rapidly. I opened a drawer and discovered an astonishing variety of forms.

"How does the army find time to fight?" I asked. "There's enough paper here to bury a regiment, after it had been properly equipped, armed and fed, of course." I contemplated a life spent counting buttons and bayonets and shuddered.

"I say, what do you think you're doing? This office is restricted." The speaker was a diffident, owlish fellow with pale blue eyes that bulged disconcertingly in a round, flushed face. He sported the insignia of a captain on his sleeve.

French straightened from his perusal of the colonel's desk. "I'm Major French of the Forty-second, seconded to the prime minister's office. Who are you?"

French's recitation of his credentials had had the desired effect. The captain blinked.

"I am Captain Bernard Welch. In the absence of Colonel Mayhew, I am in charge of this department today."

"Well, Captain, you may not have heard the news yet but you will soon. Colonel Mayhew is dead. I was asked to look into the matter." French was running a pretty bluff, but as he had no official standing in the investigation of the colonel's death I figured it wouldn't be long before someone who did would meander along and start asking difficult questions.

Captain Welch's mouth had flopped open, almost resting on his chest. He stared at French in disbelief. "Dead? What has happened? Has there been an accident?"

"The colonel has been murdered."

I hoped the rest of our military lads were made of sterner stuff, for the captain swayed and had to grasp the back of a chair for support. "Good Lord," he whispered. "Murdered, you say? When? Why?" His flushed cheeks had grown pale.

"He was killed last night, or early this morning. It's your last question that interests me. You say you're in charge here." French brandished a sheaf of paper from Mayhew's desk. "I gather that the colonel was responsible for the supply of provisions to our troops."

The captain swallowed. "Yes, sir."

"And you work for him?"

"I do, sir. I mean, I did. I handled all the correspondence, draughted orders for his signature, traveled with him on depot inspections and that sort of thing." The captain was regaining his composure as he spoke. "I do apologize, sir, but I must ask you again what you are doing here. You said you represented the prime minister. Why isn't this matter being handled by Scotland Yard, or military authorities? And you, ma'am? May I ask why you are here with the major?"

French smiled approvingly. "I can see you're an astute fellow. You must have served the colonel well. You're quite right to wonder why I'm here, and why I am accompanied by this young lady. Her presence is an accident. Mine is not. But I'm afraid I cannot tell you anything more about the prime minister's interest in the colonel's death. A matter of state security, you understand, which I am not at liberty to disclose. Scotland Yard will be along directly to sort out the criminal matter. In the meantime, I must ask you some questions."

It's a good thing the army spends a fair amount of time hammering the duty of obedience into its recruits, for French's crisp tone and assumption of authority overrode Captain Welch's suspicions.

"What can you tell me of Colonel Mayhew? Was he a solitary man? Did he have friends here at the War Office?"

The captain gave that a think. "He was a quiet fellow, sir. I know he lived alone, because he mentioned his landlady once or twice. Just in passing, sir, nothing inappropriate. The colonel was a great one for the rules, sir. God help the sergeant who turned in a jumbled report, or didn't complete a form properly."

"And his friends?"

"None that I know of, sir, but then I wouldn't. I saw him here at the office, that's all."

"Was he a pleasant man? A difficult man?"

The captain shrugged. "Pleasant enough. As long as you did your job he had very little to say to you. If you didn't, well, the colonel could have a sharp tongue."

"A professional soldier, then, and not a sociable fellow."

"I would say that sums up the colonel perfectly."

You'll notice that I hadn't said a word up until this point, and didn't plan on saying any after this point either. I could have peppered the young fellow with questions of my own, but I reckoned that French's rank would be more effective in eliciting answers from Captain Welch. Mind you, I believe I should receive some credit for having the wit to stay out of the proceedings.

French removed his hunter from his pocket and checked the time. He knew as well as I that Inspector Allen could arrive at any minute and finding the two of us here conducting our own investigation might annoy the chap.

"Had you noticed any change in the colonel's demeanour recently?"

A frown of puzzlement crossed the captain's face. "What do you mean, sir?"

"Was he upset or angry about anything?"

"He didn't appear to be."

"Was he apprehensive, or nervous?"

"No, sir. He was just the same as usual."

"Had he argued with anyone recently? Another officer, perhaps?"

The captain blushed at the prospect of gossiping about his superiors. "No, sir."

"Did he seem at all afraid or fearful?"

The captain looked shocked at the idea of the stolid Colonel Mayhew succumbing to fright. "Oh, no. He was not the type to scare easily."

French looked impatient and I could hardly blame him. We hadn't learned a thing from Captain Welch and we needed to vacate the premises.

"Thank you, Captain. That will do. I'll finish looking through the colonel's desk and then we'll find our own way out."

Captain Welch blushed pinkly. "I'm sorry, sir, but I can't let you do that. Not without proper authorization."

"You'd like a note from Lord Beaconsfield himself?"

I feared French's sarcasm would be wasted on the earnest captain, and I was proved right. Though his blush deepened, the young officer braced himself and said, "I'm afraid that if there is any question about your jurisdiction, sir, I shall have to refer you to my superior officer. You do understand, Major, that I must follow protocol, especially in the matter of murder."

We were beaten and we knew it. French chose not to bully the lad and I was glad of that; I do feel it's demeaning to bluster when you've been soundly thumped. We withdrew with an air of having gotten what we came for, leaving the captain staring after us, and beat a hasty retreat down the back stairs and out through the rear door.

"That was not our most successful foray," I said as we hurried down the pavement in search of a hansom.

"We at least learned the extent of the colonel's responsibilities. If he's assigned to the quartermaster general then he had his fingers in moving supplies, some of which might be transferred pursuant to a bill of lading."

"But as you pointed out, the tools that were shipped could have been purchased in India. Why buy them here? And why single out that one bill of lading? And why send it to Lotus House?"

"There are too many questions. Let's summon a cab and get cracking. I want to find some answers."

We returned to Lotus House to find that Vincent had dropped by for a visit and was dozing on my sofa. Now I am fond of

Vincent, though I would never admit as much to him, but the lad hasn't bathed in a very long time (if ever) and smells stronger than a donkey's carcass left to rot in the Nubian sun. You will understand, then, why I rapped on the sole of his boots with the poker and ordered him off my furniture. He woke with a yawn and feigned indifference to the rather discourteous means I had employed to relocate him. I reflected that the next time I needed to dislodge Vincent, I'd whack him on the head. He may have saved my life on occasion (well, at least three that I can recall), but the little bugger is getting entirely too comfortable in my study.

Vincent scratched an armpit vigorously and I wondered how many fleas were now cavorting in the cushions of my sofa. "Any chance o' gettin' a bite to eat?"

"I'm famished," French agreed.

"If you want to take your chances at being poisoned, I can ask Mrs. Drinkwater to bring us something."

"I'll risk it," said French.

Vincent was studying us critically. "What the devil 'appened to you two?"

I excused myself to arrange something to eat. A nuisance, that, as first I had to wake my cook from her usual Sunday afternoon stupor. Mrs. Drinkwater always has "a little lie down" on Sunday afternoons, "to recover from the stress of the week." You'd have a lie down too, if the night before you had ingested a quart of the infamous "blue ruin" gin so potent you could preserve anatomical specimens in it.

Vincent's eyes were shining with excitement when I returned to the study, so I assumed that French had shared the details of Colonel Mayhew's death with the scamp. Vincent is a bloodthirsty creature.

"Somethin's fishy, guv." The lad shook his head and looked solemn.

"Thank you, Vincent. French and I are aware that something is amiss. Was it the three thugs who convinced you, French, or the colonel's body?"

Sarcasm is wasted on Vincent.

"Wot are we gonna do about this?" he asked. Naturally, he directed the question to French, a habit of Vincent's that I am determined to break.

I cut in quickly, before French could issue orders. "You are off to the docks, to look for the *Comet*. She'll be sailing on the evening tide tonight, so you'll need to find her quickly." I could see that Vincent was mulling how he would single-handedly highjack the ship. "Don't you dare go aboard until French and I get there."

"And what will we be doing?" French sounded amused.

"We'll be visiting the premises occupied by the Bradley Tool Company."

"It's Sunday," French objected. "There won't be anyone around."

"Perfect. No one will disturb us as we go through their files. I trust that your training encompassed basic lock-picking skills? Should I loan you a hairpin?"

French announced he had a report to prepare for the prime minister and busied himself at my desk with pen and ink while Mrs. Drinkwater bustled about in the kitchen, producing a nourishing repast of rock-hard biscuits and weak tea. French completed his task and we tucked in, discussing our plans and arranging a time and place for a rendezvous. Then each of us had a belt of brandy to steel ourselves for the afternoon's work.

Vincent hurried off in the direction of the Thames and French and I strolled until an empty hansom came rattling along. French raised a languid hand and waved it down. We settled in and I opened up the artillery barrage on fortress French.

"If the marchioness has known of my existence all these years, why did she wait so long before she tried to find me? And why didn't she attempt to locate my mother?"

French looked pained, as well he might. We were a good fifteen minutes away from our destination and India Black can inflict a lot of damage in a quarter of an hour.

"I don't know. As you're in communication with her, why don't you ask her?"

"I've been trying to pry some answers out of her for ages. Do you think I'd bother asking you if the marchioness would part with her secrets?"

"Perhaps if you asked politely—"

"I've been bloody polite. And deferential, and firm, and threatening. Nothing has worked. She's been deuced evasive. Believe me, I sympathize with the old bat. I can well imagine that most elderly ladies would be shocked to discover that their long-lost great-niece is a—"

"India, stop!"

My word, the man is touchy about my profession.

"The marchioness had her reasons for sending me to find you. But she must be the one to tell you those reasons. And she'll answer your other questions, as well, if you only give her some time. You must see that this situation is also difficult for her."

"Pish. If you hadn't interrupted me a moment ago, I'd have told you that while some ancient types might be swooning right now, the marchioness is as tough as old boots. She isn't the kind of woman to go all faint and fluttery at the news that I own a brothel." Cue French's distressed expression, which I ignored. "Frankly, I'm tired of dancing with the woman."

"Please, one more letter. And I'll write to her as well."

"And if she doesn't reply, or brushes off our requests?"

"Then we shall go to Scotland and demand answers."

"You won't get any," I said. "She'll retreat to her room and refuse to see us."

"She'll see me."

I thought he sounded smug and told him so. But when I asked why he was so bloody sure the decrepit witch would admit him to her house, he gave me a cryptic smile and refused to speak about the matter, which of course annoyed me greatly.

"Very well, French. We'll play this match as you suggest. I'll write the confounded vulture once more, and then I'm finished playing nicely. You'd better hope the marchioness tells me the truth, or we'll be on the first train to Scotland and it's a damned long journey."

This alarmed him, as I knew it would, and wiped the smile from his face.

"We're still a few minutes from Salisbury Street," I said. "Plenty of time for you to tell me how you found me."

He squirmed uncomfortably and looked out the window. Then it dawned on me.

"You didn't really find me, did you? I mean, you might have been looking but it was sheer bloody luck that you stumbled across me. If poor Latham hadn't died at Lotus House, the marchioness might still be waiting to find her great-niece."

Sir Archibald Latham, former customer and clerk in the

War Office (otherwise known as "Bowser" to the tarts for his soulful eyes and tendency to hump anything in sight), had clocked out of his earthly shift at Lotus House in the middle of a session with one of my bints. Archie had been carrying a secret memo describing the state of Britain's armed forces (appalling, I suppose, best described it), and Russian agents had nabbed the deceased clerk's case and made a run for the Continent. The prime minister had dispatched French to shadow the tsar's agents and keep an eye on Latham, and that, I suspected, had led French to my door.

I laughed. "Good God. What are the odds? Eight thousand whores in London and Bowser chooses Lotus House in which to die. It must have been a shock to learn that the woman you'd been dispatched to find was the madam there."

French looked at me sourly. "I was on your track already, but I was bloody surprised to find that Latham frequented Lotus House. His death and subsequent developments certainly altered my plans for approaching you."

"Subsequent developments?" I affected an air of nonchalance. "Ah, yes. You mean the way you blackmailed me into helping you get that memorandum. By the way, did you explain to the marchioness just how you manipulated me? I can't think that she'll appreciate your methods of extortion." Privately, however, I reckoned the old trout would have done the same or worse. From experience, I knew the marchioness did not concern herself overmuch with trifles such as the Christian virtues. I must admit, I rather admired her for that view as my own philosophy regarding principles is equally elastic.

By this time, to French's great relief, we had reached our destination. We swung out of the hansom into a short street of offices and shops. The pavements were deserted, the premises shuttered. After the sound of the horse's hooves had died in the distance, the stillness was absolute. For my money, there's nothing half so eerie as an uninhabited thoroughfare on a Sunday afternoon in London. I'd rather stroll alone through the rookery in Seven Dials in the wee hours of the morning (with my Bulldog revolver in my pocket, naturally) than wander down this desolate street. Every doorway seemed to hold menace, every window a shadowy figure that traced our progress down the pavement. Of course, I'm not the skittish type, but this utter silence was disturbing. I like the sound of loud voices and thrumming wheels. It sounds like money to me. The calm of this quiet afternoon was unnatural and disturbing. On the other hand, it was a first-rate opportunity for rummaging through offices without fear of discovery.

"What was the address?" French asked.

"Number twenty-eight."

"Across the street, then."

We set out across the boulevard, for once without fear of being ridden down by a coach or an omnibus. We walked slowly, searching the doorways for the street number. We found the address of the Bradley Tool Company and stood on the pavement in front of the building, giving it a lengthy perusal.

"You're sure this is the right number?" asked French

"Yes."

It belonged to a tobacconist's shop.

# FIVE

"An accommodation address," said French. The practice was prevalent in London, with the large number of folks arriving daily from the provinces and lacking a permanent address at which to receive their mail.

Nevertheless, I found it odd that a commercial enterprise like a tool company was using a mail drop. "My suspicions are aroused," I announced.

French shrugged. "There might be an innocent explanation. Perhaps the owners' main office is elsewhere, but they want to give clients the impression of a bustling enterprise with a London location."

I was skeptical and said so. "Who cares where shovels and picks are manufactured, as long as the price is right?" That's the trouble with these silver-spoon chaps; they've no experience in the world of commerce.

"I merely suggested a motive for the firm maintaining an accommodation address."

"Another motive might be that there's no such firm as the Bradley Tool Company at all." I conned the street furtively. "Shall we break in and have a look round?"

"We might as well, as I won't have a moment's peace if I suggest that we return tomorrow and speak to the proprietor."

I must be making progress with French, as he is improving at correctly gauging my moods.

So I played sentry while French busied himself with the lock. It seemed to take an inordinately long time for the prime minister's trusted agent to pick a simple mortise lock but finally the door swung open and we piled inside, closing the door quietly behind us. We took a moment, letting our eyes adjust to the gloom until we could discern the layout of the shop. It was a tiny place, barely wide enough for two gentlemen to walk abreast, which cheered me no end as it meant that we wouldn't have to spend much time searching the premises. A wooden counter occupied the wall to our left, with row upon row of glass jars containing loose tobacco neatly labeled in copperplate script and arranged on ledges. On our right were freestanding shelves displaying a variety of pipes and boxes of cigars, matches, pipe cleaners and cigar cutters. The rear wall was bare, save for a closed wooden door.

I stepped behind the counter while French exercised his skills on the door, which presumably led to an office. I hoped it led to an office and not to the owner's living quarters.

I rummaged through the contents of the counter, composed of last week's newspapers, a couple of filthy pipes, and a half-empty bottle of cheap brandy.

"There's nothing here," I called to French, and received a muffled reply. He'd succeeded with the second lock and I joined him in the cramped closet that did indeed serve as the owner's office. There was room only for a chair and a small desk, where French had seated himself and was now rooting through the drawers.

"Ledgers," he murmured, "business correspondence regarding the shop, orders from customers. Ah, here's a packet of mail." He drew out a stack of letters and shuffled through it quickly. He extracted an envelope and handed it to me. It was addressed to Peter Bradley of the Bradley Tool Company and bore a return address in Calcutta for the South Indian Railway Company.

I inserted a nail into the flap.

"Stop," said French.

"Don't you want to know what's in here?" I asked.

"Naturally, but if it's only another mysterious bill of lading we won't have advanced our knowledge by much and we'll have alerted the owner of the shop that someone's been trifling with Peter Bradley's mail. If there is something dodgy going on, then the men behind this affair will disappear and we'll be none the wiser."

"But there might be a clue in here." I brandished the envelope.

"There may be. But wouldn't you rather get a look at the fellow who comes to collect it?"

I hadn't considered that, but then patience is not my strongest virtue. In fact, I'd be hard-pressed to characterize my adherence to any particular virtue as strong. I'm more of a vice woman, myself. But I digress.

And I did have to concede that his nibs had a point, though I wouldn't admit as much to him. Undoubtedly it would be better to suss out the character who visited the shop to pick up the mail and perhaps learn something of greater value.

"Well, you may be content to loiter about all day, or have that scamp Vincent do it, but I've got a business to run and I can't be wasting my time watching a shop door."

"You're not terribly busy during the day, India. But if you want Vincent and me to track down these fellows, we will."

Confound it. Of course I didn't want to be left out of anything, and he knew it.

"I don't mind lending a hand when I'm needed," I said, and turned away before the quirk of French's lips developed into a smirk.

We tidied the office and shop so as to leave no trace of our visit, and hurried off to meet Vincent at our rendezvous point. Even on a Sunday the docks were bustling, for as the saying goes, "Time and tide wait for no man." There were tens of thousands of heathens around the world who, though they were unaware of this fact, were desperately in need of England's products, and thousands of British folk who wouldn't be able to face Monday morning without drinking a cup of China tea, laden with West Indian sugar, while lounging in their dressing gowns. So the docks of London hum like a beehive at all hours of the day and night, and the workers here do not observe the Sabbath. The wharves and piers are a rough place, for the men who work there are a crude lot. On the other hand, they do appreciate beauty when they see it, for I received more than my fair share of appreciative comments as French and I proceeded to our meeting with Vincent.

This did not sit well with French. "Curse it, India, why must you attract attention like this? It's damned awkward when we're trying to slip around unnoticed."

"You might as well ask why the stars shine at night. I'm a force of nature. And my appearance might be useful in extracting information from these fellows. They're much more likely to talk to me than to a swell like you."

Vincent had loped up, just in time to hear my comment.

"She's right, guv. But I reckon more of these lads will talk to me than either of you."

"It's not a contest," I said, irked that Vincent was probably correct. "And will you two stop nattering like a couple of old women? Where's the *Comet*?"

"If hit was a contest, I'd win," said Vincent. "I already talked to the blokes who loaded 'er out. They finished a couple 'ours ago. She'll sail with tonight's tide, which ain't that long from now so if we're gonna take a gander at 'er, we better get after hit. She's docked at the east pier, in St. Katharine Docks."

The location of the *Comet* required a short stroll from where we had met. I used the time to question Vincent.

"Did you ask the navvies what cargo she carries?" I asked.

"A bit o' everything. Pig iron, oak lumber, wool, and"—he glanced slyly at us—"about a dozen crates o' shovels and rakes."

"Well done, Vincent."

"Save your praise, French," I said. "All Vincent has accomplished is to verify that Mayhew's bill of lading was correct."

Vincent looked injured. I'd thought the ragamuffin impervious to slights, but I had wounded him with my comment.

"I mean, well done, Vincent, for confirming that information."

"'Tweren't nothin'." Vincent sniffed.

French cut in. "Do you know if the captain's aboard?"

"Aye, he's there alright."

"Then I believe I'll have a conversation with him. You two wait here."

"Not on your life, French. I'm coming with you. The captain may prove susceptible to my charms."

French looked sour, but could not dispute the truth of my assertion. "Very well. Vincent, tag along and talk to your friends again. See what more you can learn. Have the navvies loaded any other crates from the Bradley Tool Company on other ships? Did Peter Bradley oversee the loading of the crates? You know what to ask."

Vincent darted off, with one last sulky glare in my direction. He hadn't forgiven me, but I was untroubled by this fact. Vincent being Vincent, I'd soon bring him round with a few glasses of my Rémy Martin.

French and I set off for the pier at a brisk pace. We had to dodge piles of rope and keep our eyes peeled for laden cargo nets swinging overhead. More than once the dockworkers shouted abuse at us for walking where we shouldn't. There was a tang of salt in the air, which meant the tide had flowed from the Atlantic up the Thames and would soon be flowing out again, carrying upon it a score of ships, including our quarry.

The *Comet* proved to be an iron-hulled monstrosity sporting two funnels from which grey smoke eddied, to be snatched away by the river breezes. She was rigged for sail, as well, and sported paddle wheels.

Noting them, French said, "A regular visitor to Calcutta,

I'd wager. Those paddle wheels allow her to sail up the Hooghly River. It's too shallow for screws."

"You surprise me. I wouldn't have tagged you as the maritime sort."

"The army has to travel, and along the way I've picked up a bit of knowledge about local conditions."

"You've been to India, then?" I was going to have to get this fellow drunk and pry his secrets out of him, after I'd had my wanton way with him, of course.

"Yes," he said briefly, and sidestepping a navvie carrying a sack of sugar slung over his shoulder, offered me his arm as we ascended the gangway.

A stout cove with a bristling red beard and narrow eyes was defending the ship against all boarders. We stepped onto the wooden deck to be confronted by this Viking, clutching the ship's manifest.

"May I help you, sir?" He was courteous, but his manner made it clear that we were there under sufferance and we'd need a bloody good reason to stay on board.

"I am here to see the captain," said French, nodding at the man with that supercilious air he occasionally adopts and which I find insufferable.

The ginger fellow was not impressed, either. "What's your business with the captain?"

"I should prefer to discuss that with him personally."

The bearded fellow cocked his head. "He's a busy man, our captain. We'll be sailing soon. I reckon if you want to see him you'll have to tell me why, or he'll have my head for wasting his time."

"I am with the prime minister's office."

"And my old pa is the Archbishop of Canterbury."

French gave a pained smile, reached into his pocket and extracted a small square of paper, which he handed to the man.

The fellow studied it for moment. "Wait here," he said and disappeared down the nearest hatch.

"What the devil was that?"

"A note from the prime minister, requesting that I be afforded every courtesy."

"Why don't I have one of those? And when did you get it? Why didn't you trot it out for Captain Welch when he questioned your authority?"

French waved his hand vaguely, ignoring the latter two questions and answering the first. "I haven't seen the necessity of getting one for you."

"*You* haven't seen the necessity? I'll have a word with Dizzy the next time I see him."

The ginger-bearded chap reappeared in the hatch, followed by the very prototype of the English sea dog. The captain was a grizzled veteran of many voyages, with a seamed face the colour of walnut and straggly white hair peeking out from his cap. He had a pipe clamped between his teeth, which gave him the appearance of an angry canine with a tobacco habit.

"I'm Captain Tate. What the devil do you want?" He thundered at French in a voice that nearly sent me over the rails. I suppose he was accustomed to bellowing orders above a roaring gale. He spared me a glance, and then treated himself to a longer second look. With difficulty, he tore his gaze from my bounteous charms and addressed French again. "Well? Ralph here says you're with the government."

"The prime minister's office," muttered Ralph through his flame-coloured beard.

"Oh, aye, so it was. And what do you do for the prime minister, mister—"

"It's *Major* French, and I'm here to verify some information regarding one your clients, the Bradley Tool Company. I understand you're carrying cargo for them."

The captain shrugged. "So I am. Tools, if I remember correctly." He consulted Ralph. "Do I remember correctly?"

Ralph thumbed through the documents in his hand. "You do, Captain. Ten crates of various tools to be delivered to the South Indian Railway Company."

"Have you carried freight for the Bradley Tool Company before?"

The captain scratched his chin. "Name of the company sounds familiar."

"Have you met Mr. Peter Bradley?"

The captain's forehead furrowed as he squinted into the sun. He cast a critical eye at the tide. "Might have done, once. Yes, I reckon I have. An old chap come aboard the first time we shipped for the company."

"Can you describe him?"

"What's this about, Major? This bloke hasn't done anything illegal, has he? If so, you'll need to speak to my employers. All I do is ship what they tell me to ship, and make sure it arrives on time. You should talk with Mr. Winston down at the office. He won't be there today, it being Sunday, but he'll be in tomorrow. Now then, I'll bid you good afternoon, for I'm a busy man and we'll be hauling anchor in a few hours' time."

"One moment, captain. Please describe the man from the tool company and I'll leave you to get on with your work."

"He was just a man. Nothing peculiar about him." The

captain sucked his pipe, frowning. "The far side of sixty, I'd say. Grey hair and a beard. Well-dressed and well-spoken." The old salt looked irritable at having to expend mental energy in describing something other than wind and water.

"Thank you, Captain. We've taken enough of your time." French tucked my hand into the crook of his arm and drew me away. Behind us Tate harrumphed and I heard him stump away across the deck.

"That wasn't particularly helpful," I hissed in French's ear as we descended the gangplank. "You let him off too easily."

"What did you expect me to do, haul the man to the Tower and put him on the rack?"

"I'd have gotten more out of him," I said, serenely confident. "If he weren't sailing soon, I'd come back here tonight and have his life story by midnight. I've a gift for getting information from men." Well, it's been true of every man I've ever met with the possible exception of French, who was as silent and inscrutable as the bloody Sphinx. I considered that my theory might need revision, but rejected the notion as ridiculous. French might prove a tougher nut to crack, but given enough time I was sure I'd wrest his secrets from him.

We waited for Vincent in a doorway for a good thirty minutes. I was getting restless, anticipating a drink of whisky and an early night, preferably early enough to give French a bit of instruction in interrogation techniques, when the odiferous lad turned up. French related our encounter with the captain and as he spoke a sly grin appeared on Vincent's face, which grew broader as the story neared its end.

"Oi! There's somethin' afoot, alright. I went back to those blokes who loaded the crates and they said they do it regular-like. The ship sails to India every two or three months, and for nearly a year, they been stowin' tools from this Bradley company on board." Vincent's smile was now triumphant. "And they say that ever' time they load, the same bloke comes down to watch 'em put the crates on board, and then the captain takes him down to the Jolly Tar and they have a pint and a chin wag."

"An elderly man, with grey hair and a beard?" asked French.

"Not 'ardly. 'E's a young bloke with blond hair."

The fact that the captain had been less than honest with French and me did not surprise us. After all, we are agents of the Crown and we're accustomed to a certain amount of subterfuge and obfuscation in our line of work. And then I'm a whore, so I'm well acquainted with the probity of the average man, which, I can tell you, is in short supply. Tate's deceit, however, did prompt a few more questions in my mind.

"I'll lay odds that the captain sends word to the blond bloke that we've been asking about him," I said. "Do you really think it was a good idea to produce that note from Dizzy? Now the blackguards will know that government agents have an interest in their affairs."

"A moment ago, you wanted your own note from the prime minister," said French.

"Wot note?" If Vincent had been a terrier, his body would have quivered. "'Ow come I ain't got a note from ole Dizzy? Wot's it say, anyway?"

"The city would not be safe if you carried around an imprimatur from Dizzy. You'd plunder the place in a week," I told him.

Vincent smiled wistfully. "Wouldn't that be sweet? Oh, the fings I could do."

"Will you two forget about the bloody note? If you must know, I wrote it myself and forged the prime minister's name."

"I find that shocking, French," I said. "What sort of upbringing did you have? How did you get your hands on the prime minister's letterhead? Is it a good likeness of Dizzy's signature? Could you write a letter of recommendation for me and sign it with his name? I'll hang it on the wall at Lotus House."

French gave me that steely eyed gaze of his, which he knows very well has absolutely no effect on me. "If we could just return to the matter at hand—"

"Certainly, French. Let us apply some logic to the situation. If the captain gave us a false description of the man who consigned the tools for shipping, then the captain must be involved in this conspiracy, or fraud, or whatever it is we're investigating."

"Or he might just be the cautious type, who doesn't want to disclose any information about his clients to two strangers, even after one of them trots out a note from the prime minister."

"Either way, I would guess that he'll try to contact the blond fellow to let him know that someone is asking questions about his business."

"I agree," said French, which was a pleasant surprise as he usually finds fault with most of my suggestions. "But will the captain send a messenger or deliver the news himself?"

"The ship will be sailing soon," I pointed out. "Would the captain leave the *Comet* at a time like this?"

"I don't know. I suggest we watch and see if anything happens."

We had a natter about who would watch whom and who

would follow whom and finally decided that if the captain left the ship or dispatched a fellow to communicate with Bradley, then French and I would follow. Vincent was deputed to remain at the docks, keeping an eye on the ship to see if anything untoward developed, a situation that did not please him as it did not involve trailing a shadowy figure through the streets of London and thus did not fully employ his native abilities.

"Someone needs to stay here, Vincent. I'd prefer it be you. You've got a knack for getting information out of these navvies if you see something suspicious. They're not likely to talk to India or me. It's better if we follow any messenger the captain sends." French gazed round at the bustling dock. "Though there are dozens of men here. We'll be deuced lucky if we recognize the captain's errand boy."

"You won't 'ave to worry about that," said Vincent. He pointed at the *Comet*. "Ain't that the captain?"

It was indeed the ship's master, trotting down the gangplank with a worried expression on his face.

"By Jove, we've flushed him." French was triumphant. "Off we go, India."

"Oi, 'ow long do I 'ave to wait 'ere?" Vincent asked in a plaintive voice. He looked downcast at the prospect of loafing quayside while the action moved elsewhere. I can't say I blame him, but that lad has no appreciation for the hierarchy involved in this espionage game. He's the low man on the totem pole, a fact that he consistently fails to realize. Come to think of it, I'm not sure French does either, for he has a distressing tendency to try to relegate me to the role of fetching and carrying just when things get interesting. I usually have to bully him into letting me in on the exciting bits.

We left Vincent with hasty assurances that one or both of us would return just as soon as we learned the captain's destination, and scuttled off in pursuit of our quarry. We'd almost left it too long, for the skipper was vanishing around a corner and we had to quick march after him. And here I'll just mention, once again, how bloody unfair it is that women are saddled with skirts. I'd like to see a chap try to conduct surveillance or spar with a thug while wearing a dress. You can bet the directive abolishing frocks would go out posthaste. I've been threatening to have a pair of trousers made and one of these days, I will. In a suitably dashing style, of course. A pair of trousers might prove a boon in other ways as well. Men find me hard to resist as it is. Just imagine the effect of yours truly in a pair of form-fitting britches. But I digress.

The sea dog was trundling along, moving at the pace of a man who'd consumed a bad sausage for dinner and wanted to get home to the comforts of the lavvy at the back of the garden. We'd left the docks behind and entered the warren of streets that spreads out from the river. Tracking the captain was proving a dicey proposition as there were few people on the pavement and we could not lose ourselves in a crowd. We hung back, skipping from doorway to doorway so as to have a place to dodge into if our prey turned round. Then Captain Tate would turn a corner and we'd rush forward to keep him in sight.

It's dashed odd how invigorating espionage can be. My line of work has its own excitements, but they're nothing in comparison to slinking after a fellow with your heart in your mouth, praying that he won't look over his shoulder. Our captain, however, seemed oblivious to the thought that we might be on his trail. He hurried along, emitting a steady stream of smoke from his pipe, which gave him the appearance of a locomotive carving through the countryside. You could see he was on a mission and working against the clock, as he had only a little time to spare before he had to be back on board ship and ready to sail. I was glad the cove had a deadline to meet, for it worked to our advantage. He was fixed on getting to his destination and paid no attention to his surroundings.

The captain crossed to the other side of the street and made for a tavern in the middle of the block.

French pointed to the sign. "The Jolly Tar," he said under his breath, and drew me into the entrance to a nearby shop. The skipper jerked open the door to the tavern and marched inside.

French frowned. "That's strange," he said. "Do you think the captain had time to send a message to Bradley to meet him here? Or did they have a prearranged meeting?"

"Or is Captain Tate just downing one last pint of British ale before he sails for India?"

Our exchange of rhetorical questions was disrupted by the emergence of a tall, gawky youth from the pub. He broke into a gallop and shot away down the street.

"Athletics training, or did the captain send him on an errand?" I asked.

"As he's already disappeared into thin air, we'll never find out." French swore loudly. "We've missed our chance to follow him."

"No surprise, that. He ran like a scalded cat. We'd never catch him, and we'd make ourselves conspicuous if we tried. We might as well wait a little longer. If he returns to the tavern, he might have a message for the captain. We could tackle the lad after Tate goes back to the ship and find out where he went."

"It's as good a plan as any."

I despise wasting time, unless I'm choosing how to do it. That is to say, lolling in front of a fire on a misty autumn day with a decanter of brandy at hand is a perfectly acceptable way to pass the hours, as is imbibing a flute of champagne on a warm summer's evening. But standing hunched in a shop entrance endeavouring to blend into the woodwork is hard going. I'll thank you not to point out that if the exercise was so deuced dull, why had I been the one to suggest it? You will recall that we had damned few clues to follow in this business. If I am honest (though I don't as a general rule strive to be), we had none except the gangling fellow who might be delivering a note to Peter Bradley at the moment. And then there was the fact that Inspector Allen seemed to think French and I might have spent the night torturing poor Colonel Mayhew. Under the circumstances, it seemed reasonable to suggest we hang around the Jolly Tar for a bit. That did not mean I had to enjoy the experience.

I confess to daydreaming a bit, planning a quiet evening with French, and wavering between the idea of dragging the fellow off to my boudoir or beating him over the head until he confessed all he knew about the marchioness's search for me, when I felt the object of my thoughts stiffen beside me. I do not mean that in the biblical sense. French snapped to attention and I heard his quick intake of breath. I peered around him to see what had aroused his sudden interest.

The cloddish youth had returned and hot on his heels was

a tall, well-built dandy. As they entered the tavern the chap swept off his hat, revealing a shock of wheat-coloured hair.

"Bradley," said French, sounding pleased. I was not pleased. This was going to be bloody awkward. You see, I knew the blond dandy. And I do mean that in the biblical sense.

# SIX

Peter Bradley, handsome devil, gentleman thief and former lover of yours truly, when I was a mere slip of a girl. Back then, he'd been using the name "Philip Barrett." I've no idea which, if either, was his real name. But knowing Philip as I do, and that would be intimately and in every sense of the word, I had no trouble believing he might be involved in something shady. In fact, his presence here confirmed that something illicit *was* in the cards. This was hardly the time, however, to enlighten French as to my history with Philip.

Bugger. What to do now? French was staring fixedly at the door to the Jolly Tar. I reckoned I didn't have much time, as it wouldn't take long for the captain to relate the story of our visit and then return to the ship and Philip would bolt for cover, only I could see from French's posture that he had no intention of letting the chap go anywhere without a chat about Colonel Mayhew and the bill of lading. I spent an uncomfortable five minutes gnawing my thumbnail and debating various schemes for extracting myself from this situation without undue suspicion from French. I've a quick wit and a great deal of experience at wiggling out of tight places, as you might expect from a tart, but I'll be damned if my wits hadn't taken the express to Liverpool and left the rest of me on the station platform. I was still weighing my options when the tavern door swung open and the captain scurried away in the direction of the river. We sank back into the shop's entrance and plastered ourselves against the display window, but the skipper was in a hurry to catch the tide and he strode off without so much as a glance at his surroundings.

As Tate's footfalls faded in the distance, French stuck his head out the entrance. His hand reached back to grip mine. "Bradley is leaving." His body tensed to take the first step in pursuit.

I pulled him back. "What do you intend to do?"

French looked puzzled. "Why, follow him, of course. And if the opportunity arises, I may have a word with the fellow."

Confound it. The first course might prove harmless provided Philip didn't discover us lurking after him, but the second would be disastrous. One look at French's scowling face and I knew that he would not settle for merely trailing Philip around London. He was remembering the scene in Mayhew's room. In truth, it would be deuced hard to forget what little I'd seen there, but I knew that Philip wouldn't have done such a thing. When it comes to the dirty work Philip will be found on the sidelines, buffing his nails. Someone else had done in the colonel, of that I was sure.

French was tugging at my hand impatiently. "Curse it, India! Let's move."

I followed him reluctantly into the street. Ahead of us Philip strolled down the pavement, as if he hadn't a care in the world. He'd always been a cool fellow and he looked completely relaxed at the moment.

French increased his pace and I hung back as best I could. He looked round at me once, frustrated at my slow gait, and I tottered a bit on my heel. I grimaced and gestured down at my boot, which did nothing to slow his momentum but rather more to annoy him.

"Do hurry," he commanded, "or we'll lose him."

My plan exactly, but I took a few quick steps so that French would think my heart was in this chase. No doubt you're wondering why it wasn't. It's a bit complicated. I knew that Philip was up to his sandy eyebrows in something. He had been a thief when I'd known him and I doubt that he'd changed his spots since then. There was some connection between him and Mayhew, and no man deserved to die as Mayhew had. Yes, Philip was a wrong 'un. But we had a history, albeit a chequered one and I was loath to throw the man under the wagon wheels just yet. I might at a later date, mind you, but for the moment I'd rather let him go and find him, without French in the vicinity, which I had no doubt I could do easily. There was the further complication of my past relationship with Philip, which I would prefer to reveal to French in my own fashion and at a time of my choosing. And then there was Lotus House. Philip, you see, had been responsible, in a peculiar way, for providing the capital for my venture into brothel ownership. Oddly, I felt I owed him something, if nothing more than a private chat before French ran him to ground. It's a funny old world, but there you have it. I had a number of reasons to handle Philip by myself.

Which explains why I did what I did next. Despite my efforts at slowing French's headlong rush, we'd gained ground on Philip. French put on speed and I realized that I couldn't drag him back and stall the proceedings much longer. So I tripped him. It was dead easy. One minute we were cruising along and the next I'd wobbled a bit, clutching at him, and then as I exclaimed "my boot!" I stuck that article between his legs and he went flying, sprawling headlong onto the pavement. The fall drove the air from his lungs and he grunted. For verisimilitude, I pitched down beside him, grasping an ankle and moaning loudly.

"Christ," he muttered, when he'd drawn breath. He sat up and struggled to untangle himself from my skirts, which had quite inexplicably become entwined with his legs. I told you the damned things are a nuisance. He flailed about, flinging my skirts in a way that I might have found arousing in other circumstances, until he was finally able to struggle to his feet. He stared down the street but Philip had walked on, oblivious to the drama being played out behind him and all for his benefit, the ungrateful bastard. French, usually so calm and detached, raged up and down the pavement, alternately cursing our bad luck and my clumsiness.

"Thank you," I said. "I can get up by myself."

Begrudgingly, he extended a hand and hauled me upright. I brushed myself off and noticed a small rent in my skirt, and my scuffed boots. Well, some sacrifices are necessary if we are to avoid humiliating encounters with previous lovers.

"Damnation!" French said, rather more loudly than necessary. "Bradley could be anywhere by now. What the devil happened?"

I feigned an examination of my boot. "I believe the heel is loose. My ankle twisted and I fell." I looked at him, cow-eyed. "I *am* sorry, French. I know you wanted to catch that fellow. But we'll find him again. I'm sure of it."

"Just how do you propose we do that?" French growled. "He's been warned by the captain that we're on to him. He won't use the mail drop at the tobacconist's shop again. It's too dangerous now."

"You'll think of something. You always do." I'm not above soothing the male ego from time to time, especially when I've been the cause of its disquiet.

French dusted the knees of his trousers and offered me an arm. "Well, no use crying over spilt milk. Let's go back to the dock and see if Vincent has anything new to report."

Vincent did not, except that the *Comet* had weighed anchor and was just now disappearing down the Thames, bound for Calcutta. He was incredulous that French and I had managed to lose our quarry and when French explained that the reason for our ineptitude was a sartorial malfunction on my part, Vincent's disgust knew no bounds. I could see that I'd gone down in the smelly little runt's estimation but I had other things to worry about at the moment.

French was not in a pleasant frame of mind that evening. He declined to share with me the joint Mrs. Drinkwater had burned, and took himself off sulkily. I was sure he was angry at losing track of Philip, considering that an egregious professional mistake for a man of his experience. But he gave me a long, searching gaze as he departed that left me wondering if perhaps my dramatic efforts had been too enthusiastic. In any event, I watched him stalk off with a faint feeling of apprehension that only increased as I sat down to draught a missive to the marchioness. French had been in no mind to stay and discuss genealogical matters with me, but I'd remembered his insistence that the marchioness must be the one to tell me why she had sought me out, so I penned a short note to the old bag along the lines of "I know you're my great-aunt so stop larking about and tell me why you've hunted me down." Then I took a glass of whisky to the bath and lay in the hot water, thinking about my next move with regard to Philip Barrett.

As I said, years ago, when I was a young tart, Philip had been a customer of mine. Indeed he'd been more than a customer; we'd taken to walking out together though my abbess at the time, Mrs. Moore, was not best pleased about it. I can't say that I blame her, for I was the star attraction at her house and she didn't want me spending too much time with one client. I've never been good at obeying instructions and besides, it was difficult resisting the fellow. Along with those blond locks he had hazel eyes flecked with green, a wickedly charming smile and a physique one might describe as heroic. He was a smoothboots, and though Mrs. Moore preferred he only come by when his pockets were lined, he could always get round her with some flirtatious nonsense.

Those were halcyon days, when Philip and I strolled through Hyde Park and laughed at the pretentious bints parading along Rotten Row in carriages purchased for them by their aristocratic lovers. While I've never been a romantic, I had entertained the notion that Philip and I might grow senile together, provided Philip could come up with the ready to make my dotage comfortable. You see, he was the second son of an impoverished family, and had to make his own fortune if there was to be one. And that is why he'd invited me along on a week's visit to the country to masquerade as his wife and charm a rich and randy American goat named Harold White. I was to put my energy into enchanting the old fool while Philip finagled a lucrative contract out of him. Now the best-laid plans, et cetera, so you won't be surprised to hear that it all ended in tears.

For Philip, that is. His idea of gainful employment was relieving the great and good of their jewels. He'd been using me as camouflage while he plotted to steal White's prized possession, a dirty great ruby worth a good deal of money. I'd discovered his nefarious plan and turned the tables on him, lifting the ruby from him and secreting it in a London bank until Philip had hied off to the Continent with White on his scent. I waited a year, and then I pawned the ruby and purchased Lotus House with the proceeds.

Now you would think I'd be perfectly happy for French to collar Philip and connect him to some sort of criminal enterprise, seeing as how the chap had deceived me and left me to shoulder the blame for the theft. But to tell the truth, I've always felt just the tiniest bit of guilt at doing Philip out of that jewel. Certainly he'd set me up, but you can't blame a fellow for trying to get ahead in life. I might have done the same under the circumstances. And then there's the fact that Philip is so confoundedly handsome. His smile had the most unusual effect on me. In fact, I hadn't felt quite such a frisson until French had entered the picture with his handsome, brooding face and those dark, wavy locks. The men didn't bear the slightest resemblance to each other, except that under rather quiet exteriors ran a deep current of excitement that I found enticing. I've always been drawn to rakehells, you see, and it was just my luck that a certified one in the form of Philip Barrett had reappeared in my life just as I was prying open the lock on another fanciable chap. What's a girl to do?

First and foremost, I needed to find Philip before French did. Oh, I had no intention of telling the scoundrel what I knew and why I was searching for him. No, I intended to be as subtle as a serpent, wheedling information from Philip and then deciding on a course of action. It would be hard going, as subtlety is not my strong suit, but then I'm capable of doing most anything and I had complete faith in my ability to crack open Philip like a nutshell. I'd only hurt the bloke if necessary.

I was contemplating the effort of rising from the warm bath and preparing for bed when Mrs. Drinkwater rapped on the door. I knew it was she, for I'd heard footsteps staggering uncertainly down the hall, tacking from side to side until she reached the door, where she stood outside breathing audibly until she managed to announce herself.

"What is it?" I asked.

"A gennelman. From Scotland Yard. He says."

"Oh, bother. Tell him to go away and call again tomorrow."

"He said you'd say that. And he said to tell you he ain't going nowhere until you come down and talk to him."

"Did the gentleman give you a name?"

Mrs. Drinkwater hiccupped. "Inspector Allen."

"Officious twit," I said and rose from the bath. "Tell him I'll be down in a minute, and if a woman in a dressing gown is too much for him, he'd better take himself off now."

I could picture Mrs. Drinkwater staring quizzically at the

door, trying to decipher my message. I took pity on her. "Just tell him I'll be down shortly. And don't tell him that I called him an officious twit."

"Right." I heard the uneven cadence of Mrs. Drinkwater's footsteps receding down the hallway and with a sigh, rose and toweled myself. Then I draped myself in a peach silk dressing gown that showed my delightful figure to fullest advantage and eased my feet into a pair of soft leather slippers. Let us see how Inspector Allen handles the undiluted effect of India Black, I thought. Well, a woman must have every advantage she can when dealing with the opposite sex.

I found the inspector in the study, rummaging through my desk drawers.

"Looking for a price list, Inspector? I doubt you can afford any of the services here. They're beyond an inspector's salary, I should think." I ran the risk of angering the little tick, but I think it's best to get on the front foot immediately with the peelers.

He straightened up and shut the drawer he'd been searching.

"You're probably right about the prices, Miss Black. But then, I've no interest in the wares you flog here."

"Oh, you're that type. You should have said so. I can fix you up easily enough. There's a house down the street that caters to—"

"Nor am I interested in your laboured attempts at comedy. I'm investigating a murder, a most horrific one, I might add, and I've no time for verbal fencing. Let's get down to brass tacks."

"That suits me," I said, sashaying over to the sideboard where I keep my liquor and pouring myself a generous brandy. I did not offer the inspector a drink. "I've had an exhausting few weeks on assignment for the prime minister and I need my rest."

"Pah," said the inspector. "You've got gall, saying that. And I don't care if Major French *does* work for the prime minister. *He's* got a nerve walking around with his dolly bird on his arm. That's shocking, that is."

"Spare me your official disapproval." I looked at him intently. "Or is it personal? I've often found that men who are sexually repressed or suffer from an unhealthy conjugal relationship with their wives are prone to the most exaggerated expressions of moral outrage when it comes to tarts. Which is it in your case?"

I haven't gotten where I have by being intimidated by men like the inspector. I've met his sort before and bested better men than he. I'd pricked him with my comments, as he had swelled up like one of those American opossums and was baring his teeth at me.

"I'd watch my tongue if I were you. You're in no position to cross swords with me."

"Oh, but I am. Ask your questions and then leave. You are a tiresome man."

That might have been one comment too many, but under the circumstances I think you'll agree that I was entitled to be cranky. I'd merely broken up a nest of anarchists, captured a Russian spy, been beaten in my own home, seen a horrific crime scene and encountered a prior lover from whom I'd stolen a valuable jewel, all in a little over twenty-four hours. I was incapable of being charming and obsequious after that. Well, I'm never capable of being obsequious.

The inspector jammed his hands in his pockets and regarded

me balefully. "You lied about your relationship with Colonel Mayhew."

"I don't believe I described my relationship with the man."

"Not in so many words, but Major French said that he was an acquaintance of the colonel and that you were his cousin. I don't know if the major told the truth about the colonel, but I know damned well he didn't tell the truth about you."

I shrugged. "You should take up that matter with Major French."

"I intend to do just that. But I'm speaking to you at the moment. You didn't deny the major's depiction of your relationship."

"Why should I?"

"And furthermore, you had a connection to the victim. Colonel Mayhew patronized your establishment here. I've been checking into your background, Miss Black. You're known to the local police. I've talked to some of your girls. They knew Mayhew. So tell me, just what were you and Major French doing at Mayhew's lodgings this morning?"

"We certainly weren't killing him. You saw that room. The killer or killers would have been covered with blood. You might have noticed, if you had been paying attention, that French and I were spotless."

"I noticed you'd both been in a fight, and it's clear from the scene that the colonel fought for his life. I reckon you two got those cuts and bruises from Mayhew."

"It would make no sense at all for us to have done the deed, bathed and returned to the scene of the crime," I scoffed.

"Criminals aren't always logical," the inspector said stubbornly.

"Neither are the police, apparently."

"I think you had better explain just what Colonel Mayhew got up to here at your place of business."

"I can't vouch for his personal proclivities, but I should have thought that you'd understand the purposes of his visits in at least general terms. If you want the details, I'll have to summon the last girl with him, but now that I think of it, it's been weeks since the cove was in here and I'll have to ask around."

"You didn't service him yourself?"

I laughed scornfully. "Certainly not. I own this establishment. I don't work in it."

The inspector was wandering through the room, picking up an object and examining it, then replacing it and moving on to the next. He had reached my desk and I saw his eyes light up at the sight of the silver dagger I used to open envelopes.

"What's this?" He snatched it up and waved it at me triumphantly.

"I'd have thought a man in your line of work would have recognized a knife when he saw one." I said it calmly, but I was getting deuced annoyed with the fellow.

Allen hefted the dagger in his hand. "I'll tell you what I think."

"At least you won't waste much of my time."

He ignored me. "I think I'm holding a murder weapon in my hand."

"You think *I* murdered Colonel Mayhew? Why on earth would I do that?"

"He was blackmailing you. He knew something about you that you wanted kept secret." The fellow was talking rapidly, as if to convince himself. "He threatened to expose you."

"Expose me?" I laughed. "Inspector, it took you all of three hours to find out I run a brothel. I don't exactly operate on the sly. It would be damned hard for customers to find me if I did."

"Oh, I'll grant you that you might not care about the average bloke finding out about you, but I'd wager that you might not want Major French to know whatever Mayhew knew. You think he's your ticket out of here, don't you? The handsome Major French." He was mocking me now, the bastard, and I'd had enough.

"Is this what passes for deductive reasoning at the Yard? As you've pointed out yourself, Major French knows what I do. What did you call his appearing with me on his arm? Shocking?"

That set the inspector back on his heels, but only for a moment. "Alright, then. Maybe Mayhew threatened to tell someone else. Like the prime minister, eh?" He paused to gloat. "That's it. We can't have one of our government chaps running around with a tart, can we?"

I shook my head wearily. "Dear, dear. For a policeman, you are singularly unimaginative. Government chaps are rather prone to consorting with fallen women. Indeed, they're some of my best customers, which is something you should probably consider if you insist on pursuing this line of enquiry."

Inspector Allen was still stroking his pet theory. "Or maybe Colonel Mayhew was considering sharing the news with Major French's family. He comes from good stock. I doubt he'd be pleased at having his liaison with you paraded in front of kith and kin."

That hit rather closer to the mark than the previous barbs the inspector had flung at me. I couldn't argue with Allen's premise, but I disliked having this wretched fellow state it quite so baldly. I did not expect French to trot me off to meet his pater and mater, but I'm not accustomed to hiding my light under a bushel for very long. At some point French and I needed to sort out the business of managing our association or relationship or whatever you would call it. I was bloody well provoked at having an insect like the inspector remind me that the sorting needed doing.

"Major French and I are agents of Her Majesty's government," I said. "You may confirm that with Lord Beaconsfield, the prime minister. And I would suggest you ask Major French if he is concerned with our acquaintance becoming known among his circle. I can tell you nothing on that score. And now, unless Colonel Mayhew scrawled my name in blood or you have a witness placing me at the scene, I would suggest that you have no reason to remain here disturbing me with your conjectures. If you wish to speak with me again, you will make an appointment. If you intend to turn up here at the drop of a hat just to harass me, I shall be forced to speak to some of those 'government chaps' you mentioned earlier. One of them will have a word with your governor. You will kindly see yourself out."

I spun on my heel and marched out of the study, not waiting for a reply. What a maddening fellow. I did not need him lurking around every corner, keeping an eye on me while I tried to find Philip. Not for the first time, I wished that Colonel Mayhew (God rest his soul) had left his envelope with the landlord at his local. That bill of lading was turning out to be an infernal nuisance.

You would think that after the events of the last twenty-four hours I would trundle off to bed and enjoy some well-deserved rest. Indeed I did have a kip, but only for a few hours, for I had a mission and unfortunately it could not be accomplished in the light of day. London's criminal class works nonstop round the clock but most coves prefer the cover of darkness. I wouldn't find Philip strolling the streets, of course. Fellows like Philip—the cracksmen, burglars and attic thieves who plied their trade in the West End and Portman Square—would be up on the rooftops after dark, breaking into the garrets and upper floors of the fashionable homes to be found there, lifting the precious stones and jewelry of the occupants. I wasn't hoping to find my former paramour in the flesh. I was planning to put out the word that I'd heard Philip was in London and wanted to see him again. That should be a simple enough task, requiring only a bit of legwork and a few coins.

I dozed in a chair and woke when the bells of St. Martin struck midnight. I dressed quietly and slipped down the stairs to my study, where I collected my revolver from the desk drawer and tucked it into my purse. A woman alone would be presumed to be a prostitute (an astute observation, since she usually was) and could expect a bit of rough language and less than subtle propositions. I've found that chaps are less inclined to pester me when I show them the business end of the .442 Webley.

Once I'd locked the door to Lotus House I made for the Strand, that roaring thoroughfare that never sleeps. At this time of night, the street would be humming with life, most of it of the low variety, which suited my needs perfectly. It's not a long walk from Lotus House, and I rather enjoyed striding along in the cool evening air. I wandered over to Haymarket and walked south to Pall Mall, then angled down Cockspur Street, passed Trafalgar Square (scene of one of my greatest triumphs) and turned left onto the Strand. The noise along the street was deafening. The swells were out in abundance in swallowtail coats and top hats, ambling along with their walking sticks under their arms and smirking at the girls working the streets. An army of dippers and mutchers, men, women and children would be out tonight, relieving these rich fellows, the "square-rigged swells" they called them, of their money and their watches. The tricksters would be working the crowd, fleecing fellows with card tricks and games of skittles. The tipsters and bookmakers would be doing a roaring trade before the evening's entertainment began in the alleys off the Strand—the dog matches, the prizefights with human contenders, and the ratting exhibitions. It's not a world for the delicate flowers of society.

You may be wondering why I'd venture out alone into such a heathen place. In truth, I was at very little risk. I had my Bulldog revolver in the unlikely event that things went bad, but I wasn't worried about sauntering along the pavement without a male companion. Certainly a single female would attract attention along the Strand, and when you're as delicious as I am, you can expect a fair amount of attention from the male of the species at any time. But at this time of night, single women walking the Strand were common. The troopers and ladybirds would be working the lower class, and the toffers would be trolling for the nobs. With my sophistication and beauty, I'd be taken as an adventuress, a *demimondaine*, and the only thing I'd have to worry about was a drunken swell pawing me on the street while his friends egged him on. I was quite capable of handling that sort of situation. I'd been doing it all my life. The trick was to avoid trouble but still keep the fellow as a potential customer. There's a technique to that, but I digress.

Near Adam Street I spotted a barefoot youngster with a
shapeless cap and threadbare clothes. I stopped to have a
word with him, whispering my instructions. When I dropped
a few coins in his hand he accelerated away, bound for the
rookeries that lay just a few blocks north. I'd spent quite
enough time there during my idyll with the anarchists and I
was thoroughly tired of the filth and foulness to be found in
the Seven Dials area. I'd sent the boy to spread the word that I
was looking for an old friend, describing Philip and using the
name I'd known him by rather than "Peter Bradley." I didn't
expect Philip to be staying in such a seamy part of the city, but
the blocks teemed with cheats and card sharps, punishers and
palmers—in short, with every type of criminal. The rookeries
were cramped, squalid, dingy and tortuously narrow. The
police preferred to stay well clear and leave them to the unde-
sirables. Someone in the area would know Philip and I had no
doubt that word would reach him that India Black sought his
company.

But I had other stops to make that night, and so I ambled
along to the Gaiety Theatre on Aldwych and had a chat with
the manager of the Billiards Room there. Philip enjoyed a
game now and then and the Gaiety's hall had been a favourite
of his. I dropped a discreet word in the ear of the maître 'd at
the Gaiety's restaurant, and to the barmen at its several saloons.
Then it was back into the night air for a stroll to Romano's,
for Philip had been fond of dining there, and then on to Wil-
tons as Philip had always had a passion for their oysters and
stout. I visited a few more restaurants and taverns along the
Strand, and when I'd completed these rounds I traversed a
dark and twisting alley to a door set well back into a brick
wall, with a dimly lit lantern glowing feebly above it. I knocked

and waited. A panel in the door slid open and light spilled into the alley. I heard an exclamation and the panel slammed shut, then the door opened and I was enveloped in an embrace.

"India Black! What the hell are you doing here, my girl? This ain't your part of town no more."

"Nat, you old villain," I said. "It's bloody good to see you."

The old villain wore a rusty black suit and an ancient beaver hat that had been made before I'd been born. Nat sported a splendid mustache and a bristling pair of muttonchops. Between the brim of his hat and the soup-strainer, a pair of beady black eyes gleamed at me.

"Haven't seen you in ages," he said.

"Haven't had a ruby to fence in ages," I said.

His belly shook and the black eyes twinkled. "Don't stand out there in the dark. Come in and have a drink with me."

I stepped into Nat's establishment and looked around. I'd been here before, on the day I'd pawned the Rajah's Ruby. I'd known Nat for years before I ever did business with him. He had a reputation for honesty (well, relatively speaking) and was circumspect, a man who paid top dollar and dealt with his accounts promptly. I'd been more than pleased with the price the old Shylock had paid me for the ruby. I had no doubt he'd sold it for a substantial profit, but I didn't begrudge the man his mite.

Nat ran a flash house, where, as alert readers will have gathered, stolen goods were fenced. But a flash house was more than that, being a combination of a club and a school. Palmers arrived with the goods they'd shoplifted and the fingersmiths kept Nat in a steady supply of pocket watches. They were always welcome to sit down to a glass of rum or brandy and share the latest gossip, and the young ones were allowed to hang around the edges of the group and imbibe useful knowledge, such as how to ask a passing toff to help you with a drunk friend while you lifted the swell's wallet. There were dozens of these enterprises around the city, but I'd only crossed the threshold of Nat's.

He had a crowd tonight which was not what I wanted, so I drew him aside and asked for a quiet word.

He nodded sagely and shouted at the group of fellows gathered around the fire. "Drink up, boys. I'll be with you in a minute."

That bunch needed no encouragement, for they were downing the liquor at a fast pace. There was a lot of good-natured ribbing and a few ribald comments, which is only to be expected when I walk into a room, but Nat shushed them with a glance and led me down a dark hall to his cramped office. The room was blue with smoke. Nat had been at work, as I could see by the open ledger and the weighted scales on his desk.

He offered me a chair and a drink, and I spun him a story about the old friend I wanted to find. I didn't ask Nat outright if he knew Philip. The old duffer was tight-lipped when it came to his clients, but I reckoned that one of London's best fences would know most of the jewel thieves who plied their trade in the city. I do believe Nat was a romantic at heart, for he heard me out with a sympathetic expression and patted my hand and told me not to give it another thought: If Philip Barrett was in the city, Nat would find him for me.

I walked home well pleased with my night's work.

# SEVEN

After my late night I treated myself to a lie-in. I was reclining in bed with the morning papers and a cup of coloured water Mrs. Drinkwater had delivered to me with the announcement that it was "tea." There was some evidence that she was correct, as I espied a shred of limp brown vegetation at the bottom of the cup. I'd have to have a word with my cook as I suspected that she was allocating the weekly provisions allowance somewhat differently from what I intended, i.e., in the increased purchase of alcoholic beverages for herself and the decreased procurement of just about everything else on the list.

As expected, the reporter Johnnies were having a field day with Colonel Mayhew's death. The headlines were breathless and the prose ghoulish. Inspector Allen was quoted copiously, with frequent allusions to "solid leads" and "quick resolution to the case."

Around eleven o'clock French breezed into the room, slapping his gloves against his thigh, and plunked down in the bedroom's only chair.

"You're getting rather familiar considering that we haven't been familiar yet," I said, snapping the paper closed in irritation.

"Plenty of time for that later," he said. "Get dressed. We're going out."

I looked at him with some pity. "Really, French. Surely by now you know that the only effect of that peremptory tone of yours is to ensure that I will do exactly the opposite of what you command."

"Inspector Allen's been round to see me. He thinks that you and Mayhew were conducting a torrid affair and in a fit of jealousy I carved up the colonel."

I burst out laughing. Callous, I know, but the image of French getting worked up enough to slash a chap to death was ludicrous.

"You find the fact that I'm a suspect amusing?"

"Yes, I do. But then I know you rather better than the inspector. And when he dropped by here yesterday, he accused *me* of being the killer. He hypothesized that Mayhew was blackmailing me over some indiscretion and I had killed him when the colonel threatened to tell you."

"Clearly the inspector has his lines out and is fishing for all he's worth. You didn't mention the bill of lading, did you?"

"There are times when you annoy me more than others, French, and never more so than when you imply that I am an idiot."

He smiled fondly at me. "Your eyes blaze like blue stars when you're angry, India. It's a most stimulating sight."

That was more like it. I leaned back invitingly against the pillows. It was about time the poncy bastard fixed bayonets and charged the line.

He leaned forward until we were tantalizingly close and I could smell the bay rum from his morning's ablutions. His eyes were dancing as he looked into mine. I felt an uncharacteristic fluttering in my stomach.

Then he seized my tea cup and drained the liquid from it.

"Five minutes," he said, standing. "Vincent is waiting downstairs."

I swatted him with a pillow and he retreated, laughing. Well, a playful French was an improvement over the stuffy, dour type who'd first presented himself at Lotus House last fall.

Couple that with French's declaration of interest or love or whatever it had been, and I felt there was a good chance we'd tumble onto a mattress sometime in this century.

I took my own sweet time dressing, as any self-respecting female would, and sauntered down the stairs thirty minutes later. I found Vincent, French and Mrs. Drinkwater in the kitchen. My cook was pottering about happily among her pots and pans and piling inedible buns and biscuits in front of French, who was making a valiant effort not to wince at the sight. When Mrs. Drinkwater's back was turned, Vincent spirited away the offerings and stuffed them into his pockets. He mumbled a greeting to me through a mouthful of crumbs.

"I assume you have a task for the three of us," I said to French.

"We're off to the docks again."

"The *Comet* sailed last night."

"Other shipping companies might have carried cargo for the Bradley Tool Company. It seems our only chance of catching up to the fellow, since your clumsiness prevented me from getting my hands on him yesterday."

I ignored that jab. "Do you have any idea how many shipping companies operate in London? It will be like finding a needle in a haystack."

"So you'd rather do nothing about those fellows who burst in here and delivered a good kicking to us? I'm not ready to forgive and forget just yet. I'd like another crack at them. But if you want to stay here where it's safe, I understand."

"I know exactly what you're doing, French. You're manipulating me, or attempting to, and doing a damned poor job of it. India Black is not easily provoked by shallow taunts."

At this remark, French lifted an eyebrow and he and Vincent exchanged a smirk.

I pressed on. "And I am especially not swayed by such a feeble attempt at machination as you just produced. I'm embarrassed for you, French." He attempted to look chastened and failed. I suppressed a smile. The fellow's finally learning how the game is played.

I turned to exit the kitchen. "When you two have finished stuffing yourselves, kindly let me know. The sooner we get to the docks, the sooner we'll solve this mystery and repay those chaps who split my lip."

It was a bright morning, with a breeze from the sea blowing the smoke from the tanneries and mills upriver away from the city, and making a visit to the wharves an almost pleasant prospect. Gulls plummeted from the sky to snatch bits and bobs from the brown waves. God knows what they were eating as I don't believe there's a fish alive that could survive the filthy water of the Thames. Small craft were bobbing about on the swells and the air was redolent with the smell of hemp, tar and fish, overladen with a briny tang. The docks had been busy on Sunday afternoon, but Monday morning had brought a new level of activity to the wharves.

In fact, I'd never seen such activity. Despite living within a few miles of London's docks all my life, I'd never troubled myself to set foot on them. Why would I? Consequently, the sight that now greeted my eyes was brand new. A forest of masts stretched away on the horizon. Workers in jaunty peaked caps and canvas smocks dodged nimbly about, wheeling barrows and humping bales of cotton and wool. Watermen plied the river in small craft, ferrying passengers and cargo upstream and down. Dozens of filthy creatures of indeterminate age and sex, London's "mud larks," prowled the tidal flats, looking for anything that might fetch a few pence.

The odor was overwhelming. On the morning breezes wafted the smell of coffee and sulphur, tea and molasses. We wandered past warehouses stuffed to the gills with cured hides and crates of horn, which emitted a stench that made me clamp my handkerchief to my nose. I took a shallow breath and inhaled a lungful of air laden with the scent of cloves and nutmeg, coal smoke, human waste, tar, lumber and rum.

If the smells were bewildering, the variety of men was stupefying. We passed labourers in rough clothes, their faces dyed blue from the indigo they'd been handling. Lascars roamed the wharves, dark faces shining in the pale river light, the Mussulmen among them sporting white turbans. Massive African sailors, with hard, ropy muscles and chiseled faces stalked among the bales and barrels, wicked-looking knives thrust into their waistbands. By comparison, the British seamen seemed small and gaunt, with faces tanned the colour of a fine saddle. Here and there, among the seafarers and the stevedores, strolled men of commerce, with tall hats and cigars in their hands, and trailed by frazzled clerks clutching sheaves of paper.

Did I mention the noise? Empty barrels clattered over the planks of the wharves as they were rolled back to warehouses to be refilled. The Africans chanted harsh melodies as they worked and our jolly Jack tars sang ribald songs to pass the time. The streets rang with the sound of hundreds of wagons jouncing along over the stones and the shouts of their drivers as they jockeyed for position. The chains from the cranes rattled ominously overhead. The sound of hammering was incessant, as ships were refitted and made ready for sail. Oars splashed in the water, captains shouted orders and here and there a goat bleated or a horse neighed. Men cursed, coughed, laughed and spit.

"Excellent idea you had, French," I observed gloomily. "We'll make short work of this. Why, there are only acres of docks to examine and hundreds of warehouses and ships. We should be finished by teatime."

French pivoted out of the way of a workman bearing a keg of nails, then had to swerve back to avoid being run down by a handcart. He took my arm and drew me to the relative safety of a nearby wall. Vincent followed and we huddled there, looking with dismay at the chaos that surrounded us.

"I may have underestimated the difficulty of this task," said French. "I'd planned to visit the warehouses to see if any cargo was being shipped by Bradley, but that would be a labour fit for Hercules."

"Who?"

"Never mind, Vincent." I was feeling rather irritated at having been dragged down to the docks on this fool's errand, and I was snappish. "We can't stand about here all day, French. What do you propose to do?"

"We find out wot ships are sailin' for India and then we find out if they got any cargo on board from that tool company."

"There are hundreds of ships on the river, Vincent."

"I can bloody well see that, India. But wot can you tell just by lookin' at 'em?"

"I don't follow you."

"Well," he said, with an exaggerated patience that put my teeth on edge. "If their masts and yards are shipped and their riggin' slack, they ain't goin' anywhere. We walk right past 'em wifout even stoppin'."

"Wonderful. You've just eliminated half our work. It will still take us days to investigate the rest."

Vincent blew out a long breath. "Wot's the matter wif you, India? This spy business ain't all fun and games. You can't shoot a Cossack every time you set foot out your door."

Being lectured by French is annoying; enduring the same treatment from Vincent is cause for rebellion.

"I'm going back to Lotus House."

"No, you ain't," Vincent said firmly. "Did you ever stop and fink that those 'ooligans know you opened that envelope and seen that bill o' ladin'? They know you're on to 'em and they may fink it's safer if you and French get the same treatment they give Mayhew. If that piece o' paper was worf killin' the colonel over, you and French might get your gullets slit."

"That is a far-fetched notion, Vincent." I gathered my skirts in my hand, in preparation for my dash through the chaos of the docks in search of a cab.

"He's right, India. We're in this up to our necks already," said French. "The best way to remove any threat is to uncover whatever fiendish plot is afoot."

"Good God. You're talking like Wilkie Collins now."

"Alright, then. Wait at Lotus House if you wish. Vincent and I'll do the hard work. Don't spare us a thought while you're relaxing with a cup of tea in your hand. We'll just be down here at the docks, combing through—"

"Oh, stop your gob, French. I'll stay and flail about with you."

"Stop bickerin' and listen up." Vincent tugged down his cap and assumed an air of authority. "'Ere's the plan. I'll round up some of me mates and we'll find out which ships are bound for India in the next fortnight. You two can visit the shippin' agents." He gave us a gap-toothed grin. "I doubt they'd let me in the door, anyway."

"There must be dozens of agents," I interjected.

Vincent sighed. "You could've visited six of 'em while you've been standin' 'ere complainin'."

Sometimes it's best to let the male creatures have their way. I don't recommend this course of action often, but it can be useful on occasion. You are then free to trot out your cooperation at a later date and extract something useful in return. With this stratagem in mind, I graciously assented to the division of labour that Vincent had proposed. French wanted to accompany me on the rounds of shipping agents, but I pointed out that we could cover twice as much ground if we split up. Besides, I had no doubt I'd have better luck at prizing information out of the clerks than French would, hampered as he was by the absence of breasts and a dazzling smile.

We arranged to meet back at our present location in a few

hours' time, and then Vincent hightailed it in search of his mates while French and I divvied up the docks. We wouldn't come close to visiting them all today, but we had to start somewhere.

I shall not bore you with a description of the mind-numbing hours that followed. Should I ever become a full-time member of the prime minister's staff, I shall insist on being assigned a fresh young lad, eager to prove his abilities and therefore apt to pant like an eager hound at the prospect of spending the day roaming in and out of warehouses and offices, repeating the same yarn ad nauseam and leaving no stone unturned until he'd accomplished his task. My ficti-tious young fellow would have to be made of sterner stuff than I. After two hours I had wearied of introducing myself as Ethel Perry, who desired to ship a large crate of furniture to her dear brother Frederick, stationed near Calcutta. This per-son had briefly met a Mr. Peter Bradley, who had confided that he frequently shipped cargo to Calcutta and that she could rely upon him to help her find a shipping agent to handle the transaction. Unfortunately, Mr. Bradley was out of the coun-try at the moment. Did this agent, perhaps, handle shipments for Mr. Bradley's firm, the Bradley Tool Company? At this point I had to endure not only a negative reply to my question, but also a sales pitch of astonishing duration and force, advis-ing me of the merits of the agent I had approached and the advantages of using the same to send my crate to India. Extracting myself from these conversations was a lengthy process. As I said, I had wearied of the matter only two hours into it, but I stuck it out for several hours more until I dragged myself back to my rendezvous with French and Vincent.

"Any joy?" asked French as I arrived. In addition to being

stubborn, men are so frequently unobservant. I was limp, sticky and footsore, and certainly did not look like a woman who'd had any success.

"No," I said tersely. "You?"

"Nothing."

"Me neiver," said Vincent. "But the boys are on it, and we'll see what they can turn up."


It had been a hard day's work, but in the hansom on the way back to Lotus House I found myself feeling oddly cheerful. Granted, I was bone-tired from walking the wharves and bored witless with the exertions of the afternoon, but at least we were a step closer to finding Mayhew's killers and the three coves who had used French and me as punching bags. And though I'd just spent the last few weeks dodging death and mayhem at the hands of those anarchist devils, I felt ready for action. There's nothing like the prospect of a mystery to stir the loins of a government agent. The existence of a few chaps who don't scruple at beatings and killings of the most savage variety adds an element of danger and a pleasant frisson to the situation. I was highly motivated to settle scores with the rapscallions who had invaded Lotus House and killed the poor colonel.

I must learn to guard against my irrational exuberance, for it's Sod's Law that just when there's a satisfactory prospect in the offing, something will turn up to remind you that man's lot is a dismal one and all ends in dust and ashes. In this case, it was not something but someone who arrived to remind me of that immutable lesson.

The hansom turned the corner and Vincent leaned out the window. "Oi. Are you movin' 'ouse, India?"

"What the deuce are you talking about?"

"There's a gang o' workers carryin' boxes and parcels into Lotus 'Ouse and a wall-eyed cove directin' traffic." Vincent's brow wrinkled. "And where'd them dogs come from?"

"Dogs?" I pushed him to one side and craned my neck out the window. There was indeed an unusual amount of activity surrounding my front door. A hired carriage was parked by the stoop and the driver, a portly gentleman with a red face, was standing dejectedly on the pavement while four collies pranced and shied about him, twisting their leads round his legs. Behind the carriage a cart was parked and three men laboured to remove a mountain of trunks and boxes and carry them into Lotus House. The wall-eyed cove Vincent had mentioned was barking orders at the workmen like a regimental sergeant. That seemed appropriate under the circumstances for it would require military efficiency to oversee the transfer of all this materiel, it being roughly equivalent to the amount Napoleon had needed for his invasion of Russia. The wall-eyed cove noticed our arrival and called a halt to the activity while he waited for us to disembark from the hansom, stalking over to greet us. At least I hoped he meant to greet us, as his visage was anything but welcoming. He was a villainous-looking fellow, with a pinched face and lips and one pale grey eye that stared straight at you while the other gazed off over your shoulder. It was deuced difficult to figure out whether the man was looking at you or admiring the scenery behind you, and I had to fight the urge to glance round to see if perhaps an attractive woman had hove into view.

He mumbled something inaudible. Well, I might have heard it but for the frenzied yapping of the collies.

"I beg your pardon?"

Then an eldritch screech slashed the air like a scimitar.

"You bloody bitches, pipe down! Fergus, stop dawdlin' and get my luggage inside. Good God, man! *I* could have had these bags inside by now. It's time for my tea and I'm bloody hungry and the bloody cook here seems to have lost her wits, if she had any to start with." A demented cackle echoed down the street.

"Blimey," said Vincent.

"Dear God," said French.

As for me, I was speechless. The Dowager Marchioness of Tullibardine had arrived at Lotus House.


The marchioness's major domo suppressed a smile. "Aye, it's her. Come down from Tullibardine to see Miss India Black. That'd be you, I suppose," he said, one eye boring into me. "I be Fergus, Her Ladyship's . . . " He paused for a moment as he considered how best to describe the relationship. I hoped he would be discreet for I wasn't up to contemplating the marchioness sharing a bed with this fellow. Not with his looks. Nor hers, for that matter. Fergus found the word for which he'd been searching. "Manservant," he concluded. His gaze shifted to French.

"How-de-do, Major."

"Hello, Fergus. Are you well?"

"Alright, considerin', you know." He cast a suggestive glance at the marchioness, who had wobbled out of the front door and was watching us intently. She's a doughty old bird, not much bigger than a flea and nearly as maddening. She looked much as I remembered her: the wizened face with the powder pressed into the cracks and a streak of rouge across each cheek, which gave her the appearance of a Sioux chief on the warpath. She peered at us through eyes cloudy from cataracts and her mouth hung open, showing the stumps of a few discoloured teeth.

French removed his hat and bowed stiffly. "Auntie."

*Auntie?*

"And how's my Sassenach nephew?" asked the marchioness.

*Nephew?*

"Ye two look like ye've been in the wars. Come in and have a drink. It'll buck ye up."

I recovered my composure. "I don't believe I need an invitation to enter my own home," I remarked, not without some asperity.

The marchioness hooted with laughter. "Still full o' spunk, are ye?"

She disappeared into the house and the rest of us trailed in after her, with varying degrees of enthusiasm. Fergus issued a set of instructions to the workman unloading the cart and started after us.

"'Ere," roared the carriage driver, over the yelping of the collies. "Wot am I supposed to do wif these 'ounds?"

Fergus stumped off and retrieved the pups, which proved to be a difficult task as the carriage driver had assumed the appearance of a maypole and it took a while to unwind the leads from the poor chap. Then, to my horror, Fergus led the dogs up the steps.

"Not in the house," I said, barring the door with my arm. The marchioness had disappeared. French and Vincent had gone into the study, from which I'd soon be evicting Vincent as he had no right to be privy to the family secrets I felt sure would be revealed now that the marchioness was in town. Fergus was poised in the open door with the collies milling about his feet and panting at their leads. I caught sight of Mrs. Drinkwater, her mouth frozen open in horror. The bints had come spilling down the stairs in their dressing gowns, which reminded me that in an hour's time I'd have a houseful of customers and the prospect of loosing four dogs and the marchioness on my clientele almost caused my heart to stop beating. I drew a deep breath.

"I will not allow those dogs in my house," I repeated.

The marchioness elbowed me to one side. "O' course they're comin' inside. Where do ye expect 'em to sleep? On the street?"

"I don't care where they sleep, as long as it's not in the house."

"Now if ye had a proper kennel . . ." mused the marchioness.

"Why would I have a confounded kennel?" I snarled.

"Don't snap at me. 'Tis your own fault ye dinna have the facilities to care for my pups." The old trout patted me on the arm. "Dinna fret yerself, my girl. They'll do alright on the bed with me. Now then, where's that pea-brained cook of yers? I want my tea and I want it now."

"I'll thank you to show a bit of respect for my servant," I said. The fact that I never accorded Mrs. Drinkwater the slightest courtesy was beside the point. She may be a pea-brained cook, but damn it all, she was *my* pea-brained cook and if she was going to be abused, I'd be the one doing it.

The marchioness headed for the kitchen and I foresaw bad things, very bad things, happening there if I did not head off the assault on Mrs. Drinkwater's domain. I scurried after the marchioness and that bloody Fergus took advantage of my absence as gatekeeper to shoo the dogs inside and drag them into the study. I checked my advance to deal with this development, but I heard raised voices from the kitchen and decided that the dogs must wait. Mind you, all the while this domestic drama was being played out, a curious group of dollies, eyes like saucers and tittering like a group of schoolgirls, was ranged up the stairs. The fleeting thought that things were spiraling out of control crossed my mind. I sent the bints upstairs with some roaring curses and dashed off to the kitchen.

Sure enough the marchioness was inspecting the place, lifting pot lids, muttering under her breath and cursing a blue streak. Mrs. Drinkwater had elected to retreat to a corner (very sensible of her, I thought) and had adopted an air of dignified restraint, leaning against the wall with her arms crossed. Or perhaps she'd merely propped herself up after an afternoon down at the local. In any event, she did not look happy.

The marchioness slammed down a lid. "Christ on his cross. You dinna expect me to eat that swill, do ye? Fergus!" The marchioness would have done well in the Royal Navy. You could have heard that voice in the crow's nest on a foul night in the roaring forties.

It was time I assumed command, but damned if I could figure out how to do it.

Fergus arrived, sans dogs. Now what could he have done with those four canines?

"Fetch us some tea, Fergus. I'm parched from my travels and there ain't a crumb worth eatin' in this godforsaken hole."

Mrs. Drinkwater came out of her corner like a prizefighter

who'd taken a few punches but wasn't to be counted out yet. "Listen here, you wicked biddy. This is my kitchen and I'm the cook here and if you want something to eat, you'll ask for it polite-like and be grateful for what you get."

I've never had occasion to be grateful for anything from Mrs. Drinkwater's kitchen, but I had to admire the old lush's spirit at defending her territory.

"Pipe down," muttered the marchioness, combing through some pantry shelves. "There's no jam here, Fergus. Not a drop. And not a biscuit to be seen."

"What do you call these, if not biscuits?" Mrs. Drinkwater produced a plate of blackened wafers and waved it under the marchioness's nose.

"Lord save us, I thought it was the coal for the stove. Here's some money, Fergus. Fetch us some provisions. And get a haunch for dinner tonight. I'm in the mood for a hearty meal after that dreadful journey."

"Are you going to allow this addled crone to come in here and take over my kitchen?" Mrs. Drinkwater demanded.

"Are you going to let this drunken sow fix my tea?" the marchioness demanded to know.

I've faced down Cossack guards and Russian spies and Scottish assassins, but confronted by these two withered beasts with fire in their breasts, I had to admit defeat. I turned on my heel and fled, back to the relative sanity of the study, where I found French trying to coax one of the collies off the delicate silk upholstery of a Queen Anne chair and Vincent attempting to pull one of the beasts out from under the sofa. The other two animals had made themselves at home *on* the sofa and were now having a nap. I sank into a chair and put my face in my hands.

"Where'd that bloody Fergus fellow get to?" Vincent asked. "These damned curs ought to be whipped."

"Fergus has gone to buy something for the marchioness to eat. Mrs. Drinkwater and the marchioness have squared off in the kitchen. I predict bloodshed. I just haven't decided who to murder yet."

French laughed. "You wanted answers, India. You'll get some now."

"I wanted a letter," I corrected him. "I did not expect that creaking, haggard, liver-spotted woman to appear on my doorstep. What am I to do with her? I can't put her up here."

"Why not?" asked the marchioness, who had tottered unnoticed into the study. "This is a whorehouse, ain't it? If there's one thing a whorehouse has plenty of, it's beds. I've already found a room to my likin' and had Fergus take up a few things."

I raised my face from my hands and stared at her in horror. "Not the room at the top of the stairs."

"You can't expect me to hike up and down these halls every day? Yes, the one at the top of the stairs will do nicely. It's charmin', what with all that blue damask and the silk drapes. Even got some pretty drawin's on the wall. In truth, I hadn't expected a brothel to be so attractive, but then I confess, I ain't ever set foot in one. Just goes to show ye, the world is full of surprises."

I agreed with her assessment, for I had not expected to return home today to find that the marchioness had arrived from Scotland with the intention of exercising the right of eminent domain over my bedroom, nor that my mahogany four-poster would soon be hosting a pack of flea-bitten hounds. Yes, the world is a surprising place.

"Ow," Vincent howled, sucking his thumb. "That bloody dog bit me."

"Serves ye right, ye stupid boy, for pullin' on her leg like that." The marchioness squinted at him. "Do I know ye, young feller?"

"I was up at that castle last winter, 'elpin' save the Queen from them hassassins."

The marchioness displayed her few teeth and a great deal of mottled pink gum. "So ye were. Ye got your skull split open, if I remember rightly."

"That I did," said Vincent proudly. "'Urt like the devil, too."

"Weel, weel. Glad to see ye again, ye young cub. Ye acquitted yerself weel in that affair. But don't be pullin' on my Maggie's leg, do ye hear?"

Vincent nodded. "Sorry 'bout that, M' Lady. 'Twon't 'appen again."

"I'm sure it won't, my boy. Yer a smart lad and don't need tellin' twice."

The street Arab and the Scottish aristocrat (and I use that term loosely) beamed at each other. I could swear they'd formed an alliance of sorts. Dear God, could it get any worse?

"Ye've got to be very careful with my Maggie. She's about to whelp."

Yes. Yes it could.

# EIGHT

This is the last time you'll hear me say such as this, so pay close attention: India Black folded. Usually, I'm two-thirds grit and one-third pepper but I didn't have the stamina to go even one round with the marchioness. I just sat back and let the wave that was the marchioness crash over me and plant me face-first in the sand. When Mrs. Drinkwater waltzed into the study in high dudgeon, complaining that Fergus had taken over her kitchen, I told the cook to feed the girls and then take off the rest of the night. At full pay, mind you. I was that upset. I sent Vincent up to Clara Swansdown's room to tell her to run the house for me tonight and under no circumstances to interrupt the cozy gathering in my study. Then I pushed one of those Scottish curs out of my favourite chair and sank into it, exhausted.

The marchioness and Vincent talked a blue streak, reliving our adventures at Balmoral and our success at preventing Her Royal Porcinity (that's Queen Vicky to you lot) from dying at the hands of fanatical Scottish nationalists. French chimed in from time to time, casting anxious glances at me all the while. I expect he thought I'd bite off his head if he enjoyed himself, but I was too shattered to make the effort.

Fergus returned and spent an hour in the kitchen, producing a tea the likes of which I'd never enjoyed before in Lotus House. He brought in a tray with a mountain of sandwiches, buttered toast and soft-boiled eggs. He apologized that he hadn't had time to whip up a cake or a batch of biscuits, then soothed the marchioness's complaints with a jug of fresh cream and a jar of Dundee marmalade. His tea was fragrant and hot. I had a taste, just to be polite, and then found myself wolfing down bread-and-butter sandwiches and toast with the rest of them.

"Glad to see ye eatin', India," said the marchioness. "Ye were lookin' a bit peaked."

"It's been a long day," I said. "And I've had a bit of a shock."

The marchioness cackled. "I assume yer talkin' about me."

"And Fergus, and Maggie, and the rest of them." The dogs were quiet now, having dined on the mince that Fergus had brought back with the other provisions. They were curled on the floor near the marchioness's feet, except for Maggie, who'd been given dispensation to sleep on the sofa, being on the verge, as she was, of popping out a litter of mewling pups.

The marchioness sat back with a satisfied yawn. "That was a proper feed, Fergus."

"Thank you, My Lady. I'll clear up now. May I get you something before I go?"

"A glass of whisky wouldn't go amiss. And my snuff box, Fergus."

I stiffened. I'd spent a hellish few days in the draughty castle at Balmoral during a Scottish winter, pretending to be a lady's maid to the marchioness, a situation arranged by French, which (now that I think of it) warranted some retaliation on my part. The worst of my tasks had involved dealing with the marchioness's snuff habit. She was fond of the stuff, but after ingesting it was prone to sneezes loud enough to set off avalanches in the Cairngorms. She produced a fair amount of moisture with those sneezes, and I'd toweled off the old woman and everything in the near vicinity too many times to recall. Then there was her vision, which was dicey when it came to distinguishing snuff from powder or salt or any other granular material. In short, the news that the marchioness wished to partake of snuff sent me dashing to the kitchen for an armful of linen.

The marchioness had her fingernail in a porcelain snuff box when I returned. I bolted across the room, intent on swaddling the old gal's face until the inevitable sneeze occurred, or I smothered her, whichever event might occur first. She inhaled heartily and her face screwed in preparation for soaking my study and I flung myself forward in desperation. As I passed Fergus he reached over and dexterously extracted a square of linen from my arms, which he deftly draped over the marchioness's countenance. A muffled explosion echoed through Lotus House. The marchioness blinked and Fergus rubbed her down briskly with the towel. Well, he was a damned sight quicker and more adept at this sort of thing than I had been in Scotland. I relaxed a bit for the first time since the dowdy aristocrat had materialized on my doorstep.

It occurred to me that I had been slipping unconsciously into the role of the marchioness's lady's maid, and that strategically that would place me at a significant disadvantage with the old trout. I needed to regain the initiative and letting Fergus tend to the marchioness's needs was a start. Consequently I dumped the load of linens into his arms and settled myself in a chair with a glass of brandy at hand. I had a stiff jolt of the medicinal liquid and immediately felt better.

The feeling lasted less than five seconds.

The marchioness made herself comfortable. She had of course occupied my favourite chair, closest to the fire. "Weel, now. I reckon it's time I told ye why I've left the comforts of hearth and home and come to London. 'Twas a dreadful journey for a woman of my age and infirmities and I hope ye appreciate the trouble I've gone to just so ye'll stop sendin' me those bloody letters."

"There's a modern invention you may not have heard of up there among the sheep. It's called the Royal Mail. You could have answered my questions in writing and saved yourself the trip."

The marchioness chuckled, which sounded like a maddened hen was trapped in the study, seeking escape.

"Aye, I could ha' done. But I dinna think that matters of importance to the family should be handled from a distance."

"Family matters," I said faintly. "What family matters?"

"Dinna be dim, India. I am referrin' to our family, o' course." She nodded at me, and then shot French a look that made him sit up and smooth his hair.

"You and French and the old lady are kin?" Vincent found this notion incredible.

So did I, although I'd already made the connection between

the marchioness and myself. She was surely the great-aunt who'd taken in my mother when she'd been banished from her home. French had introduced me as his cousin and the marchioness had referred to him as her "Sassenach nephew," which must mean that somewhere in my family tree, his branches intertwined with mine. The poncy bastard had actually spoken the truth.

It was a bit much to take in, frankly, like learning that fairies are real or that some politicians are indeed honest fellows. I couldn't quite believe that I had a family, let alone that it included a demented, snuff-inhaling, collie-loving marchioness from Scotland and the poncy bastard who'd irritated and attracted me in equal measure since the day I'd met him.

"Blimey," said Vincent, which reminded me that the odiferous lad was still present and there was no reason for him to be, unless the marchioness was about to disclose that Vincent and I were cousins or half brother and sister or something equally repugnant to contemplate. Even the Old Hirsute Character Upstairs wasn't that cruel.

"I believe it's time you left, Vincent," I said.

"But, hit's just gettin' interestin'," he protested.

The marchioness issued a maniacal laugh. The stumps of her ancient teeth winked in the firelight. "No need to shove the boy out the door, India. We dinna have a thing to be ashamed of, save the usual half-wits and nitwits. Just a reg'lar family."

I had no idea what constituted a regular family, or indeed any type of family, and told the marchioness so in a curt voice. "And why the devil have you kept this knowledge from me for so long? You've known I was your great-niece for months now." God help me, I sounded hurt. And desperate. India

Black is never hurt or desperate. With some effort, I smoothed my face and regarded the marchioness with a stony expression.

"Have another drink, India, and settle yerself. I'll tell ye the whole story."

Sound advice. I downed my glass of brandy and poured another. Then I subsided into my chair and resigned myself to listening to the old girl meander through the ancestral grounds. I no longer cared that Vincent was still in the room, drinking my good brandy and petting that damned collie bitch that was due to give birth any minute. Apparently, the two of them had made friends after the leg-pulling incident.

The marchioness's mouth flopped open and she stared at the ceiling, gathering her thoughts. I thought this might take some time, but to her credit the old girl waited scarcely a minute before launching into her tale.

"French tells me that ye've done some diggin' and found out about yer mother and that groom feller."

"Yes. The Earl of Clantham told me about that. We lived with him when I was small." I had tracked the old reprobate to his home on Portman Square a few weeks ago and wangled from him a version of the truth. He'd been quite open about hiring my mother, who'd been beautiful and sophisticated, as his companion and allowing me to live with the servants, though he'd been less keen on that part of the arrangement. He'd also taken pains to absolve himself of any responsibility for throwing my mother and me into the street when she had become ill and ugly, and of no further use to the man. I still seethed at my interview with the fellow, and amused myself with the idea of dropping by unexpectedly and throttling the man one night while he snuffled uneasily in his sleep. But that was a matter for another day.

The marchioness sighed, and to my surprise, her expression was melancholy. "She was a good girl, yer mother. And lovely, oh, my. The boys come runnin' from miles away, just for the chance of catchin' a glimpse of her. She was spirited, too, was Isobel. And willful. Much too willful, that girl. When Thomas Black took the job o' groom, she fancied herself in love with the feller. There was no talkin' to her. She set her cap for him and had to have him, even if it went against her father's wishes."

"You're speaking of my grandfather?"

"Aye. My brother Duncan. A good man, though stubborn. That's where Isobel got her spirit. And ye too, I reckon. I couldn't blame Duncan for wantin' more for his daughter than a bloody groom. After all, she was the heiress."

"'Eiress to wot?" asked Vincent, fondling Maggie's ears. "Women don't in'erent nuffink."

The marchioness smiled indulgently. "Not usually. Not here in England. But the peerage o' Scotland is different. Scottish titles pass to the heirs general, not just to male heirs, unless the charter from the monarch says that only menfolk are eligible. In my view, it's a fine thing that women can inherit. They're a lot less likely to throw away their estates on horses or dice, though it's been known to happen, o' course. Anyway, that's the way things are in Scotland. We do things different up there, my boy. That's why we're a superior breed to you Sassenach."

"And so my mother was the eldest daughter of your brother Duncan?"

"Your *grandfather* Duncan. Aye."

I stole a glance at French. Here was an interesting development for the poncy bastard, I thought smugly. I was an heiress. Then it occurred to me that he might already know this. I would have to apply some persuasive methods to his nibs when I got him alone.

"Your grandfather was the seventh Earl of Strathkinness," the marchioness said. "Until Duncan's time there had always been a male heir to inherit the title. But Duncan and his wife didn't have a son."

"Only Isobel," said French. "Your mother."

"And that's when the whole bloody thing went wrong," muttered the marchioness, swilling whisky and waving the empty glass in the air. Fergus appeared silently at her side and freshened her drink.

"Isobel decided she was in love with that damned groom and Duncan sent her off to me so she'd get over the bloody feller. Only by that time, the damage had been done. She was with child. Poor Duncan. The news nearly killed him. He banished your mother and told her not to set foot on the estate again. Then he locked himself away in his study and drank himself to death."

"What about my grandmother?"

The marchioness pursed her lips grimly. "She was a weak 'un, was yer granny. She should've kicked Duncan in the tallywags and told him to take the news like a man and see that the title went to Isobel, but she didn't. She was half scared of Duncan's temper, and a bit of a ninny. I'm pleased to see that ye ain't a bit like her, India."

"You can call India a lot of things, but 'weak' ain't one of 'em," said Vincent loyally. I felt the prick of a tear at the boy's devotion, but I knuckled it away. It was just as likely that the little mercenary was already anticipating how he could get his hands on a portion of my inheritance. I'd have to keep an eye on him or he'd be haring off to Scotland to help himself to the family jewels. Assuming there was an inheritance, of course. After all, the marchioness had referred to me as an heiress. This being the most interesting feature of our conversation to date, I thought it time to press the matter.

"You're telling me that I am the heiress to the estate and title of the Earl of Strathkinness?"

"Wot do you call a lady earl?" asked Vincent.

"Countess," said French.

"India a countess?" Vincent found the notion so ridiculous that he burst into laughter, clutching his stomach and hooting loudly. Maggie raised her head and looked at him severely, as did the marchioness. Frankly, I found the whole scenario so surreal that I began to laugh. The marchioness directed her steely gaze at me, and while Fergus and the collies might have quailed before such a look, I'm afraid I found the old bag's severity a new cause for mirth.

"You're having me on," I sputtered, though for the life of me I couldn't quite figure out why the marchioness would do such a thing.

"Pull yerself together, lass. I know it's a bit of a shock, but yer the rightful owner of a fair parcel of Scottish land and a big house and ye need to start behavin' as such."

I shot a glance at French to see how he was coping with this fantastical nonsense and caught him grinning broadly. I should think most women will understand what I felt when I saw that smile: an irrational anger. We're complicated creatures, we females of the species, and while I suspected that French's pleasure was genuine, I was furious that he'd known this information for some time and failed to acknowledge the fact. Not to mention that he'd involved me in a number of dicey situations in which the current Countess of Strathkinness might have become the deceased Countess of Strathkinness. A murmured warning just as we were going into battle against Russian agents or Scottish assassins wouldn't have gone amiss. "Careful, India," he said. "Remember that you're a member of the ruling class now and shouldn't take unnecessary risks if you want to live to enjoy that title of yours."

Consequently I rounded on the chap.

"You poncy bastard." That wiped the smile from his face. "Exactly how long have you known this?"

"Och, settle yerself, India." The marchioness intervened. "I told the boy it wasn't his place to tell ye the truth."

"Then why didn't you? You had plenty of opportunity, while I was reading you to sleep each night up in Scotland. And I've written you a half-dozen letters. You could have replied to at least one of them."

The marchioness looked uneasy for a minute, sucking her few remaining teeth noisily. "Much as it pains me to admit it, I was wrong. I should ha' told ye after we finished our work at Balmoral."

"Our work? So you *were* working for the government."

The marchioness looked at me slyly. "Oh, 'twas nothin' formal, ye understand. I was just helpin' out my nephew. And ye."

God, a more vexatious woman had never lived. I was about to retort that her assistance had been unnecessary and that she'd created more problems than she'd solved, but then I remembered that there was more the crone could tell me.

"You've known of my existence for twenty-eight years. Why did you wait so long to start looking for me?"

The marchioness looked away from me, into a darkened

corner of the room. Her chin trembled and there was a fine tremor in her hand as she raised the glass of whisky to her lips. She drank unsteadily, and wiped her mouth on her sleeve. She looked every inch the broken old woman.

I wasn't buying that pap. "Well?" My voice was cold.

"Yer mother told me that she and Black were goin' up to London. She promised to write, and for a while she did. But after Black died of the typhus, the letters trailed off until they finally stopped entirely. I sent a man to London to find her, but he couldn't. She'd gone to ground; there was no trace o' her to be found. Knowin' yer mother as I did, I dinna think she wanted me to know what had become of her. She was proud, ye see. I let it be. There's things on this earth ye can't change. Ye can only endure 'em."

"You gave up on my mother, yet you tried to find *me*. Why?"

"Because yer the countess now. Yer granny died a year ago, and the title has been vacant too long. Ye need to claim it. If ye don't, there'll be fellers jumpin' on it like a dog on a bone. There's a few already sniffin' around. 'Twouldn't be right if some gormless young idiot got the title and the estate. We're an ancient family, India, and I need ye back in Scotland. Then ye need to marry as soon as we can find ye a suitable mate and ye need to start whelpin' bairns."

Now put yourself in my shoes for a minute and ponder the situation. In the past twenty-four hours I'd put up with a lot: anarchists, Russian spies, a beating, the blood-spattered corpse of Colonel Mayhew, the arrival of the marchioness with a pregnant collie, and now the news that I was a countess who needed to marry and produce an heir and a few spares with all possible speed. What would you do under the circumstances?

Right. I can see you're the sensible type and would do just as I did. I got drunk.

I woke with a splitting headache and the impression that a herd of camels had paraded through my mouth. My spirits were not improved when I noticed that I was not sleeping in my own bed but in a spare room down the hall, fitted out with the bare necessities of a whorehouse: a bed, a washstand, a plain wooden chair, and a thick rug so the chaps wouldn't have to put their bare feet on the cold floor. My clothes lay neatly over the back of the chair and someone had managed to stuff me into one of my nightgowns. I do hope it wasn't Vincent.

I staggered to the door and bellowed for Mrs. Drinkwater. That estimable lady appeared in a thrice, bearing a medicinal glass of brandy. It appeared she'd been in need of physic herself as she reeked of alcohol. For once, I didn't mind that she was half pickled, so long as she was capable of fetching me a cup of coffee and a gallon of water.

"That bloody woman . . ." said Mrs. Drinkwater.

I collapsed onto the bed, having expended all my energy in summoning my cook. "Whatever you're going to say about the marchioness, I agree with you. Now, please, I beg you. Bring me some coffee."

Mrs. Drinkwater tottered off, muttering under her breath about "Scotch bitches" and "confounded dogs."

The marchioness poked her head around the door. "So yer up, are ye? 'Bout time. I had a devil of a time dealin' with your customers last night."

"What?" I sprang off the bed in alarm, and immediately

wished I hadn't. I grasped the back of the chair but the room persisted in spinning. "Don't tell me . . . You didn't . . . Surely to God, you couldn't have . . ."

The marchioness grinned dementedly. "I handled things for ye. Not to worry. We took in a barrel full of money last night."

*We?*

"If I'd known the trade was this lucrative, I might have set meself up in it years ago. I'm in need of a new carriage and at this rate I could pay for it before Candlemas."

I pinched my temples between my thumbs, and then massaged my face with my palms. "French?"

The marchioness waved a hand. "I sent him away, naturally. He looked shocking bad, with that eye of his. Didn't want him scarin' off the punters, did we?" She paused in this astonishing recitation to eye me critically. "Come to think of it, it's probably a good thing that ye weren't around either. Ye look like death served cold."

"That's considerably better than I feel."

"That's hardly a surprise, is it? Ye drank enough brandy to drown a draught horse."

"In my defense, I had some startling news yesterday."

"Aye," the marchioness said complacently, as if she'd had nothing whatsoever to do with delivering the information that had set me off on my binge. "I could see ye were jolted."

I looked at her sourly. "Wouldn't you be?"

"To learn that I'm a member of one of the most ancient and noble families in all of Scotland, with a title and an estate? Och, I'd be devastated at that news," she said, in a voice that dripped with sarcasm.

Mrs. Drinkwater hooked a foot around the door and popped it open with her hip while the china rattled ominously on the tray she carried. She sat it down on the bed, studiously ignoring the marchioness. I noticed the cook had brought only one cup. She'd have to do better than that; a shortage of china would not discourage the marchioness. Which reminded me that I'd better seize the single cup before the marchioness latched onto it. I did so with alacrity and poured myself some of the thick slurry that Mrs. Drinkwater optimistically refers to as coffee. This morning, the foul brew tasted like ambrosia. I downed a cup of the stuff as quickly as I could and poured myself another. The marchioness regarded me with a look of amusement.

"Do ye drink a lot, India? Yer grandfather loved the bottle, and it was the ruin of him."

"I usually exercise some restraint. There are exceptions, however, such as when the bloody Dowager Marchioness of Tullibardine appears on my doorstep. When are you leaving?"

The marchioness cracked a grin. "Don't ye worry, India. I wouldna dream of runnin' off and leavin' ye to deal with the situation by yerself."

Just what I had feared.

"As soon as ye've put things to rights here, we'll pack ye up and move ye home."

That was a bit of a facer. Lotus House *is* my home. I had no intention of moving to the land of heather and bagpipes. I am not fond of the Great Highland Warpipe and the prospect of listening to the sounds of cats fighting for the rest of my days did not appeal. I said as much to the marchioness.

She grinned. "Aye, ye've built a nice little nest for yerself here. But ye can't have the title and the estate unless ye come to Scotland and claim it. Yer a bright lass. I'll give ye time to think it over, and then we'll head north."

She patted my hand and wobbled out of the room. My head was gyrating, and I didn't think it was due solely to last night's drink. I swallowed the rest of my coffee and tried to remember what life had been like before French and Dizzy and the marchioness had entered it. I didn't have much time to ruminate on those tranquil days for Mrs. Drinkwater returned, huffing from her climb up the stairs.

"There's a gennelman to see you."

I groaned. It was far too early in the day to transact business and while I hadn't seen a mirror yet, I suspected my appearance was far from enticing. "Send him away, Mrs. Drinkwater. With my compliments, of course. Ask him to come back this evening around seven."

"After all these years, I cannot wait even a few hours more to see you, my dear." The voice was a deep baritone, husky and attractive, and belonged to Philip Barrett.

# NINE

Now my first thought was that this was a deuce of a time to be caught at a disadvantage. My hair was tangled, my vision slightly blurry, my lip bruised and cut, and my nightgown was wrinkled and looked as if a drunk woman had thrashed around in it during a fitful night's sleep, as indeed had happened. But if I've learned one lesson in life it's how to put on a show. I jumped from my bed and threw myself into Philip's arms, smothering his face with kisses which he returned with increasing enthusiasm. Mrs. Drinkwater gaped at us. As if noticing the cook's presence for the first time, I stepped away from Philip and smoothed my hair. Then I gestured languidly at a chair and cocked my head discreetly in Mrs. Drinkwater's direction. Philip caught my signal and smiled.

"Do have a seat," I told him. "Mrs. Drinkwater, please bring more coffee for my guest and fetch my dressing gown and slippers for me. And, Mrs. Drinkwater? See that we're not disturbed." I gave her a meaningful look and she shot me one of dismay, and possibly terror, at the prospect of restraining the marchioness from barging into the room to meet my gentleman caller.

I gave Philip a radiant smile. "You're looking well. The Continent must agree with you." I'd caught just the merest glimpse of him at the tavern when he'd met Captain Tate. Today was my first chance to really observe my former lover. He did look a peach. His golden hair was bright from long months in the sun and his face was smooth and tan. The hazel eyes were still full of mirth, and his shoulders bulked large under the elegantly tailored jacket he wore. A thick gold chain dangled from his watch pocket and his boots were shined to a gloss. He looked very prosperous and I told him so.

"I've a few things going," he said, with more than a hint of pride. Ah, pride. Every man's downfall. I'd soften him up and then find out what sort of projects he had working. By the time I'd flattered and flirted, he'd be dying to tell me just what a success he'd become. But first things first; we had a bit of history between us and it's best to either clear the air or obfuscate matters completely so as to move on to the present.

He was staring at me with some concern. "I say, India. What's happened to your face? It almost looks as if someone has struck you."

"It's my own fault. I took a tumble on the stairs the day before yesterday." I needed to distract him, so I allowed my gaze to wander admiringly over him. "It's been a long time," I said. "I've missed you."

He smiled roguishly. "You must have. You've been looking for me. How did you know I was back in London?"

It wouldn't do to confess the truth, so I lied without the slightest hesitation. "One of my customers must have mentioned that you were here. You know how it is; if you want to find out the latest gossip, visit the nearest brothel."

"Ah, yes. Which customer was that?"

I wagged a finger at him playfully. "I never kiss and tell. But he did me a service. I was distraught when you had to leave England."

"Not as distraught as I was." He laughed, but gently, as though the memory of fleeing to the Continent after his failed attempt to steal the Rajah's Ruby had been an adventure rather than a disaster.

"I had hoped you'd come back sooner," I said, which was patently untrue but I said it with conviction and I do believe the chap bought it.

"I would have done so, but that damned Harold White proved to be a confounded nuisance. He bore an almighty grudge against me, even if I didn't steal that gem of his. I tried to slip into England several times, but he had a man in every port. I made it to Portsmouth once and had to turn right around and catch the next ship back to France to avoid being arrested."

"But White has given up the pursuit?"

"He has. I've heard from one of my contacts that he finally returned to America."

"So you're a free man?"

"For the moment." He smiled at me and my stomach fluttered. Damn, but the fellow was attractive.

He gazed around the small room. "These are humble surroundings for the madam of the house."

His eyes caught mine, and I could see a challenge there. I had known from the moment that I'd begun to search for Philip that he would learn that I was no longer a mere tart. Some helpful fellow would have told him that India Black was looking for him and Philip could find her any day of the week at Lotus House, for she was the madam of that august institution. Well, the helpful fellow probably wouldn't have phrased it that way, but you get my drift. Philip would set to contemplating how a beautiful (albeit clever and ambitious) whore had found the dosh to open such a fine establishment. He'd remember that the last time he'd seen the Rajah's Ruby it had resided in his case, which was separated from my room by an unlocked door. And he'd certainly recall that I'd been struck suddenly with a horrible illness and demanded that he go in search of a maid to assist me, thereby leaving me alone for several minutes with Harold White's jewel just a few feet from my sickbed. In Philip's place, I'd have been, shall we say, skeptical. Allaying Philip's suspicions would take a bit of finesse, but it was nothing I couldn't handle.

"Indeed, they are. But this is not my room." Mrs. Drinkwater returned with my robe and slippers and I donned them, not at all abashed that I'd been sitting around in my nightgown blathering with Philip. He'd seen the goods before, and on more than one occasion. "I've taken in an old abbess who is down on her luck. She's staying in my room for a few days." Mrs. Drinkwater snorted. I skewered her with a look that sent her scurrying out of the room.

"That ancient mother downstairs who's ordering the girls around?"

His words struck a chill in my heart. I was going to have to do something about the marchioness and soon. At the moment, however, downstairs and out of my hair was the safest place for her.

I summoned a weak grin. "She's a firecracker, isn't she?"

"A bloody cannon, more like. If you're not careful, she'll be running the place soon and put you back to work." He crossed one elegantly trousered leg over the other and looked at me appraisingly. "You've done well for yourself, India. I knew you were a goer, but I never thought you'd pull together the ready to buy a place like this."

I prefer these direct attacks. No need to waste time on feinting and darting hither and yon; just open up with the artillery and charge. Easy to repel, though, if you know what you're doing.

"I had a patron," I said. "Harold White."

Philip's face lost some of its smooth composure. He blinked. "White?"

I thought that would throw him. I pressed the attack by shrugging apologetically. "He took a shine to me, after that visit to his house. He used to come up to see me in London. When he told me he was going back to St. Louis, he offered to set me up here."

"White paid for this house?" Philip asked, incredulous.

"Yes," I said. Well, it wasn't quite a lie as the American millionaire *had* paid for my brothel, though he hadn't known it. I'd used the proceeds from the sale of his precious ruby to fund the purchase of the building and the contents and to set up business.

I stood up and walked over to Philip, whose mouth still hung agape. I plopped down in his lap and ran a hand through his hair. He responded automatically by putting his arm around me but I could see his heart wasn't in it. Yet.

"I am sorry, Philip. I knew White was hunting you, but I was sure he wouldn't catch you. You're far too intelligent to be caught by the likes of him. And I did my best to point him in the direction of that Ashton fellow."

As expected, this news cheered Philip immensely, as he'd thought Rupert Ashton had snatched the gem from under his nose. Ashton was a jewel thief, you see, like Philip, and he'd wangled an invitation to White's house in Devon, just as Philip had, for the sole purpose of relieving White of ownership of the Rajah's Ruby. There was no love lost between the two men, and that's to my advantage. I knew that the mention of Ashton's name would anger Philip. It's all complicated, I know, but the important bit is that I ended up with the ruby and Philip had to hightail it to the Continent wondering whether Ashton had stolen the gemstone from Philip's case or I had been involved somehow. I'd given some thought as to the story I'd tell Philip if ever he reappeared in my life, and now I'd laid it out for him. When I'd concocted it, I had thought only to offer Philip an explanation and brush him off. But his involvement in this Mayhew matter had changed the situation and now I needed him to believe my tale and to trust me, at least to the point that I could penetrate his defenses and learn exactly what that involvement might be.

I leaned my cheek against his and sighed deeply, just to show the chap how pleased I was that he'd returned to the Big Smoke. He patted me absently, still mulling the information I had shared with him. It was time to bring him back to the present.

I fingered his gold chain admiringly. It was attached to a handsome timepiece, which I pulled from his pocket. I whistled softly. "Ooh, look at you. That's a work of art you've got there. Cost a pretty penny, too. Are there any jewels left in France?"

He smiled. "A few."

"And did you leave any virgins in *L'hexagone*?"

That made him laugh, and he gave me a squeeze. I relaxed a little at that, for it signified that we were moving back to our old ways together.

"I've been saving myself for you," he said, burying his mouth in the hollow where my neck met my shoulder.

I know I've been wittering on about French and how anxious I was to get the poncy bastard in my bed, provided he could be persuaded to forget that precious fiancée of his, but I'll be damned if Philip's lips didn't arouse a powerful feeling in me. I won't apologize. It's unnatural for a woman of my youth and vigor to behave like a nun and French had been no help at all in that department, given his propensity to act like a virgin on her wedding night. Philip's touch aroused a lust I hadn't felt for some time and I grasped his head between my palms and angled it so that I had a clear field of fire. Then I pressed my mouth to his. His lips were as soft and pliable as I remembered, and I spent a good deal of time reacquainting myself with every tasty morsel of that delectable mouth, nibbling on his lower lip and easing the sting of my teeth with soft caresses from my tongue. He cinched his arms around me and hugged me tighter. There was heat building between us, and suddenly Philip stood and carried me to the bed. He dropped me rather unceremoniously, which in the old days would have been merely the prelude to greater athletic endeavours from us both, but today the shock of hitting the bedcover served as a reminder that my dalliance with Philip was duty, not pleasure.

I needed information, not to scratch an itch that had been building since I'd met French. The thought of French returned me to my original objective in locating Philip, namely winkling information from him about the stolen arms.

Philip launched himself at me but as he did I rolled sideways off the bed and sprang to my feet. He looked up at me in astonishment.

I gathered my dressing gown around me and stood panting, a pained smile on my face. "Dear boy, you've quite swept me off my feet."

"Have I? Then what the devil are you doing out of bed?"

"As much as I'd love a frolic, I've got to attend to some business."

"You own the place, India. Tell that old bird downstairs to handle things for you."

He reached across the bed for me and I took a step back. I smiled hastily, for I didn't want to discourage the chap.

"Now that you're back in London, we've plenty of time to get reacquainted."

Philip winked at me. "I should like to start now."

I took his hand. "As would I. But I've got to leave here soon and I must bathe and dress."

"You look inviting to me just as you are. Rather sleepy and rumpled."

I smiled at him fondly. "What a smoothboots you are. Tell me where I can reach you and I'll send word when I've finished my business and sorted out the girls and the customers. Then we'll have a proper rendezvous." This last I said in a husky voice that was full of promise. I've worked on that voice and it's been very effective with men, if I do say so myself.

Unfortunately it did not elicit the desired response from Philip. I'd been fishing for an address. I'd planned to hire a few street urchins to stake it out and report to me on Philip's movements. But Philip sidestepped my enquiry with ease.

"I'm afraid I've some affairs of my own to see to this week. It would be best if I contacted you."

I pouted a bit, to show him how unsatisfactory this arrangement was, but the chap held firm. He wasn't going to trust me yet. Wise man.

"What's your business?" I asked him. "A house in Belgravia with an absent owner and a safe full of gemstones?"

Philip stood up and adjusted his clothing, tightening his cravat and arranging the creases in his trousers. "I've given up that work for the moment. I'm into something else. Much less dangerous than climbing around on rooftops. And I can stop praying that the old butler won't come charging into the room with a service revolver while I'm cracking a safe."

"Oh? What are you up to now?"

He put a finger to his lips. "Can't say much, my dear. Even to you. But it's as close as anything can come to being a sure thing. I'm piling up the dosh. In a few months, I plan to set up my own empire. I'll hire the best cracksmen and fingersmiths and put them to work. I'll plan the operations and fence the goods and if things get hot, I know where to send my boys and how to get them there without a hitch. Running from White was a useful exercise, actually. I know how to avoid the police in a half-dozen countries. I'll make a fortune and live like a king." He smiled dreamily, in contemplation of the criminal monarchy he proposed to establish.

"You'll need a queen," I observed.

"Have you someone in mind?" He shot me a teasing grin.

"You'll want someone bright and ambitious and beautiful, of course." I put a finger to my chin and pretended to think.

"Are you saying you might be interested in the position?" asked Philip. He swept a hand around the room. "You'd leave all this behind?"

"Who says I have to give it up? You want an empire, don't you? There isn't any reason we couldn't expand operations and build a score of Lotus Houses around the country. And in Paris and Berlin and Brussels." I knew the idea would tempt Philip and I was rather proud that I'd thought of it. In fact, I wish I had earlier. Things were now complex, given French's newly declared interest in me, my role as a British agent and the fact that I was an heiress, though I had no idea what that meant. There are heiresses and then there are heiresses, and I'd want to see the size of the house and accounts of the estate before I gave up Lotus House, regardless of what the marchioness might think. Her idea of a proper house was probably a hovel with a kennel for a hundred hounds attached.

"I say, you might be onto something." Philip looked thoughtful.

"We have a great deal to discuss when we meet next."

Philip looked sly. "Perhaps we could talk another time. There are other things I'd prefer to do at our next meeting than converse."

I smiled and hoped to hell that Philip couldn't see that the prospect that seemed so pleasing to him left me feeling singularly nonplussed. My word, this was getting convoluted. Well, you can worry or you can work, so I hustled Philip out the

door with a lingering kiss and the promise of another day and
went off to have a bath and a think.


I was hoping to have a long soak in the tub, scrubbing away
the effects of last night's binge and pondering my next move
with respect to Philip. I'd known I wouldn't be able to pry his
secrets from him at our initial meeting, but future assigna-
tions with the fellow would be fraught with danger. Oh, I
don't mean the throat-slitting kind of danger. No, I mean the
peril posed by a handsome blond chap with hazel eyes, a lazy
smile and absolutely no morals at all, one who would expect
us to pick up right where we had left off. And I will admit that
I'd led him to believe we would. I sighed. Perhaps that had
been unwise. Perhaps I should have chosen a different tack
with Philip, though for the life of me I couldn't think of an
approach more likely to loosen a fellow's tongue than a tumble in the hay. You might even say it was my duty to bed Philip,
though I suspect French would disagree.

Dear French is such a different creature from Philip. I suppose I'm rather drawn to French's public-schoolboy persona,
with his code of honour and principled behaviour, until the
same ethical standards collide with my desire to sweep him
off his feet. But I've always had a fondness for rascals and
rakehells, and Philip qualified as both. What made the situation even more untenable for me was that Philip appeared to
be involved in some nasty business this time. Philip's kiss
could not erase the vision in my mind of Colonel Mayhew's
blood-spattered room. There was also the matter of those
three thugs charging into Lotus House and pummeling me.
At this very moment, Philip might be sitting down to a glass

of beer with those fellows. And then there was French, who was surely the better man, only I might never know that for certain if the poncy bastard insisted on being such a ruddy gentleman.

I was lying half asleep in my now-tepid water, thinking about the dilemma I faced, when Mrs. Drinkwater barged in.

"She's a terror," complained Mrs. Drinkwater as she poured a pail of scalding water into my bath.

"I don't suppose you're talking about one of the girls?" I asked gloomily.

"There's not a whore alive who could cause as much trouble as that confounded woman."

I suspected Mrs. Drinkwater's assessment of the marchioness was an accurate one. "What's she done now?"

The cook snorted. "What ain't she done? Them dogs of hers has the run of the house. The girls traipse into your study anytime they want just to have a natter with the witch. And that chap she brung along? What's his name? Angus? Douglas?"

"Fergus," I answered.

"He thinks he runs the kitchen. He won't even let me boil water. Says I couldn't make a proper cup of tea if my life depended on it."

This happened to be true, but I didn't think that now was the time to break the news to Mrs. Drinkwater.

The litany of complaints continued. "And that march's nest, or whatever she calls herself? This morning she ordered me to fix her hair for her. *Ordered* me, she did. I told her I don't fix hair. I'm the cook and the housekeeper and I don't lift a finger when it comes to hair. I guess she got that through her head. She had one of the girls do it for her, not that it looks like much, because there's not a lot to work with, if you understand me."

I did. While portraying the marchioness's maid at Balmoral, I'd waged war against her frazzled locks more times than I cared to remember.

"I'll have a word with her," I said.

"It'll have to be more than a word. It'll have to be a whole damned sermon. How long is the old bag staying?"

I was curious about that myself.

Mrs. Drinkwater lingered for a few minutes more, grumbling incessantly until I asked her to rustle up some sandwiches for me.

"Alright, but don't you be surprised if that awful man interferes again. If the sandwiches aren't fit to eat, it won't be my fault."

I cheered up a bit at this news, remembering the tasty tea Fergus had provided. If I could only figure out a way to send Mrs. Drinkwater north with the marchioness and retain that inestimable man.

The cook disappeared, to be replaced by Clara Swansdown, formerly known as Bridget Brodie from Ballykelly. Clara's my most reliable girl and if I have to be away from Lotus House for an evening, I trust her to run the show for me. She marched in and shut the door behind her, upended the pail on the floor and sat down on it.

"Sure, and by now you'll have heard about last night," she said, frowning at me.

My heart sank. For a moment I contemplated putting my head underwater and drowning myself.

"The marchioness?" My voice was faint.

Clara nodded vigorously.

"What happened?"

"She sent Sir Alfred packing."

"Packing?"

"Threw him out the door," Clara confirmed. "Landed on his bum in the middle of the street."

"The marchioness tossed Sir Alfred down the steps?" This was difficult to believe, as Sir Alfred was a podgy bloke and the marchioness, soaking wet, weighed about as much as a six-year-old.

"It was that Fergus chap who done it. He may be old, but he's strong."

"Ye gods," I said, pinching the bridge of my nose. "What did Sir Alfred do to deserve such treatment?"

"Said the Scots were an ignorant bunch of savages who were so stupid they couldn't even think up trousers."

"I see."

"Sir Alfred said he wouldn't be back here, and he'd tell his chums not to visit here again either."

I groaned. "Thank you for telling me, Clara. I'll send a message to Sir Alfred right away and smooth things over. I suppose it'll cost me a few free hours with his favourite girl. That's Molly, isn't it?"

"Yes, ma'am. Ma'am? The marchioness is a grand gal and all the girls like her, but she's got a tongue on her like a razor. Some of the customers aren't used to that. Is she going to be here long? If she's staying for a bit, you might want to have a word with her about being a little kinder to the gents. I mean, I know you're related and all, but still, this is your house." Clara blushed.

"How'd you know we're related?"

"She told us you were. Said you were her favourite niece."

"I'd hate to see how she treats her least favourite," I grumbled as I reached for the towel.

The marchioness was sprawled on the sofa in my study, snoring softly, with Maggie the bitch curled around her feet. Fergus was asleep in one of the chairs, snuffling like a buffalo with his head tilted back and his mouth agape. The other three dogs had made themselves at home on the furniture. One lifted its head as I came into the room and curled a lip at me. I curled a lip right back, then slammed the door. If I had it to do over, I wouldn't. The slamming door woke the rest of the dogs, who erupted into a snarling, barking frenzy, dashing about looking for something or someone to bite. Fergus sprang to his feet and fetched the poker from the stand by the fireplace, turning to brandish it at me and shouting some kind of Gaelic war cry. The marchioness mumbled something I could not hear over the cacophonous roar and turned over in her sleep.

"Aye, it's you," said Fergus, lowering the poker and glaring at me. "You shouldna wake us like that." He made a feeble attempt to quiet the dogs.

I closed my eyes. "That noise is giving me a headache. How can the marchioness sleep through that?"

I knew the answer to that question from my days as lady's maid to the marchioness up at Balmoral. She never slept when people usually did. She'd be up half the night, demanding to be read to from the Bible or drinking whisky into the wee hours. No wonder she needed a nap during the daytime.

"Did you toss one of my customers out into the street last night?" I asked Fergus.

"Aye, I did. A fat bastard who insulted the marchioness."

"I'll thank you never to do that again, Fergus." My voice was like iron.

Fergus looked sullen. "I willna let anyone ridicule the mistress."

"No doubt she deserved the abuse," I snapped. "That fat bastard is one of my best customers."

The marchioness opened one eye and stretched luxuriously. "He's a rude bastard, as well as fat. Why d'ye tolerate the feller?"

"This is my house, and I'm the one who decides whether a customer is welcome. I'll thank you both to keep your noses where they belong. If I'm not here to run things, then Clara Swansdown is in charge, and you'll do as she says." By this time I was nearly shouting. "And in heaven's name, what the devil were you two doing hobnobbing with the clients anyway?"

The marchioness pursed her lips. "We were just lookin' for some entertainment, y'see. What's the harm in a glass or two with the chaps? Everything was goin' splendid until that idiot mouthed off about the Scots."

"And then you had to defend your honour?"

The marchioness nodded vigorously, completely missing, or perhaps ignoring, my sarcasm. "Precisely."

"In the future, I'll thank you to stay away from the clients. Go to the theatre, or the music hall. Read a book. Pet your damned collies. But whatever you do, do not step foot out of this study."

"How am I goin' to get to me bed?" asked the marchioness innocently.

I gave her the look I usually reserve for tarts.

She gave me her toothless smile. "Ain't it time for tea yet? I'm famished. Fergus?"

But her loyal retainer had already slipped from the room. Mrs. Drinkwater would not be happy and I suppose I should have pattered off to the kitchen and sent Fergus packing, but I was hungry too, and reckoned my chances of an edible meal to be substantially greater with the dour Scot in the larder.

French arrived, which set the dogs to barking again, and then Vincent breezed in, his ugly mug breaking into smiles that stimulated the canines once more. By the time they'd quieted down and the marchioness and French and Vincent had exchanged pleasantries, Fergus had returned with the tea tray and we all fell on it like starving wolves. If I allowed this to continue, Mrs. Drinkwater was likely to storm out and I'd have to look for a new cook and housekeeper, a prospect I did not relish. Have you ever tried to hire household staff for a brothel? Good servants are hard to come by, and those who can do their work while ignoring naked women and priapic gentlemen are rare as hen's teeth. I pondered just how rare they were as I savoured a flaky scone slathered in butter and dressed with a generous helping of plum jam.

"I got news," Vincent announced. Through a mouthful of cake, per usual. "One of the boys says the *Sea Lark* is loadin' for India, and some crates from the Bradley Tool Company went aboard this afternoon. She sails tomorrow mornin', on the tide."

"Well done, Vincent. Pity we weren't there to see if Bradley accompanied the cargo." French's praise made the young scoundrel blush.

"'Tweren't nuffink to do wif me. I just know who to ask."

The marchioness had been listening with interest. "What

are you lot up to? Is somebody else tryin' to kill the Queen? I'll bet you ten quid it's the damned Irish."

"Not this time, Aunt Margaret." French explained the events of the preceding two days. I'd have let the old woman die of curiosity, but then French did not have to worry about the marchioness interfering with his business. Now there was a thought. I made a mental note to apply the screws to French and persuade him to invite the marchioness and Fergus *chez* French. After all, he was the marchioness's nephew and thus by all rights he should have the pleasure of at least half of her company while she was here in London.

The marchioness sputtered with indignation at the report of the attack on French and me and the theft of the envelope. She clucked in sympathy over the description of Mayhew's body, and, damn her wretched soul, she looked thoughtful at French's bitterness at having lost the trail of the handsome blond Peter Bradley, due to India's defective boot heel. The marchioness cut her eyes in my direction, her lips pursed. Damn and blast. Philip had seen her when he'd come to Lotus House this morning. Had the marchioness caught sight of him? She must have, or she wouldn't be giving me the fisheye at the moment. I was beginning to doubt whether I'd be able to keep all the plates spinning in the air while this game played itself out.

"What'll ye do next?" the marchioness asked French.

"Vincent and I will visit the *Sea Lark* tonight and attempt to get a look inside the crates."

"And what do you suppose I'll be doing tonight?" I asked. "Knitting a shawl for Her Ladyship? I'm coming with you, French."

French looked pained. "I wish you'd reconsider, India. We'll have to climb aboard the ship and search the hold. Vincent and I can move about more easily than you can in your skirts."

"An excellent point, but one that can be easily addressed," I said. "I must acquire some trousers."

# TEN

I've mentioned several times how deuced inconvenient it is to perform one's duties as a government agent when one is encumbered by yards of cloth hanging from one's waist. I'd been meaning to have my dressmaker fit me out with trousers for some time, and had spent more than a few moments contemplating her shocked expression when I requested a pair. What with one thing and another, I hadn't had time to go to her premises. I announced my intention of going there immediately. I already had in mind what I wanted: a pair of smart woolen trousers in a charcoal colour so dark it was almost black, and lined with crimson silk. It would look fetching with a white silk blouse and my red jacket with the silver braid and pewter buttons. Very military it was, though shockingly masculine, but when you've a figure like mine, you can pull off such things. I described my plans to French, who hooted with laughter and then, when he'd brought himself under control, advised that my planned ensemble might draw attention at the docks. Bugger, he had a point.

And a solution, as it turns out. It appears that Her Majesty's government keeps a fair amount of old theatre costumes and discarded clothing around so that agents who have to don a disguise will have ready access. French planned to outfit himself from the stockpile and offered to bring me a few items that would not stand out on the wharves. I have a firm rule about letting men choose clothes for me, but then I have a firm rule about keeping my sluts in line and the marchioness was proving no help at all in this endeavour. Consequently I provided French with a list of measurements and sent him off with instructions that if the clothes could not be fashionable, they must be clean. I had faith that French would abide by this directive as he's as fastidious as a cat about his own appearance. Vincent, being an authentic specimen, needed no assistance in dressing for the part of a ragged dockworker.

I spent the rest of the afternoon dealing with the minutiae of running a first-class brothel that has been invaded by Scottish hordes and their wolf packs. The dogs needed mince and Mrs. Drinkwater and Fergus were at loggerheads over who would fix dinner. My cook, while exercising her housekeeping duties, had collected enough dog hair to knit a large blanket. The girls were getting lax, as I had expected, wandering into the study to enquire if the marchioness was about and coddling Maggie with tidbits from the kitchen. The hag herself was out of sight, tucked up in my bed, snoring like a stevedore with a ferocious cold.

An hour later, French returned with several sacks of trousers and jackets. I rummaged through them and found a suitable outfit for the evening. The breeches were coarse wool and would have to be held up by string, but their baggy fit covered the natural curve of my hips. I chose a loosely woven cotton shirt, a tweed jacket of ancient vintage and a striped scarf to wind round my neck. French handed me a flat cap such as half of London's labourers wear, and with my hair tucked up inside I looked, well, not particularly masculine, but I could pass as an adolescent boy. The clothes, as promised, were clean, though they'd seen much wear. I swaggered around the study in my costume, marveling at the ease of movement in my trousers. I'd have to have more than one pair of these made up, when I found the time.

The evening passed pleasantly enough. Among French, Vincent and me, we managed to keep the marchioness occupied during business hours that night. Fergus dealt for us and we played hand after boisterous hand of *vingt-et-un*. The marchioness wanted to play for cash, and to appease her we did, although I had to stake Vincent as he didn't have a penny. Once, my ancient houseguest stood up and wandered about the room, coming close to the doorway into the hall, but French was up on his legs in a hurry and succeeded in cutting her off and herding her back to the table, where she made short work of us at the cards.

Near midnight, I shut down the casino, leaving Vincent to protest that he had had no chance of making back his money and it wasn't fair. I had to point out to him that it was my money he'd lost, which did little to cheer him up. Possession is nine points of the law, in Vincent's opinion. The marchioness cackled and promised to give him another crack at her. Then she wished us luck and said she'd be waiting up for us. As we left, I heard her ordering Fergus to fetch her a drink and bring the Bible, as she was in the mood for the Book of Judges tonight. The three of us set out to find a cab to carry us to the river. French had a pack slung over his shoulder containing a few implements we would need for the night's work. I'd slipped my Bulldog in the pocket of my jacket.

The *Sea Lark* was anchored in the Regent's Canal Docks on the north side of the Thames, where the river curves between the Lower Pool and Limehouse Reach. It was a long drive from Lotus House to the edge of the Limehouse district of the city. The area is teeming with foreigners who find casual employment on the wharves. Lascars and Chinese roam the streets and every other dilapidated building houses an opium den or a brothel. Life is cheap in this part of London and I was glad to leave the street behind and scramble out onto the great wooden piers.

It was a perfect night for skullduggery. A half-moon hung in the sky, casting the faintest of silver light. A thick mist rolled up from the Thames. There was much activity on the wharves and quays, for London's docks are never quiet, but the noise was muted by the fog, and the oil lanterns that burned at warehouse doors and in the cabins of the many ships gave off a viscid yellow glow that dissipated only a few feet from the source. We made our way cautiously along the wharves, stepping smartly to avoid the workmen who appeared out of the thick brume bearing heavy loads on their shoulders. We had to dodge around the ladders propped up against the warehouse walls while chaps scrambled up and down them carrying sacks of grain and chests of tea and tobacco.

We reconnoitered our target first, strolling down the busy quays to where the *Sea Lark* rode low in the water, heavily laden with her cargo. It was nearing midnight now. High tide would occur in just over eight hours, so we had plenty of time to creep aboard and do a thorough search. The steamship was an ungainly-looking vessel, broad of beam with a large funnel set amidships. Three lifeboats were roped to either side of the deck near the bow, and a low superstructure contained cabins, from which light glowed through the portholes. The cranes had been rolled away from the quay and the hatches to the cargo holds had been battened down. It was clear that the ship's consignment had been stowed away for the voyage. This was good news for us, as we should be able to trundle about in the hold without any interruption. Now we just needed to find a way on board, and that proved easier than you might think.

We'd considered our options and had debated hiring a small boat upriver and floating downstream until we reached the docks, then rowing up quietly to the *Sea Lark*. French would toss the grappling hook he carried in his pack over the rail and would shinny up the rope, securing it safely so that Vincent and I could scramble up after him. I wasn't keen on this plan, involving as it did a lot of luck on our part (no one would hear the sound of the grappling hook on deck, no one would wander aft to find yours truly floundering up the side of the ship, etc.) and no little skill.

Our second choice, and my preferred one, was to walk boldly aboard. That posed far less risk to us as the gangway was busy with coves carrying on provisions for the voyage. A steady procession of men was unloading supplies from a fleet of wagons parked on the quay. We need only equip ourselves with a basket of bread or a cask of rum, avert our faces from the bloke who was standing on the wharf at the bottom of the gangway marking his list, and we'd be on the deck. And so I found myself with French in the shadow of an archway leading into a courtyard, rubbing a handful of coal dust into my face and along the backs of my hands.

"Not so much, India," French said, spitting in his palm and scrubbing my cheeks. "You look like a bloody blackamoor. You need only appear grimy, as if you've been working all day."

I enjoyed the feeling of his warm palm against my cheek. But never let it be said that India Black is easily distracted from the work at hand. "I do hope this disguise is adequate."

"Keep the sack you're given on the side of your head close to the bloke with the list, and don't speak. If he asks you a question, just mumble. And remember you're supposed to be a bloke, so mumble in a deep voice. Ready?"

I tugged my cap over my eyes and produced an alto murmur. French chuckled.

Then he and I and Vincent strode confidently into the throng of men who moved between the wagons and the *Sea Lark*. Vincent took the lead and I followed him, with French bringing up the rear. We took our place in the line of men waiting to pick up provisions and shuffled forward.

"Don't worry," French whispered in my ear.

I nodded, but I confess to being nervous. I'm a dab hand at playing maids and shepherdesses and maidens without sin, but this was my first appearance as a man and I found it a bit unsettling. There was nothing to be done but to put my back into the performance, so I spit and slouched and scratched and prayed I'd pass muster.

Vincent reached the wagons and put out his hands expectantly. An obliging cove in the wagon bed dropped a sack of flour onto Vincent's shoulder. "Ten pounds flour," said the cove, and "ten pounds flour," echoed the fellow with the list, labouriously marking the paper with the stub of a pencil. Vincent walked off briskly.

I took my place by the wagon (careful to keep my chin tucked and my cap pulled low over my eyes), reaching up with my smudged hands. A moment later and a bag of flour descended onto my shoulder, emitting a fine cloud of white powder that enveloped my head. I had taken a breath when the weight of the bag had hit my shoulder and now I inhaled a quantity of the white stuff. My nose itched. I balanced the bag with one hand and scratched my nose with the other. It was no use. I tried, Lord knows I tried, but I couldn't help myself. I sneezed. I'd half stifled it, but the half that escaped sounded high and girlish, which I suppose is how nature intended it to sound.

The cove in the wagon paused in the act of lifting another sack of flour. The cove with the list looked up from his paper. Vincent, halfway up the gangway, froze. I heard French suck in his breath. I ducked my head, hefted my sack and marched off. Behind me, I heard French say, "Bloody man always has a cold." Then the gangway was vibrating under my feet and the fellow in the wagon said "ten pounds flour," and his compatriot with the checklist echoed his words. The gangway shook as French stepped on it and followed me aboard.

At the top of the gangway, a solid chap in a striped jersey and knitted cap waved French, Vincent and me forward to an open hatch, where we handed off our bags of flour to be stowed in the ship's hold. We should have joined the line of workmen threading its way back down the gangplank.

Instead, we melted into the shadows at the first opportunity, where we held a hurried conference.

"We must get to the cargo hold," French whispered.

"I thought we were here for tea with the captain," I retorted.

He ignored my sally. "I don't think we can loosen a hatch on deck without being seen. Perhaps we should go below and try working our way into the hold."

"I don't know, guv. I fink we'll stand out like a donkey in the Derby, 'specially India. She don't exackly look like a bloke. Not up close, she don't. It's them . . ." I saw the shadowy movement of his hands as he carved two curves in the air at chest level.

"But there'll be so many men moving around below deck that we stand a good chance of being ignored. And India will just have to keep her head down and her mouth closed. Granted, that latter feat may be difficult for her to—"

"Stop wittering like two old pussies at the garden gate. Time is wasting. Do I need to remind you that this ship will be sailing in a few hours? And even though the thought of leaving the marchioness far behind is attractive, I'd rather go someplace other than Calcutta. Let's try the forward hatch." And so saying I slipped away from my two partners, who would no doubt have stood there until the first mate wandered by and tossed us off the ship.

I led the way toward the bow, darting from shadow to shadow and ducking under the wedges of yellow light that spilled out of cabin windows. There were one or two lads about, coiling long pieces of rope, puffing on pipes and joshing one another. They seemed uninterested in anything other than bragging about their exploits in London's taverns and whorehouses. We dropped to the deck and crawled along the planks, keeping the superstructure between us and the sailors. I marveled at the ease with which I conducted this maneuver in my trousers and reflected that it was just like men to keep such an advantage to themselves. They do natter on about sportsmanship and the like, but has any one of them bothered to inform the fair sex that movement is considerably easier in britches? No, they have not.

We scuttled like crabs to the hatch closest to the bow of the ship. A dim lantern burned at the rail, but otherwise the deck was shrouded in darkness here. I had thought the hatch might be locked, but there was only a hasp, its slotted, hinged metal plate fitting over a loop of the same material. An iron bolt was thrust through the loop, holding the hasp closed. Vincent scrabbled forward and began working the bolt from its moorings. He moved cautiously, but even the slightest tug on the bolt resulted in a rasping noise that seemed audible over the noise on the quay and the wind off the river. I was as nervous as a sheep sniffing wolf on the breeze by the time the lad eased the pin from the loop and found a crevice in which to deposit it. It wouldn't do for the bloody thing to be rolling about on the deck as the ship rose and fell gently with the motion of the water.

Vincent clambered to his knees and tugged at the hatch cover, to no avail. In the darkness, I couldn't tell whether it had moved at all. It dawned on me that this might be the end of our night's adventures. It should have occurred to one of us that these hatches were made to withstand the lashings of wind and weather on a sea voyage and were not a thin piece of wood to be moved around by an underfed street Arab, a poncy gentleman and a woman.

"Damn," French muttered in my ear. He'd reached the same conclusion about the hatch cover.

Vincent slumped down beside us, panting from his exertions. "Can't do it, guv. She's too 'eavy. I can get her up an inch but it's stuck on t'other side."

Light dawned, in the proverbial sense. "There must be a lock on that side of the hatch as well," I said.

"Even if there is, the damned thing's heavy," said Vincent.

"Crawl around there and see if there's another hasp," I directed him.

"Why don't you go yourself, instead o' orderin' me around?"

I tend to forget just how sensitive Vincent is to anyone except French instructing him to do something. One of these days he and I would have to have a chat about that. After all, I was a full-fledged agent now. Hadn't the prime minister himself given me carte blanche to run the anarchist operation as I saw fit? Vincent was just being bloody-minded. It's a state I recognize easily, being rather bloody-minded myself.

"It would be best if you went, Vincent," said French smoothly. "You're more skilled at creeping about without being seen."

Naturally the little sod went off without a word of protest, having received a pat on the head from his hero. I was extremely annoyed but being the stalwart type said nothing while Vincent eased around the coaming surrounding the hatch and went to work on the second lock. He moved slowly, lifting his head to be sure that the sailors on deck were still occupied with their conversation, but finally I heard a stealthy rasp as the bolt was withdrawn and Vincent wriggled back around the hatch to join us.

The three of us arranged ourselves as best we could in the space we had and on French's whispered count of three we heaved on the cover. It was heavy as lead but with both its hasps loose, we were able to lift it several inches. One of us would be able to squeeze through, but what of the other two?

"One moment," said French. We eased down the cover and he disappeared into the darkness, returning a moment later with what appeared to be a large needle with a sharp point on one end and an eye at the other, through which a lanyard dangled.

"Marlinspike," he whispered. "We'll wedge it into the opening and crawl through."

I looked dubiously at the thing. "It doesn't look strong enough. Will it hold?"

"It's made of iron. I reckon it will hold long enough for us to get inside."

Now, I know what you're thinking, and I was cogitating about the very same thing. "How the devil do we get out?"

"We'll worry about that later."

Just like a man—only concerned with ingress, never with egress. Had there been any way of actually exiting stage right at this point without blowing the gaff, I'd have done so. But there wasn't, and thus I joined my companions in heaving up the hatch cover once more. French groaned and cursed and shoved his shoulder under the hatch to free one hand, which he used to jam the marlinspike between the deck and the cover. We let go gingerly and waited for the confounded hatch to slam shut, but the marlinspike held.

"It'll be tricky work, sliding through the opening without dislodging that thing," I observed.

French merely grunted. "You first, Vincent. Then India goes and I'll come last."

Vincent, being as thin as your average wharf cat, slid through the opening like melted butter. I'd expected a long drop, but the hold was full and I heard a thump quite near the opening as he came to rest on the cargo. I stuck my head through the hatch. Risky that, but I wanted to know what I was getting into.

"How far is the drop? What's down there?"

"A few feet. I'm sittin' on some crates. Don't know wot's in 'em. Slide in on your belly, feet first, and you'll be alright."

"Watch out below," I whispered, and squirmed through the opening. Dealing with breasts proved a bit awkward, but by the time I'd managed to get them over the threshold, so to speak, the toes of my boots hit wood and I eased down onto a large container. There wasn't enough space to stand upright, so I stooped down and duckwalked out of French's way.

He dropped gracefully into the hold and then we all crouched together and pushed up the hatch so that he could extract the marlinspike.

With that task accomplished, I contemplated the next. The air was fetid, ripe with the smell of bilge water. It was dark as pitch in the hold.

"How the hell are we supposed to see down here?"

"I'm surprised you hadn't thought of that before now," French said. The poncy bastard was gloating. I could tell by the sound of his voice.

"Oh, do trot out your candle or whatever you've got in that pack and stop sounding so pleased with yourself." The fact that French had remembered the necessity of light and I had not was irritating. I blame the marchioness. I doubt that French would have been as prepared if he'd had the old crone underfoot and wreaking havoc. Nevertheless, I was glad that he'd had the foresight to bring along a pack. I wondered what else he had inside there.

I heard the scrape of a match, and had to close my eyes for a moment against the sulphurous glare. When I opened them again, French had lit the stub of a candle and was nursing the flame, cupping his hands around it to ward off draughts. When he was satisfied that the wick was burning brightly, he produced two more candles from his pockets and handed one to Vincent and one to me. Then he lit them for us. It was rather solemn and vaguely religious, lighting those candles while the shadows reared dark and foreboding around us.

"You look like a parson," I cracked.

He gave me a roguish grin that nearly made my candle melt. "Do you like parsons?"

"You two can do that another time," Vincent said crisply. "Let's hotfoot it through this ruddy place and get the 'ell out of 'ere."

"What a killjoy you are, Vincent," I said. "Lead on."

French stuck the marlinspike in his belt and left his pack on top of the crates below the hatchway. "India, come with me. Vincent, you go to the other side. Remember, we're looking for crates stamped either 'Bradley Tool Company' or 'South Indian Railway Company.' Or the crates might be labeled 'tools.'"

"Perhaps I should go with Vincent," I suggested. Had French forgotten that Vincent could not read?

He had not. "I wrote down the information and gave it to the lad earlier. He'll recognize the words if he sees them."

Vincent had not lingered to hear this conversation. He had taken off like a flash to the other side of the ship, disappearing over the edge of the crates with the agility of a monkey.

The cargo had been packed solidly to fill the hold. The only space in which to move about was on either side of the stacks of boxes, chests and crates, where the curved sides of the ship had left a bit of room to maneuver. French and I crawled on hands and knees to the edge of the piled cargo.

"There are some cracks between the crates you can use as footholds," said French, and proceeded to prove his theory by dangling his feet over the edge and searching with his foot until he had found a space to wedge his toe. He made light work of it, and was soon at the bottom, standing on the deck that separated the hold from the bilge. My descent was slightly less nimble, but I made it to the deck with only a scraped elbow and one small tear in my trousers.

The space was narrow and we had to lean against the hull and shuffle along slowly. French rose on his toes to read the labels on the crates near the top of the hold, while I strained my eyes to decipher the scrawled marks on the crates near the bottom.

"Some of the tags must be facing the other way," I said. "I can't tell what's in those boxes."

"We can only do what's possible, and hope that we find what we're looking for."

On that cheery note I bent over and resumed my efforts, creeping down the side of the hull. It was damned uncomfortable down there and about as exciting as sitting through the Sunday sermon twice. We made slow progress, as the stevedores had packed the hold tight. My back began to ache and my thoughts drifted to my comfortable bed back at Lotus House, until I remembered that the marchioness was the current occupant of that berth, which made me curse under my breath.

We'd been at it for a good hour, crawling along like cater-
pillars in the confines of the cramped space, when Vincent
gave a low whistle and French and I stopped and listened.

"Oi, I fink I found somethin'."

In an instant French was scaling the mountain of crates
that towered over us, and I was right on his heels. We gained
the top and hunched down to avoid the timbers over our heads.

"Whistle again, Vincent," French commanded, and we followed the sound of the muted tone. French lay down on his
stomach and peered over the edge of the crates. I joined him
there and saw Vincent below us, the glow of his candle nearly
swallowed by the looming shadows.

"There's a bit o' paper pasted on this one," he said, holding
the candle up to the side of a crate. "'Bradley Tool Company'
it says."

"Why don't you stay here, India. It's too narrow down there
for us all, and I need room to work."

I didn't mind refraining from more acrobatic feats tonight
and I was quite willing for French to scramble down alone to
join Vincent. I lay on my stomach to watch.

"Hold my candle," French told Vincent, and took the marlinspike from his belt. French inserted it into a space between
the planks of the crate. I saw his shoulders hunch as he applied
pressure and the plank groaned. He leaned into the spike,
using it as a lever to force the board. The wood resisted and
French removed the marlinspike and shoved it into a different
position, at the corner of the crate. I heard the rasping of nails
as they were pulled clear and suddenly French and Vincent
had a plank in their hands, which they twisted persistently
until one end came away from the crate. In the candlelight, I
saw a few wisps of straw protruding from the opening.

"Careful with those candles," I whispered. French and Vincent spared a moment from their labours to inform me that they were not mentally defective and were well aware of the dangers of fire.

French thrust his arms through the opening and pulled out double handfuls of straw, dropping them at his feet. He inserted his arms again and this time I knew he'd encountered something. I heard metal grind against metal. French was fishing about, trying to get a grip on the object he'd found. He leaned back against the bulkhead and tugged gently, working his arms back and forth.

A slender cylinder of wood and steel popped out and French nursed the rest of the article out of the crate with all the care of a midwife delivering her first babe. I looked down at the rifle cradled in French's arms.

"Blimey," said Vincent. "That ain't a shovel."

French looked grim. "Indeed not. It's a .577 Martini-Henry rifle, capable of firing ten rounds per minute at a velocity of nine hundred feet per second."

"Wot a peashooter."

"It's lethal in the right hands, and those hands belong to the army. These are military-issue weapons."

I squirmed forward for a better look. "Mayhew worked for the quartermaster general's office."

"I had made the connection," said French.

"So somebody stole these 'ere rifles from the army and they're shippin' 'em to somebody in India?"

"So it appears."

"Wot do we do now?"

As so often happens in life, that decision was made for us. One moment we were gazing down at one of the British

Empire's most effective pieces of armament, and the next we were scuttling like rats for a hole. Someone had opened the door to the cargo hold and several men were now standing inside, carrying bull's-eye lanterns and cursing a blue streak while they searched for the source of the sounds of flight.

I blew out my candle to avoid being seen, and scampered for the hatch, though my progress was impeded by the fact that I had to bend over to avoid smashing my head into the timbers overhead, and the fact that it was too damned dark to see anything. I heard French and Vincent swarming up the side of the cargo and the sounds of their footsteps trailing after me. I reached the hatch and prayed that my compatriots would be there soon as there was nothing I could do until they arrived. They seemed to take a confoundedly long time, but then French pounded to a halt beside me, gulping air like a blown horse, with Vincent right behind him. We put our hands against the hatch cover.

"Push now," said French, but we needed no such instruction. We shoved with all our might. The hatch moved a fraction, but didn't open.

"Hell and damnation," French panted. "Someone put the bolts back in the hasps."

Our pursuers had climbed to the top of the crates and were advancing on us. It was difficult to tell how many there were, as their lanterns cast a flood of light before them, obscuring them and illuminating us like actors on a stage. I took a breath and tried to steady my nerves. This might be awkward. We'd no doubt be mistaken as thieves and our disreputable attire wouldn't help matters, but I felt sure we could talk our way out of this situation. If nothing else, we could pull out our trump card, old Dizzy himself, and see how long it took these chaps to tug their forelocks and apologize for inconveniencing us. So I didn't fret myself, instead using the time it took them to close on us to prepare a speech of sorts. It's always best to get on the front foot right away, and foreclose any offense by the other party.

I must admit to feeling slightly intimidated by the silent advance of the men with the lanterns. There was something diabolical in their slow, deliberate progression toward us over the boxes and chests. The lights moved forward inexorably, like the torches of some demonic clan seeking a sacrificial victim. Boots thumped hollowly on the wooden crates, and I could hear the men breathing heavily from their climb. If I'd caught someone pilfering things from Lotus House, I'd have shouted loud enough to wake the dead. These chaps, whoever they were, held their tongues. And that is when I pulled the Bulldog from my pocket.

"Stop or I'll shoot," I said.

French sucked in his breath. I heard the rustle of his coat as he extracted his Boxer revolver.

Naturally I expected a response to my command. What I heard was unexpected: a deep, throaty chuckle that did not sound at all amused. The lanterns flashed in my direction and I flung up my arm to shade my eyes. I couldn't see a blasted thing in the glare. Then one man stepped forward. He was bent over with his head crooked up to stare at us. I recognized him immediately. It was the wretched fellow who'd tripped me in the foyer of Lotus House. I did not feel sanguine about this development. Then two more men edged forward and I recognized them as the other ruffians who'd manhandled French and me. God, what a nefarious bunch of villains they looked at the moment in the quavering yellow light from the lanterns and in the shadows that moved like ominous clouds as the ship swayed.

"Drop your weapons," said their leader. "You are outnumbered. Even if you get off a shot you'll be dead in the next second."

I spared a quick glance at French, to find him looking at me. We hesitated.

"Lay down those barkers and be quick about it."

French shrugged and knelt gently, placing his revolver at his feet. I emulated him, slowly. I didn't relish the prospect of giving up my Bulldog, but we were outnumbered and there was no point in dying now when we might live to fight another day.

"I was afraid you'd become a nuisance," said the man. "We should have dealt with you earlier."

I remembered the blood-spattered walls of Colonel Mayhew's room. The thought was not reassuring.

"Tie them up," the man instructed his cohorts.

A fourth man had remained in the shadows. Now he took a step forward, but took care to remain out of the circle of light cast by the lanterns.

He cleared his throat. "What do you intend to do with them?"

My stomach clenched. It was Philip. My first instinct was to claim his acquaintance and beg for his help but it was clear that the leader of this dubious crowd was the man who had spoken first. Philip had sounded downright diffident, which was not surprising. He'd always been a gentleman thief and had never had a taste for violence. There had been a decided tremor to his voice. I locked my eyes on the maestro of the group, determined not to reveal, inadvertently or otherwise, my association with Philip.

"What I should have done before. We can't afford to leave behind any witnesses. When we've reached open water, we'll slit their throats and throw them overboard."

I wished I'd shot the fellow.

# ELEVEN

We lay in a row, our hands and feet bound tightly with stiff rope. The ruffians had gagged us, stuffing rags into our mouths and binding our faces with strips of cloth. There wouldn't have been much to talk about anyway. Our chances for escape seemed slim. I'd twisted and turned my wrists until they felt like raw meat and still hadn't been able to loosen my bonds one whit. These fellows were professionals. I doubted there was a loose knot among the three of us. They'd dumped us in a heap at the foot of the cargo, in a narrow space between the stacks of crates and a bulkhead that partitioned the cargo hold. A thin strip of amber light leaked through the panels of the bulkhead. That pale thread of light represented a passage beyond and freedom, if only we could reach it.

I reckoned we'd set sail about two hours after we'd been captured. There'd been a flurry of activity on deck, with the sound of feet running overhead and the shriek of the capstan as the anchor was raised. The boiler had been fired and the engine began to grind slowly. The ship had shuddered as she gained leeway and wallowed awkwardly with the motion of the Thames. It had taken some time to travel the length of the river, and as we bumped and swayed my heart and my hopes sank. It would not take long until we reached the mouth of the river and the engine began to throb with a full head of steam, and soon after French, Vincent and I would be flotsam.

I'll tell you candidly, I was frightened and by God, I was angry, too. Not at Philip, though I wasn't best pleased with that chap. I thought he'd looked relieved when one of the thugs shoved the rags in my mouth, eliminating my last chance at laying claim to his friendship. You can't blame a chap for being true to his nature, and I knew from firsthand experience that when things got sticky, the only sign of Philip would be the dust from his heels. No, I was angry at the Great Hairy Chess Player in the Sky. I ask you, is it fair to be told you're an heiress one day and then have the rug pulled out from under you the next? And what of French? We'd yet to resolve all our differences, but I'd planned to bed the poncy bastard soon and now he'd never have the chance to experience that bliss. Well, the way matters stood now, I'd soon have my chance to rail at the Almighty in person, which, come to think of it, might not be the wisest course of action when He's sitting in judgment of your mortal soul. I don't know what French and Vincent were thinking of at the moment, but these matters theological had my full attention. There's nothing like impending death to focus the mind.

The first I knew that something was up was when French rolled over and butted his head against mine. I rolled away, irritated by this interruption of my contemplation of my fate. But the fellow was merely alerting me to the fact that the moment I had been dreading had come. The door into the bulkhead popped open and the amber light swelled until I could see the figures of Vincent and French on either side of me. A shadowy figure stood in the door, the outline of a butcher's blade clearly visible against the light. I whimpered, softly I hoped, but I couldn't hide the fear welling inside me. We were to suffer the same fate as Mayhew before our bloody carcasses were dropped off in the dark waters of the channel. The door closed swiftly and the inky gloom enveloped us again.

"India?"

It was Philip. You'd think the bloke would remember that I was gagged and wouldn't be able to carry on a conversation, but that was a point to discuss at a later time. For the moment, I was grateful that he had come, and just a trifle puzzled. I knew he wasn't here to fillet us, but playing the hero had never been Philip's style.

I grunted through the gag. A cautious hand groped my ankle.

"India?" I made an affirmative noise, to let the bloke know he'd selected the correct captive. A blade slid between my ankles. My body tensed. Perhaps I'd been wrong about the chap, but then he commenced sawing at the rope that bound my feet together. I felt the release of pressure as the strands of the rope gave way, then Philip's hand moving up my leg to my thigh. He fumbled about, looking for my hands, and I prayed he wouldn't cut me inadvertently. He found my wrists and used one hand to painstakingly determine the location of my bonds; then I felt the cold sliver of steel pass between the thin skin on the inside of my wrists, and Philip set to work to sunder the rope. I held my breath for fear of moving my hands into the path of that blade, for it had been honed to a fearsome edge. I have to hand it to Philip, he was a ruddy expert with that knife. My shackles fell apart in an instant. I yanked off the strip of cloth that had been tied round my head and pulled the rags from my mouth.

My rescuer leaned over and put his mouth to my ear. "Are you alright?"

"I'm as well as might be expected, considering I've been lying down here ruminating about my impending death."

"I am sorry about that. My partners can be overly enthusiastic when it comes to protecting their interests."

"That is one way to put it, yes."

"What the devil are you doing here, India? How did you get involved in this?"

"It's a long story, and as we seem to be sailing away from London at a rapid clip, I'd rather tell it to you some other time."

"And how the hell did you know I was involved in this? I assume that's why you came looking for me. I didn't think you were the sentimental type."

"Also a tale for another time. Now hand over that knife and get out of here. You're running a terrible risk being down here. If those chaps find out you've helped us escape, you're likely to get the same treatment as Mayhew."

I could sense he was torn between staying to find out how I'd happened to be on the ship and returning as swiftly as he could to his cabin, where he could practice his look of astonishment when told the prisoners had escaped. In the event, he did the sensible thing, and decided to save his own hide. I'd known he would. It was what I would have done in his situation.

"You didn't happen to bring our guns with you, did you?" Well, a girl can try.

"I couldn't take that risk."

Bugger. I'd been fond of that Bulldog.

"Give me five minutes," said Phillip. "Then go through the door in the bulkhead. It opens into another part of the hold, and you'll find a companionway to the deck. Once on deck, turn left. Stay in the shadows and walk about twenty paces. There's a lifeboat secured to the rail there. Loose the lifeboat and jump overboard. There may be a commotion on deck, but the engines are running at full capacity and no one will want to stop to fish you out."

His heels grated on the planks as he swiveled to leave. Then he turned back. "Take all the ropes and the knife with you. I'd rather my friends thought you'd orchestrated your own escape."

"Sensible idea," I said.

"Good luck to you, India. And whatever you do, for God's sake, let this thing go. You're in over your head."

I thought it quite likely that the same was true of Philip. But to tell him so would achieve nothing but burn a few precious seconds of the time we had remaining before the rest of the gang arrived to toss us overboard. On impulse I reached up, found Philip's head and drew it to mine for a lengthy kiss. I'm not sure whether I meant it in gratitude or benediction, or as simply a last chance to press those soft lips to mine. Then Philip took my hand and placed the handle of the knife in my palm, and ghosted away into the gloom. Light filled the hold as he cracked the bulkhead door and slid through it. The darkness swallowed us again.

I rolled over onto my knees and grabbled about until I found French's hands. It took only an instant to part the strands of rope that bound him; then he was tearing out his gag while I freed his feet.

"Did you hear that?" I asked.

"Yes, I heard. That was Bradley, wasn't it? Why did you call him Philip? How do you know him? And why is he setting us free?"

I set about cutting Vincent's bonds. "Let's just get off this bloody boat and then I'll tell you everything. Now stuff those ropes in your pockets and let's go."

"Give me the knife," said French.

"Get your own," I hissed. "This one's mine."

"Do be reasonable, India. I've had some training and know how to use that weapon."

"So have I. Know how to use it, I mean. And I'll wager my training was more practical than yours. You probably learned to knife fight from some dandy. I picked up the skill on the street."

"Put that rag back in 'er mouf, guv," said Vincent, "and let's scarper."

As I had a knife in my hand, French did not attempt to follow Vincent's instructions. Instead he lurched to his feet, fumbled toward the bulkhead and eased open the door. I used the light that flooded in as an aid in finding Vincent's ear and cuffing it. The two of us sprang up and crowded behind French, who had his head through the opening, conning the lay of the land.

"All clear," he whispered. He opened the door carefully and we filed through, blinking in the dim light, into another section of the hold. This was filled with bales of cotton cloth, piled to the timbers of the deck above us. As Philip had said, a narrow companionway against one side of the hull led upward to a covered hatch.

French went first and I was anxious to follow him but the steps were small and the angle steep, and I had to wait until he was at the top of the companionway before I could start after him. Warily, French pushed the hatch cover open a few inches and peered out. A draught of fresh salt air swooped down the companionway and I breathed it in gratefully. Beyond the outline of French's head I could see a half-dozen stars, glowing with a faint silvery light against the velvety black of the sky.

He pushed the hatch open and clambered up the stairs and out onto the deck. I was hard on his heels. Vincent came bounding up the companionway like an old salt and the three of us scuttled into the lee of the forecastle. There was a brisk breeze blowing across the bow. Steam poured from the funnels and the thump of the boilers reverberated through the ship.

We glanced about cautiously. There were a few chaps about, gathered in a knot at the rail on the other side of the deck, about thirty feet from us, smoking pipes and watching the faint lights of the English coast slowly fade from view. My spirits soared when I saw those lights. At least we were within sight of land, and French and Vincent would be able to row us ashore in a matter of a few hours. Well, I certainly didn't intend to blister my soft white hands by paddling us home. French and Vincent would serve admirably for that purpose.

French drew us close and we held a hurried confab on the

best and most expeditious way to pinch a lifeboat and get off the confounded *Sea Lark*. A faint thread of orange light had appeared on the eastern horizon, though full darkness still enveloped the ship. Our captors would have to act soon if they were going to toss us overboard under cover of night. It was imperative that we leave the ship with all speed.

"I'll go forward and examine the lifeboat," said French. "We need to know how it's secured to the deck." He crept forward and Vincent and I huddled together, keeping a watchful eye on the sailors at the rail. As we gazed at them, one tar detached himself from the group and strolled in our direction.

"Blimey," said Vincent. "'E's liable to walk right up on the guv.""

"There's not much we can do about it," I said. "Not without raising the alarm. Let's pray that French has his wits about him and spots this fellow in time to hide."

We watched in breathless anticipation as the bloke ambled slowly up the deck, now and then kicking a line to test its tension or inspecting a davit or chock on the deck. I glanced forward and saw French's dark form against the white-painted lifeboat. He had his back to us and I willed him to pause for a gander around the deck, but he was intent on his task and paid no mind to the fellow headed in his direction.

"We've got to warn him," Vincent said.

"You go," I told him. "And take the knife. If you have to kill that bloke, do it."

Vincent seized the handle of the dagger and scampered for the lifeboat. He put a hand on French's shoulder and his nibs nearly jumped overboard. Vincent leaned in close to deliver his news and I saw French's head whip round, searching for the threat. Meanwhile, the sailor sauntered on, making his slow journey of inspection. If he continued at his present pace, he'd be within sight of French and Vincent in a few seconds. I was wondering just how to explain her nephew's death to the marchioness when French and Vincent bolted like rabbits out of the shadow of the lifeboat and back down the deck, to huddle next to me. The wash of the sea against the hull, the pulsing of the engines and the ceaseless wind covered the sound of their footsteps. The lone sailor was staring casually at the lights of England. He paused and leaned on the railing, his back to the lifeboat, but I hardly thought we'd be able to lower the cursed thing without the fellow noticing the activity on deck. It occurred to me that there was something crucial I ought to know.

"Psst, French. How the devil do you lower a lifeboat?"

"It's on a davit, a winch system which lets down the boat to the water when you turn a crank." He pointed down the deck. "See that pulley mount on deck?"

"What's a pulley mount?"

His sigh of exasperation ruffled my hair. "Oh, for God's sake, India. You and Vincent keep watch while I lower the boat."

That sounded satisfactory to me, seeing as how manual labour was involved.

Vincent had been listening to our conversation. "'Ow long will it take to get that boat in the water, guv?"

"Nine minutes and thirteen seconds."

"There's no need to be sarcastic. The lad merely asked a question," I said.

"I don't have the faintest idea how long it will take. I'm not an expert on lifeboats, you know."

"Wot about a diversion?" Vincent was determined to be

helpful. "I could go to the front of the ship and yell 'Man over-board!' Wot do you fink?"

"We'd have everyone on board ship up on deck in thirty seconds flat," I said. "Which, I submit, is not helpful if we're trying to steal a lifeboat. By the way, how do we get from the deck to the boat once it's in the water?"

"There'll be a ladder, or something," French said vaguely. "I like the idea of a diversion, but India is right. We can't draw attention to the deck. Now if we could get to the boiler room, we could do some damage."

"What about a fire in the hold?" I asked.

"Too risky. We could kill a lot of innocent people if the thing got out of control, which it could easily do with those bales of cotton cloth down there."

"Just a small fire?"

"I'm with India," Vincent announced. "We got to get off this 'ere ship wifout bein' seen. All we need is some smoke and noise, and we'll be away."

"Alright," French said reluctantly. "Vincent, here are my matches. Start the fire in the compartment closest to the stern and as far away from us as possible. When you've got it going, dash back on deck and raise the alarm. Let us pray that every-one will be so occupied with the fire that no one notices us."

It wasn't the ideal plan, but then we weren't in the ideal situation. If all went well, we'd be rowing for shore within half an hour. If the worst occurred, we might just have kindled our very own Viking funeral boat.

Vincent scurried off with French's matchbox clutched in his hand. We huddled on deck, listening to the splash of water as the hull cleaved the sea.

"I've half a mind to go down there and start winching the

boat over the rail," said French. "If we can gain even a minute of time, it would be to our advantage."

"I'll join you. More hands make less work."

"Except when the hands don't know the difference between a winch and a wench."

"Cheeky bastard." I crept off. I heard the scrape of French's boot on the planks as he followed me. We slunk along in the dark shadows cast by the ship's superstructure, stealthy as two cracksmen, but the fatal moment came when we'd have to cross the open deck to the lifeboat by the rail. I cast one last furtive glance over my shoulder and flung myself toward a large iron structure bolted to the deck and housing a toothed wheel. This, French had informed me, was the pulley mount.

"I've got to release the brake and insert the crank," French whispered, and then spent an inordinately long time mucking about and making a frightful amount of noise. He spared the time to check on the sailors on deck but they were absorbed in their pipes and their conversation. Then he crouched down by the pulley mount and gave the handle a gentle push, which produced no effect whatsoever. He shoved a little harder and I was relieved to see the handle moving. French exerted more strength and the gear began to turn, slowly but steadily, and most important of all, silently. I'd been afraid that the winch might be rusty and that one turn would result in a screech that would have the entire ship's crew down upon us, but the captain, bless him, must have been a stickler for detail for the winch was freshly oiled.

French made a few rounds with the cranks and the lifeboat had shifted a bit, moving in its cradle, when a cracked adolescent voice screeched a warning. "Fire!" Vincent shouted from the stern. "Fire in the aft hold!"

"Christ," said French. "That'll rouse the natives." He applied himself to the handle and pumped furiously. He worked manfully and I watched as the lifeboat lifted clean out of its cradle, swinging gently on the cable that held it aloft. This brought to mind another question that I had forgotten to ask French. How were we to loosen the cable once the lifeboat was in the water? I'd also been keeping a keen eye out for a ladder and I had yet to spy one. There were a number of ways in which this scheme could go wobbly, but I consoled myself (not that it was much consolation) with the thought that our options for exiting a moving ship under a full head of steam were limited.

The lifeboat was swinging freely now and the arm through which the cable was threaded had extended the boat out over the rail so that it dangled above the water. It was still a deuced long way from the lifeboat to the surface of the ocean and our position was precarious.

Vincent's alarm had certainly created a diversion. The stern of the ship now swarmed with figures running to and fro and shouting like the devil. If there's one thing a sailor fears above all else it is fire, and these chaps were rocketing about the deck, manning pumps and brandishing axes. Vincent scuttled into view. I noticed he had liberated one of the ship's axes himself.

"Hurry, French," I said, casting an anxious glance at the activity. "We haven't much time."

I paced about the deck, fretting, and watched the proceedings at the stern. For the moment, everyone was preoccupied with the fire Vincent had set, but if anyone cast a casual glance in the direction of the bow, we'd be spotted. I said as much to French and Vincent, but French was panting from his exertions and Vincent was gnawing a fingernail and neither spared breath to reply. French was pumping madly and I leaned over the rail to check his progress. I was relieved to see that the boat was just ten feet or so above the roiling waves.

My relief was short-lived, however. Someone had seen us. The bugger sent up a view halloo and suddenly every man at the stern wheeled round and stared at us. I calculated the distance between us and them and reckoned that we had only a few seconds to make good our escape. I thought it best to inform French of this, but when I turned to do so, I found he'd clambered into the lifeboat with Vincent's axe and was hacking away at the cable that held the boat suspended from the arm.

"You bloody idiot. If you cut that cable the boat will fall and you'll be in the water." I should have thought that was perfectly obvious to him, but perhaps he was a bit stressed by the situation. Perhaps my own mind was affected by the fact that a pack of men was advancing toward us up the deck, led by our three friends. They did not look friendly, nor kind, nor would I wager that one of them knew when to use the fish fork.

It's damned odd what goes through your mind at a time like this. I wondered whether the whole ship's company could be in league with Philip (of whom there was no sign, by the way) and his compatriots and decided that was a ridiculous notion. The captain could well be a coconspirator, but it was doubtful that a criminal gang would pay an entire ship's crew to cover up its nefarious doings. I found that thought comforting.

So what would the villains do now? If they confronted us, we need only tell the truth and invite the crew to view the evidence. I didn't think they'd take lightly to the idea that British guns were being used to kill our own chaps in some dusty, God-forsaken spot in India. We might get the upper hand rather easily, and end up sailing back to London with our quarry in our pockets. I bent over the railing to inform French of this brilliant idea when a bullet ricocheted off the iron railing near my head.

This required some revision to my plan of telling the truth to the crew. It would be bloody difficult to do that with a bullet in the head. Obviously the criminals were determined to finish us off before we had a chance to expose them.

"Crikey!" said Vincent.

French peered up at us. "Jump!" he commanded.

I gauged the distance between the deck and the lifeboat and did not like what I saw. "Where's the ladder?" I shouted.

"Just jump!" French screamed.

I seldom complain, unless there's good cause to do so, but I felt disinclined to launch myself off a heaving deck toward the rather small target the lifeboat offered. A ladder would have been so much more helpful.

A second shot cracked, echoing over the sound of the waves, and the wooden deck exploded a foot from Vincent. He uttered a strangled gasp.

"Are you hit?"

"Got it in the leg," he said, and dragged himself over to stand by me. "It's alright, I can make it."

"Jump!" French roared.

Vincent put his grimy, bloodstained hand into mine and over we went. I'm grateful to the pup, for I might not have found the courage to jump into that bucking lifeboat alone. We dropped like two bloody great boulders into the boat. The momentum of our weight snapped the remaining strands of cable and the boat plummeted to the waves. The first jolt, when I landed in the lifeboat, jarred my teeth and drove the breath from me. I scarcely felt the second, when the boat hit the water. Still breathless, I pitched forward and found myself sprawled in the bottom of the lifeboat, my face buried in a coil of rope that smelled of mildew.

French clambered over me, digging his heels into my ribs as he groped for the oars. He found one and thrust it into the oarlock, but that was all he had time to do before the bullets were whizzing past our ears. I looked frantically for cover and considered hiding behind French but I was too damned fond of the fellow to use him that way.

"Over the side!" French shouted, lifting Vincent by the scruff of his neck and tossing him into the choppy water. Now French knows very well that I can't swim. Indeed, on my last aqueous adventure, I'd had to be hauled from the river by Vincent. Unfortunately, the lad didn't seem to be in any condition to act as my personal lifesaver at the moment. I intended to inform French of this, but he forestalled my protest by according me the same treatment Vincent got.

The cold shock of the seawater quite took my breath away. It is not true that I panicked. I may have flailed about a bit, and sputtered, but I would never do anything as undignified as trying to climb atop French, nearly drowning him in the process, as he claims. And it is certainly untrue that he had to punch me in the jaw to get me off him. I came by that bruise naturally, from being forced to jump off the deck of a perfectly good ship into a tiny lifeboat.

French tucked an arm under my chin and towed me to the lifeboat, where he left me clinging to the edge like a limpet and with strict instructions (entirely unnecessary, I assure you) to keep my head down. Then he swam away and snagged Vincent, who had drifted a short distance away on the current. The *Sea Lark* was steaming past us but the hooligans kept up a steady fusillade, with bullets hitting the lifeboat and splashing into the water around us. We huddled together, clinging to the side of the lifeboat and keeping our heads well below the line of fire. My teeth were chattering and my legs were working like pistons. I doubted I could continue this rather strenuous activity for much longer. I managed to enquire about Vincent.

"I'm not so bad. My leg's dead but t'other one's workin' fine. I'm as cold as a corpse, though. Do you fink they'll keep movin' or will they come back and 'ave another go at us?"

Just what I was wondering. I expounded, in short bursts of speech interrupted by my teeth clacking together, my theory that the crew was likely not corrupt, and that the captain, who might be, and our knaves, who certainly were, would not want to haul us back on deck and give us a chance to point out their villainy.

"If the confounded crew ain't in league wif those rascals, 'ow come they let 'em shoot at us?"

I'd thought of this as well. "They probably told the crew we were stowaways, maybe even that we had crept on board to steal something, and that we set the fire to cover our escape. Even the most reasonable of men would take umbrage at having his ship set afire."

The shooting had subsided now, and we could see the *Sea Lark* steaming away from us, the dim figures of dozens of men gathered on the aft rail.

"I hope your theory is correct," said French. He clutched the edge of the lifeboat with one hand and Vincent's collar with the other. "If so, our friends may convince the crew to sail on and leave us here. The sailors might think casting us adrift this far from land is adequate punishment."

We watched with apprehension for any sign that the ship was turning back. The small circles of light from the portholes grew dimmer and the thumping of the screws faded into the distance. It was jolly dark out here, with only the sound of waves lapping the sides of the lifeboat. A cold wind ruffled my wet hair, and I shuddered.

"I think they're going on," said French. "But even if they come back we've got to get in the boat before we freeze to death." I wasn't sure that hadn't already happened. French placed both hands on the edge of the boat and gave a mighty kick, propelling himself up and into the craft. French hauled in Vincent and then pulled me aboard. I flopped in headfirst, with my feet waving in the air. I was damned grateful to be out of the water.

"Are you badly shot, Vincent?" I asked.

"It ain't a bullet at all." The lad sounded disgusted. "It's a big ole splinter. Must've come from the deck."

"You're sure?"

"'Course I'm sure. It's stickin' out a good six inches. You want to feel it?"

I declined.

French did not. "It'll be hours before we get to shore. I'm going to pull out that thing and bind up your leg."

"It can wait. It don't 'urt. 'Ardly."

French bent over the lad and ran a hand up the boy's leg. I heard Vincent gasp.

"Good God," said French.

"Just leave it in there." If I hadn't known Vincent as well as

I did, I could have sworn the scamp was terrified. One can hardly blame him. I shouldn't like the idea of a scrap of wood protruding from one of my appendages and the thought of having it pulled out without even a sip of brandy to dull the pain was monstrous.

"Come, come. It'll only hurt for a moment."

That, I reflected, was one of history's great lies and I would have to remonstrate with French later about trotting it out so cavalierly.

He bowed over Vincent's small, shivering figure and I saw his shoulders tense.

Vincent yelped. "Oi, guv! Don't touch it." Then Vincent screamed and French was standing, swaying gently with the motion of the boat, and brandishing a wicked piece of wood, fully ten inches long and sharp as a dagger.

Vincent had gone silent.

"Poor lad. He's fainted." French ripped off his coat and wrapped it round the boy. "We could use one of your petticoats right now, India."

"I've a scarf." I unwound it from my throat and passed it over. French deftly wrapped Vincent's leg and sat for a moment with his hand pressing on the wound.

"Bleeding?" I asked anxiously.

"Hard to tell in this light, and with his clothes soaking wet. We'll have to get him to a doctor as soon as we can. I've no way of knowing if there are any splinters or bits of his trousers left inside. If there are, they've got to come out, or there could be serious consequences."

"I suppose we should start rowing."

"Come sit by Vincent and keep pressure on his wound."

We swapped places awkwardly. French found the second

oar, inserted it into the oarlock, and set to work. I could see we were destined to spend a fair amount of time out here on the water, for the wind and the tide were against us and it was a long pull to land. French tackled it heroically. I'd expected nothing less but I wondered how long he'd hold out. Vincent's head was rocking violently with the movement of the boat. Reluctantly I slipped my arm behind his neck to steady him and scooted closer to hold him upright. I thought it unlikely that even protracted exposure to seawater had cleansed the boy of the layers of filth he'd accumulated, but I was pleasantly surprised to learn that he smelled no worse than a dog that had plunged into a viscous swamp.

Dawn was approaching. The first rays of sunlight had appeared, casting a pallid glow over the grey water. I am no sailor, but it seemed that the waves were building and the breeze had freshened since we'd clambered aboard the lifeboat. I shivered uncontrollably and Vincent, even in his unconscious state, was shaking. I could see his face now and he looked as pale and lifeless as a dead flounder.

"Will he be alright, French?"

French stopped rowing for a moment and rested his arms on the oars. "He's lost a lot of blood, I think. And these conditions can't be doing him any good."

"Tell me when you're tired and we'll change places."

He snorted. "I hardly think you're strong enough to maneuver these oars."

"I'm strong enough to thump you over the head with one, if provoked."

He laughed, then sobered and resumed his rowing. I could see him fully now in the grey light of dawn and his face was pinched with exhaustion.

"Regardless of what you think, I shall try my hand at it," I said firmly. "You'll need a rest soon."

He ignored my comments as men do when they feel their masculinity has been impugned and settled into a fluid, rhythmic stroke that would have eaten up the distance, save for the waves that hammered our small craft. We struggled on, or I should say French struggled on, battling the buffeting waves and the cold wind that streamed out of the north. Hard to believe it was May. I've been warmer in a January blizzard. The faint lights on shore had been extinguished as the sun had risen, and the English shore looked farther away than it had in the darkness.

"How far are we from land?"

French shrugged. "Too bloody far. But this is a shipping lane, and there will be vessels about. I'm hoping we can hail one and get taken aboard."

I hadn't thought of that prospect and found it cheering, especially since I had noticed that my feet were now covered with water. I pointed out this fact to French.

"Damn and blast! There must be a leak somewhere."

"Indeed," I said coldly. If we were going to continue our relationship, I must cure French of this annoying habit of his. I do not care to have the obvious continually pointed out to me.

"Make yourself useful and look for it." I believe French was growing tired for he sounded irritable.

I propped up Vincent as well as I could and plunged my hands into the icy water, groping along the rough planks of the lifeboat's hull. A splinter pierced my palm and I swore loudly. It was the first of many. By the time I'd covered the length of the boat, my hands felt as if I'd been fondling a hedgehog.

"Did you find anything?"

"No, but I suppose that's good news. It's obviously a slow leak or we'd be swamped by now."

"Is there anything on board you can use to bail the water? There should be a bucket or pail that could be used for that purpose, or to catch rainwater for drinking."

"That's an appalling thought. I hope you didn't mean to imply that we'll be out here so long we'll need such an implement."

It didn't take long to search our small vessel. It did not contain a pail. I regretted this immensely, as did French when I informed him.

"Perhaps it fell overboard when the lifeboat dropped into the water. In any case it should have been secured."

"You can inform the ship's owner of this shocking oversight when we get back to London."

"*If* we get back to London."

"Of course we will. Don't be such a gloomy puss."

Vincent stirred and looked round groggily. "Where are we?"

"The same place we were when you fainted," I said. "Correction, we're twenty yards closer to shore."

French swore.

We passed some considerable time in silence. Vincent was too ill and weary for conversation and French was disinclined to engage in civil discourse. I used the time to mull over the gang's activities, and what our next move should be. It might have been sensible to drop the matter entirely. The presence of the villains on the *Sea Lark* surely indicated a strategic withdrawal from London. Mayhew's murder would almost certainly lead to the discovery of the thefts as the police investigated the colonel's background. And our enquiries around the docks must have further persuaded the thugs that it would be wise to leave England until the dust settled. I decided that the best thing for us to do was alert Dizzy to the theft of the rifles and let him handle the military blokes, and inform Superintendent Allen of what we'd learned. My interest in finding Mayhew's killers had dissipated a bit. If the bloke was going to join forces with criminals, he'd assumed a bloody big risk and paid for it with his life. I was still chapped at having been roughed up by those three blackguards in my own home, and I wasn't thrilled to be tootling about on the Atlantic thanks to those blokes, but in the interest of a quiet life I would be willing to forgo revenge.

The only wild card in this hand was the presence of Philip. The poor devil had the judgment of a guinea fowl. Driven by greed, he was, or he'd have never thrown in his lot with these killers. Philip liked clean linen and a daily bath and good cigars. He did not go in for bloodletting, torture or murder. I feared the chap had made a fatal error and would pay for it. I pictured him enduring the fate of Mayhew if the criminals ever twigged that Philip had let us go, and I shivered at the thought. I looked up to find French rowing mechanically, his eyes fixed on me.

"Thinking of Bradley?" he asked, in a damned unpleasant tone, half mocking and half condescending. "Or should I call him Philip, as you do? You're obviously intimate friends."

"We are, and you might take a moment and be grateful for that fact. Otherwise, we'd have joined Davy Jones in his locker by now."

"You recognized him the day he met Captain Tate at the Jolly Tar." It wasn't a question. "And that's why you tripped me when I went after him."

"Yes, I recognized him. He's a cracksman and a jewel thief but he's not a killer. Before you collared him and accused him of Mayhew's murder, I wanted to find out what he was up to, using my own methods."

"I suppose those methods involve a bottle of champagne and a soft mattress?"

I bridled at that, partly because that very thing might have been necessary. "See here, French. I do not take kindly to those seamy allegations. My acquaintance with Philip goes back many years, long before a certain government agent entered my life and turned it topsy-turvy. In a way, Philip has done me a good turn." I wasn't about to reveal that I had stolen a stolen gem from the bloke. "And I thought it only fair to give him a chance to—"

"To what? Inform the rest of the gang that we were on to them? You've obviously warned him, and he's warned the rest of them and now they're sailing off to India." French was virtually incoherent with rage.

"I have not warned Philip. I had merely renewed our acquaintance and had been waiting for an opportune time to find out his connection to this whole affair." I did not think it wise to mention that I had been wearing my dressing gown at this meeting, nor that it had taken place in a bedroom.

"Oi," Vincent said weakly. "Are you talkin' about the gentleman thief? The same chap you used to spark wif?"

"So the whole of London knows about your relationship with this man?" asked French.

"I hardly think Vincent constitutes the entire city."

"You surprise me, India. The man is connected to a horrible crime."

"If you knew Philip—"

"I do not desire to know Philip, now or ever."

"Then you shall just have to take my word for it that he did not murder Mayhew."

"But his compatriots did, and he is guilty by association."

"But not by law," I retorted.

"We shall never know that, now that he's escaped justice by fleeing the country." French rowed ferociously. "Just how well did you know this fellow? Was he your lover?"

I considered shoving him overboard. "You presume too much with those questions, French. Shall I enquire into the intimacy of your relationship with your fiancée?"

"I'll thank you not to besmirch the name of Lady Daphne. She is a pure, sweet young woman."

"In contrast to me, do you mean? If that's how you feel, then I wonder why you've been hanging around me like a doting hound. Ah, could it be that underneath that supercilious manner of yours, you're nothing but a man like all the rest? You'll marry your docile lass with a title and spend your free time whoring."

He recoiled as if I'd struck him, a look of pained astonishment on his face. Then his eyes narrowed and his jaw tightened.

"How dare you accuse me of such a thing? I have never treated you like a, like a—"

"Like a whore? You can't even bring yourself to say the word. You'd be surprised how many men can't. It permits them the illusion that they are gentlemen. And I seem to recall that you had no qualms at sending me off to the Russian embassy to ply my trade, so long as I brought back that bloody memo you wanted."

Well, that caused him to clamp shut his jaws, as I expected it would. I would note, however, that anger is a fine inducement to strenuous physical effort as French rowed like a galley slave for the next several, silent hours. I did offer, three times in fact, to take a turn on the oars, but French refused by doggedly shaking his head and paddling on. Very well, if he wanted to sulk, let him. I suppose I should have been flattered that his nibs was jealous of Philip. If I were typical of my species, I'd probably drop a few comments about Philip's manly figure or beautiful eyes, just to goad French to fresh demonstrations of envy. But I've never gone in for such games. You never know when a chap's leash may break under the strain and he'll go for your throat. Besides, I had a nagging suspicion that French's taciturnity might not result from jealousy at all, but from mere anger at me for interfering with Philip's capture back at the Jolly Tar.

# TWELVE

The day wore on, and a more unpleasant day I have never experienced. It was bitterly cold in that little craft, with the wind blowing briskly and our clothes sodden with seawater. Vincent passed in and out of consciousness. In the sunlight it was apparent just how much blood the tyke had lost. His trouser leg was soaked from ankle to waist and the scarf French had wrapped round the wound was steeped in gore. With great reluctance, I unwound the thing and washed it out in the water, wringing out the excess before reapplying it to the boy's leg. Every now and then I'd catch French looking worriedly at Vincent and chewing his lip, but when he felt my eyes upon him he found something to stare at on the horizon. I occupied myself by cupping my hands and bailing out a cup of water at a time. We bobbed about like a drunkard's head, and I was half sick to my stomach, although that might have been hunger as none of us had eaten since dinner last night. By noon I had decided that it was indeed hunger and not nausea afflicting me and that I would gladly exchange French for a loaf of stale bread and a swallow of inferior brandy.

Despite French's assurances that we were adrift in the middle of a busy shipping lane and would soon attract attention, we were roundly ignored by the stream of vessels passing by. The steamships chugged past and the sailing ships looked glorious as they flew along, heeling over with the white spray flying as they carved through the waves. They were bound for the ports of the Empire, and not one of them was willing to douse the boiler or drop canvas to investigate our tiny craft. They must have taken us for a band of lunatics who'd chosen to fish in the worst possible location and they simply changed course and sailed past us without so much as a wave of the hand.

The sun was beginning to slip below the yardarm (whatever that may mean; I just know the golden orb was plummeting toward the western horizon at disheartening speed) when a fishing boat drew near and hailed us. French lifted a weary arm and I was dismayed to see the shredded flesh on his palm. It was lovely to watch the deft maneuvers of the fishermen as they lowered the sails and came alongside us. It was tricky work, standing up in that lifeboat as it rose and fell on the waves, but French and I lifted Vincent into the waiting hands of our rescuers. I reached up and felt my arms being pulled out of my sockets as three burly fellows hauled me aboard. They brought French aboard the same way, and he collapsed onto the deck. We must have looked a dreadful sight, for the sea dogs took one look at us and hurried us below deck into a dim and foul cabin, lit by a smoking oil lamp and reeking of fish. They swathed us in blankets (damp and also permeated with *eau de piscine*) and fired up a spirit stove and boiled water for our tea. In a few moments we were gulping greedily at the hot liquid and swallowing huge chunks of coarse bread. I have never had a finer meal. I'm afraid we were very impolite guests, for we all fell asleep as soon as we had eaten and spoke not a word until our odiferous angels deposited us ashore. Despite their protestations, French emptied his pockets of coins, and I kissed each one of those grizzled coves on the cheek. It was the least I could do, and if any of them thought it odd that a beautiful lass was gallivanting around in a pair of trousers, they had the grace not to mention it.

Frankly, I was surprised to find Lotus House still standing as it had been a full twenty-four hours since I had left it and God knows what the marchioness was capable of destroying in that length of time.

"Call the doctor and have him look at Vincent's leg," French said as the hansom pulled up to the pavement. It was the first time he'd said a word to me in hours, and it was just like the poncy bastard to issue an order. "I'm going to see the prime minister and apprise him of the situation. I'll be back after I've spoken to him and had a rest."

With that he snapped an order to the driver and the hansom lurched away.

"Wot's 'e so buggered about?" asked Vincent. His eyes were drooping with fatigue and he could barely stand.

"Pay no mind to him," I said. "Let's get you inside."

"It's the gentleman thief, ain't it? Wot's 'is name?"

"Philip. But you're not to worry about that right now."

"Don't *you* worry about it. I'll straighten out the guv."

I could have hugged the lad, but I'd never hear the end of that and the little sod would be expecting favors from me for the rest of his life, so instead I put an arm around his waist and dragged him up the steps and pounded on the front door.

Normally you'd expect that when you return home after disappearing for a day and a night, looking as if the dogs had dragged you in from the nearest rubbish heap and supporting a wounded comrade on your arm, your employees would jump to it, stumbling all over themselves to pour you a hot bath, fetch the doctor and administer some medicinal spirits. I only mention this as it did not occur. Indeed, no one answered the door.

"Wot the 'ell?" Vincent grumbled.

I hammered on the door with all the force I possessed and for good measure, shouted for Mrs. Drinkwater.

Clara Swansdown jerked open the door and put a finger to her lips. "Shhh."

It had to be that bloody marchioness. It would be just like the old trout to shuffle off this mortal coil while residing at Lotus House. Inspector Allen would be delighted to put me in the frame for another death.

Clara deigned to open the door wide enough so that I could drag Vincent inside. "Ooh, poor fellow. What happened?"

Explanations could wait. "Summon the doctor," I said. "Unless he's already here."

Clara looked confused. "Why would he be here?"

"I assume we've an invalid in the house. Otherwise I'll speak as loudly as I wish in my own home."

"Ah, you thought the marchioness was ill." Clara patted my arm. "The old pet is fine. No, it's Maggie."

"I don't have a bint named Maggie."

Vincent's pale face creased in a smile. "It's the marchioness's bitch. Is she whelpin'?"

Clara grinned. "She's already popped out two and the marchioness says there's more on the way."

"Let me see," Vincent demanded. He took one shuffling step forward and collapsed.

Clara, having noticed the smear of blood now covering the marble tiles, gave a little shriek.

"Forget those blasted puppies and fetch the doctor." I left Vincent on the floor. Well, what else was I to do? I couldn't carry him upstairs by myself and as not a single tart had materialized by now, I assumed they were all watching Maggie spew out miniature canines.

The marchioness's head appeared from behind the study door. "I'll thank ye to keep yer mouth shut. Maggie's havin' a dreadful time and . . ." She noticed Vincent's body sprawled in the foyer. "What the devil are ye doin' out here? Get that young feller to bed. And get a doctor to look at him. What's wrong with the lad anyway?"

I was too weary to answer. "Clara will fetch the doctor. Could you please send out Fergus? I need help getting Vincent to bed."

The marchioness withdrew, muttering. Fergus appeared, shirtsleeves rolled to his elbows. With his wall-eyed countenance, he was able to simultaneously glare at me (no doubt blaming me for Vincent's state) and look tenderly upon the young rascal. Despite being an old fellow Fergus easily lifted Vincent in his arms and carried him up to the bedroom I had been using. I resigned myself to spending the next few nights on the sofa in my study, provided the marchioness hadn't enthroned Maggie there.

The doctor arrived, a brisk, chinless young chap with a pince-nez. He handed me his bowler and proceeded to give Vincent a thorough examination. I winced as the doctor cut through Vincent's trouser leg and exposed a livid slash in the flesh, which was turning blue and puckering at the edges. When the good doctor took out a metal probe, I remembered that hot water would be needed and took myself off to find Mrs. Drinkwater.

An hour later Vincent's gash had been cleaned and bandaged, the doctor had given him a dose of morphine and the boy was sleeping soundly. Maggie had also produced seven mewling black-and-white bundles. The marchioness was crowing with delight, the tarts were arguing over the puppies' names, Mrs. Drinkwater had felt inspired to bake a cake no one would eat and I was dead on my feet. I helped myself to a few drops of the morphine the doctor had left for Vincent, stretched out on the rug by his bed and dropped into welcome oblivion.

It was dark when I awoke, stiff and crabbed. My clothes were sticky with salt and my skin felt drawn. I struggled upright. Vincent was sleeping peacefully, a small bubble expanding and contracting at the corner of his mouth. I stumbled to the top of the stairs and shouted for Mrs. Drinkwater.

Fergus stuck his head out of the study door. "Her Ladyship asked me to inform you that the puppies are nursing and sudden noises may frighten them."

"Is that verbatim, Fergus?" I glared at him and heard the old witch cackling in my study. Mrs. Drinkwater came from the kitchen, wiping her hands on her apron. Apparently Fergus was busy with his nursing duties and Mrs. Drinkwater had been restored to her position as cook. I requested a plate of sandwiches and a hot bath and after I had indulged in both, I felt considerably better. Apparently, the key to enjoying Mrs. Drinkwater's food is to refrain from eating for an extended period of time before indulging.

Afterwards I wandered back into Vincent's room and found him awake, still weak but ravenous. I procured more sandwiches and sat with him as he devoured the pile. Then he had two pieces of cake, followed by a half-dozen ginger biscuits. He swallowed the last few crumbs and threw back the covers.

"Get back in bed this instant," I said. "The doctor said you must rest."

"Where're me britches?"

"I discarded them. They were soaked with blood and the doctor had to cut them off you."

As expected, this information pleased Vincent enormously. He inspected his leg. "Crikey, that's a whale of a cut. 'Ow many stitches did I get?"

"The doctor says you'll have a scar."

Vincent flashed a gap-toothed grin. I had known he'd find that news exciting as well.

"Where's French?"

"He went to tell Dizzy about the rifles." In truth, I was beginning to wonder where French was. He'd had ample time to inform the prime minister of the scheme we'd uncovered, and he'd had more than enough time to rest. I supposed he was staying away from Lotus House to signify his displeasure with me. Very childish, that, and not at all what I expected from such an honourable fellow as French.

"'Ere, wot am I goin' to do wifout any trousers?" Vincent's forehead was puckered with worry.

"I'm having one of the girls run up a pair for you. They'll be ready soon. But you're not going anywhere until the doctor says you can."

"Not even to see them pups?"

I sighed. "I'll see if Fergus has a dressing gown he'll loan you."

Fergus proved to be accommodating, just as soon as I gave him the money for a new dressing gown. By the time I managed to turf out the marchioness, her faithful retainer, Maggie and her puppies, the other three dogs, and Vincent, I'd be destitute. I brooded over that prospect for a moment and then remembered the astonishing fact that I was an heiress and had no need to worry about how much whisky the marchioness could drink or how many sandwiches Vincent could eat at one go. I hadn't had any time to think about the bombshell the marchioness had dropped on me, and it was time I had a chat with my aged houseguest.

I clattered downstairs and into the study, where the marchioness was coaxing Maggie to nurse one of her offspring.

"I believe I'll bring all my bitches here to whelp," the marchioness said with satisfaction. "Just look at this litter! Finest litter Maggie's ever birthed." She thrust one of the tiny creatures at me. I was forced to take the thing, or it would have fallen to the floor. It immediately began to whimper.

"Puir wee thing. Put yer finger in its mouth."

"I don't even do that for customers." Nevertheless, I pried open the pup's mouth and inserted the tip of my pinkie.

"Sit yerself down and tell me what ye've been up to. Where's that rascal nephew of mine? And what happened to Vincent?"

I'm not proud of myself. I should have handed her back that damned dog and thanked her sarcastically for inviting me to take my ease in my own home. Instead, I sat promptly,

cradling the wee beast, and gave the marchioness an anno-
tated version of what had transpired since I'd left Lotus House
on the night before last. She listened keenly, now and then
stroking Maggie's head or nudging one of the pups in the
direction of the feed trough. I confess I omitted a good portion of our adventures. I skimmed over the part where Philip
had released us and eliminated entirely the angry words
French and I had exchanged in the lifeboat.

When I'd finished she looked thoughtful. "Ye say one of
those villains took pity on ye and let ye go? Now why would he
do that, I wonder?"

I shrugged.

"And where is French?"

"He's gone round to see the prime minister."

"I'd like to meet that man. Do ye think French would introduce me?"

"I'm sure he'd be delighted." Just thinking of French's face
when the marchioness made her request was going to afford
me hours of amusement.

"My Lady—"

"Och, ye can call me 'Auntie.' Ye might as well, seein' as how
we'll be livin' next door to one another."

I nearly dropped the pup. "Well, um, thank you. I suppose.
I mean, it may take a bit of getting used to, you know."

Thank God this domestic scene was interrupted by Clara
Swansdown, accompanied by the rest of the whores. They'd
come to see the puppies. I gave up mine without regret and
watched as a houseful of sluts kissed puppy heads and whispered nonsense into puppy ears. If I could get the girls to pet
and cuddle the customers like that, I'd have to keep the doors
open twenty-four hours a day to keep the clients happy. I

snapped out of my reverie at the thought of my customers. I'd been absent for two nights and I hadn't even thought to enquire about my enterprise.

I herded Clara to one side. "I'm sorry I've left you alone so much recently, Clara. How has trade been?"

"Oh, it's been grand. Never busier."

"How much did we take in while I was gone?"

Clara nodded at the marchioness. "You'll have to ask her. She's been collecting the money and keeping the accounts."

"Collecting the money?" I gaped. "You mean, she's been talking to the customers? Do we still have any?"

Clara giggled. "Well, we've lost one or two. Them that aren't sound on Scotland." She looked meaningfully at the marchioness and lowered her voice. "You know how she is. Takes offense real easy about bagpipes and kilts and all that. We just steer the conversation away from any such things. Now she's solid on dogs and stag hunting and the fellows love that sort of talk."

"The marchioness discusses stag hunting with my customers?" My tone may have been a trifle steely.

Clara looked uneasy. "Well, we found it best to let her go on about the rut, instead of Culloden, whatever that is. Sure, and she nearly has a heart attack if you mention that word."

My own heart felt weak at the moment.

"Did I do anything wrong?" Clara asked.

"No, no. You've done just fine." Well, I could hardly blame Clara for not corralling the old girl. I'd had no luck at that myself.

That did not stop me from attempting to do so now. I sauntered over and sat down beside her on the sofa. "I hear you're running the till these days."

She beamed at me, her pink gums shining. "Aye, we've done well."

*We?*

"I've a knack for this, ye see? I'm a dab hand at chattin' up the customers, and what fine fellers most of 'em are." She leaned over to share a confidence. "Mind ye, some of 'em need a stern lecture about their manners. The English are terrible snobs, ain't they? Ye'd think Adam Smith and David Hume were local boys from Sussex. But not to worry. I disabuse 'em of that notion right away."

"How many clients have we lost?"

The marchioness waved a hand blithely. "Weel, now, that I couldn't say. But I do know that if a feller takes offense at being told he's wrong about the Act of Union, then he's not worth havin' as a customer."

I squeezed my eyes shut. "Your Lady—"

"Auntie."

"Auntie," I said through gritted teeth, "we . . ." Dear God, what was I saying? "*I* cannot afford to lose customers over their political views. In fact, I make it a point to discourage talk of politics at Lotus House. It only leads to bad feelings and loss of income."

"Pish," said the marchioness.

I'm ashamed to say that I gave it up. I'm a self-sufficient woman. I've handled Cossack guards and Scottish assassins and foreign anarchists, but I'll be damned if I had the gumption to tackle one decrepit crone with a brace of puppies on her lap. What I needed was a quiet place to think over things, like how to break the ice with French, and how to eject Vincent and the marchioness at the first opportunity, and how to restore a bit of sanity to my life.

"Ye know, I've been thinkin'."

I steadied myself. "Yes?"

"I had no idea that this profession of yers was so damned lucrative."

The alarm bells began to ring. With justification, as it turns out.

"The two of us would make a formidable team. Yer spendin' way too much money on liquor. And why the devil don't ye make those girls pay for their own rouge? Do ye have any idea what that's costin' you every month? Ye turn me loose and I can have this place shipshape in thirty days."

"What about Scotland?" I bleated.

"What of it? I wouldn't say this to just anyone, but seein' as yer family, I'll tell ye. It's bitter in the winter."

"It can be very cold in London in January."

"Compared to Tullibardine, London will feel like Italy. Not that I've ever been to Italy, mind. I don't hold with foreigners."

"But what about claiming my title? I'll need your help to do that." I was so bloody desperate I was willing to consider pootling off to Scotland to rid myself of my . . . well, "guest" is hardly the word for someone who had invaded my house and taken over my business.

"Aye, there is that. We'll have to go home soon, but then there's no reason we can't come back here. To tell the truth, ye'll need some money. The house at Strathkinness needs a few repairs."

"Repairs?"

"Aye. A new roof, and the drains will have to be seen to, and then there'll be a few windows to replace."

"But what about the income from the estate?"

The marchioness's eyes skittered to the window and a

vague expression crossed her face. "There's that, of course, but a few extra bob would come in handy."

"What is the income from the estate?"

The marchioness gently poked one of the puppies in her lap. "Look at that little feller. He's prime. I'm thinkin' of givin' him to ye."

Now I knew very well the marchioness was trying to distract me, and I was not going to be played quite so easily. I was just about to tell her so when French walked in and provided a real distraction. He looked a bit haggard from his hours at the oars, and his hands were wrapped in cotton bandages.

He bowed his head to the marchioness. "Good afternoon, Aunt Margaret." He did not look at me.

"Where've ye been, ye Sassenach rascal? Have ye seen the pups yet?"

"I'll look at them later. I've just stopped by to tell India that the prime minister has requested our presence at a meeting."

"What? Now?"

"You've time to change. I'll meet you in the lobby of the Langham in an hour's time." And with his message delivered, he strode off.

The marchioness watched his retreating back with pursed lips. "Weel, he's got a burr under his saddle, don't he? What do ye suppose has vexed him so?"

I knew perfectly well, but felt disinclined to share the information with her. But from the shrewd glance she shot in my direction, I had a feeling she might have guessed.

# THIRTEEN

When the prime minister of Great Britain summons you it's best to respond promptly, even if you're in the middle of a discussion about the terms of your inheritance. I threw on some clothes, hailed a hansom and trotted off to the Langham Hotel, where Dizzy resided. He'd once had a fine London house but he'd sold it after the death of his beloved wife, Mary Anne. Hard to credit it, I know, but the crafty old Levantine had married a woman a decade his senior, and there hadn't been much money in the match. That was quite enough to shock the *ton,* but deuced if the old boy hadn't actually married out of love, a thing unheard of among the beau monde. To me, it was just another example of the old boy cocking a snook at "the quality" and I liked him all the more for it. But I digress.

The doorman recognized me and gave me a brief nod, opening the heavy door for me. French was lounging in a chair in the lobby. He got up languidly and sauntered over, managing to gaze politely at a point just over my shoulder.

"I've just seen a fellow in a top hat and an army chap making tracks for Dizzy's room." At least French was speaking to me. "Neither looked happy. I'll wager we've stirred up a hornet's nest."

"Splendid. It's so tranquil at Lotus House that I'm bored to tears."

French stifled a laugh (another hopeful sign, I thought), and we hurried up the stairs. My heart had lifted at the prospect of action, and perhaps French's had as well.

There were stalwart fellows loitering about the hall and at the door of Dizzy's sitting room. French nodded to the guard at the door, who knocked lightly to secure our admittance. A beefy chap opened the door and bowed us in. He might be playing the role of butler tonight, but I wouldn't want to argue with him about where he'd stashed my umbrella. Dizzy was getting edgy, what with anarchists swarming all over London, intent upon blowing up government officials and aristocrats. I can't say I blame him for feeling that a few lads with thick necks and scarred knuckles might be just the ticket.

The prime minister rose at our entrance and advanced on us, beaming. I was glad to see the old fellow looking well again. He'd caught a nasty cough after spending the Christmas holidays at Balmoral. The Queen likes fresh air, you see, and insists that the windows remain open even when the draughty old pile is enveloped in a bloody blizzard. Poor old Dizzy had suffered greatly from the chill, but he seemed to have recovered his health and spirit.

"My dear Miss Black," he said, catching my hands and squeezing them gently, those brilliant black eyes of his fixed on mine. The fellow is about as sincere as a three-shilling whore, but I am fond of him. I smiled back at him and told him how pleased I was to see him again.

He acknowledged French with a slight bow and then led us over to the other occupants of the room.

"Sir Hereward Digby of the India Office," said Dizzy, indicating a disgruntled chap with a tuft of white hair like an ermine's tail surrounding his bald pate, a round face and a fleshy nose marbled with blue veins.

"And this is Major General Buckley, of the quartermaster general's staff."

Buckley's career had not been spent in the field. He was broad in the beam and the buttons of his uniform coat were strained to the point of danger. Over the years, his face had assumed a permanent expression of suspicion, and his mouth was crimped and posed to pronounce the fatal word "no" to any proposal. Both Digby and Buckley shot a curious glance at me when the prime minister introduced me to them.

We all took a pew and Dizzy was kind enough to have tea and cakes brought in. We munched and sipped politely and made small talk until Dizzy signaled that it was time to discuss business by clearing his throat and depositing his cup and saucer on the table.

"Just so that we are aware of how things stand, let me apprise you all of certain facts. Mr. French and Miss Black are agents in my employ." At this revelation, the general jumped as if he'd been spurred and the chap from the India Office choked on his Earl Grey. Dizzy ignored the interruption and carried on. "Mr. French has advised me that they have learned that British rifles are being shipped to India under false bills of lading, and that a certain Colonel Mayhew, assigned to the quartermaster general's department, has been murdered, most likely as a result of his association with this matter."

Dizzy cast a sidelong glance at French and me and we nodded to confirm his statement.

"Consequently, I made enquiries of the army and General Buckley has confirmed that large numbers of rifles and a great amount of ammunition have gone missing from military armouries over the last few months." Dizzy turned a grave visage toward Buckley and the military wallah nodded unhappily.

Dizzy continued on, relentlessly. "It appears that the armaments were transferred by written order to the Bradley Tool Company, which was in turn responsible for shipping the arms on to our military depots in India."

"That is highly irregular," said French, in a mild voice, but all the same Buckley shot him a vicious glance.

"Indeed," Dizzy concurred gravely. "The army may consign certain items to private companies for transportation to foreign ports, but never weapons. Those are carried by Her Majesty's Royal Navy."

"Who signed the orders?" I asked.

"Colonel Mayhew." It was General Buckley who spoke. He leaned forward in his chair, his hands on his knees. "In each case, the colonel issued instructions to deliver the weapons to this fictitious company. In fact, this arrangement began to occur only after the colonel joined the quartermaster general's staff."

"Was he responsible for these sorts of arrangements? The transport of weapons, I mean." I was careful to keep my voice neutral.

"It was within his purview, yes. Otherwise, the orders would have attracted attention. But since Colonel Mayhew was the officer responsible for such matters, no one thought to question him."

French withdrew a cheroot from his pocket. "May I?" he asked the prime minister.

"Certainly. Tobacco is a powerful stimulant to the mind. We shall need the use of all our faculties to resolve this matter."

French smiled tightly. "Am I right in assuming that this matter goes beyond mere theft? I doubt Sir Hereward is here to discuss the army's deficiencies."

The general bristled at this and Dizzy cut in smoothly to prevent an outburst. "You are correct, Mr. French. Just after you brought the matter of the stolen rifles to my attention, a memo from Sir Hereward crossed my desk. By the way, my esteemed colleague here keeps an eye on the princely states of India. It is a tiresome job, as there is always some rajah or rani arguing over the amount of the British subsidiary allowance they are receiving, and the Mussulmen are always disputing with the Hindu, and there's usually a revolt brewing somewhere, which brings us to the matter at hand." Dizzy waved a hand at the India Office bloke. "Perhaps you would be so kind as to explain."

Sir Hereward would. "As Lord Beaconsfield has said, I am responsible for all matters relating to the princely states. I, ahem, assume that you are all familiar with this term." Naturally, the chap was looking at me.

I looked vacant and put a finger to my mouth. "I say, aren't those the little kingdoms and such that some Indian prince pretends to run, only really we're in charge of the whole circus? And they've got such exotic names, those little chaps.

Maharajah and nizam and nawab. I'm sure I don't know how you keep them all straight. Where was I? Oh, yes. We keep the ruler sweet by paying him off and in exchange we get to collect all the tax revenue and pocket the profit from the state's exports. And then when the chap bites the dust we refuse to acknowledge his heir and claim that the kingdom has reverted to us. Have I got that right?" I looked around innocently.

Sir Hereward was not amused. "We provide valuable services to the rulers of these states, ma'am, and their subjects benefit. You must remember that these people are little more than savages. Without us, they would have no wells or irrigation, or any roads to transport their crops to market. And as for the reversion of the kingdoms to the British government—"

"I believe we are straying from the point, Sir Hereward," Dizzy said soothingly. "The rifles?"

If it had been anyone other than the prime minister, I do believe the India Office chap would have stayed on his soapbox. As it was, he looked hurt for a moment and rubbed his hand over his bald pate.

"Yes, of course. For the past few months, we've been dealing with a troubling situation in the state of Ganipur. The rajah there had assumed the throne on his father's death and had seemed an excellent fellow. The British resident at the court thought the young man was shaping up nicely, listening to the resident's advice and treating his people well. But two years ago, the rajah began to act strangely. He began to ignore the resident's counsel, then the rajah became rather rude and offensive and finally, and after a few months, he told the resident to pack up and leave. When our chap refused, the rajah had his cavalry escort the poor devil to the border and left him there with his luggage in a heap by the side of the road. Well, we couldn't have that."

"No, indeed," I murmured. French's elbow dug into my side.

"What caused the disruption in the relationship?" he asked, to distract Sir Hereward.

Sir Hereward's fleshy face darkened. "Someone has been pouring poison into the rajah's ear."

"Russians," Dizzy hissed. Lord, that man hates the Russians, which I suppose is natural as Dizzy's every waking moment is spent trying to keep the greedy bastards from weaseling their way into the British Empire. The Ivan is always poking about in Afghanistan or India, probing for a soft spot in the British armour so the Russians can stir up some discontent and make a few friends among the locals. I'm not overly fond of those Russian buggers myself but my hatred is rather more personal, having spent some time as a prisoner of those treacherous thugs.

I braced myself for a lengthy diatribe from Dizzy against our Slavic foes, but Sir Hereward wasn't ready to yield the floor.

"Yes, the tsar has sent an agent to stir up things in Ganipur, and he has succeeded admirably. In fact, the rajah has taken up arms against us and the army has been battling his troops for several months."

General Buckley, armchair strategist, gave the India Office chap a sour look. "Why the devil have we been fighting some jumped-up little heathen for months? We should have wiped out his forces and hanged the wretch by now."

Sir Hereward remained cool. "You'll have to take that up with your associates at the War Office. I gather the rajah has rather a lot of troops, General, and our forces are stretched thin at the best of times. And he doesn't stand and fight, you know. He attacks our supply chain and raids our camps, but he doesn't collect his army in one spot. Ganipur is a hilly region, sir, and the rajah and his boys can disappear into those hills for weeks at a time." Sir Hereward shifted in his chair and I could see that he was sharpening a lance point for General Buckley. "And then there's the matter of the rajah's arms. His army is not equipped with the usual motley assortment of ancient muskets and old swords. He's contrived to get his hands on several hundred Martini-Henrys, straight out of England's armouries."

Ooh, I would hate to have been on the receiving end of that stab.

General Buckley subsided in his chair. "The stolen rifles have been delivered to the rajah of Ganipur?"

As Sir Hereward had just said so, in plain English, I thought the general rather slow on the uptake.

"Good God!" he exclaimed. "It can't be."

"I'm afraid so, General. Two weeks ago we fought an engagement with the rajah's forces and took a dozen prisoners. They were all equipped with Martini-Henrys."

"I don't suppose they could have ambushed our brave lads and taken the rifles from the boys they cut down?"

Sir Hereward shook his head. "We questioned the prisoners. To a man, they claim the rifles arrived at their encampment in crates, and they were each issued a new weapon and ammunition."

A bead of sweat appeared on the general's upper lip. "I say," he sputtered feebly, "that's a damned bad show. Just wait until I get my hands on the blackguards who've done this—"

"You're quite right, General. The situation is intolerable," said Dizzy. "The question then becomes, how do we remedy it?"

"We've got a man in India who's looking into the thefts," said Sir Hereward. "He's chasing a lead or two, but I'm afraid I've nothing more to report than that."

"The India Office is investigating the matter? Why hasn't the quartermaster general's office been notified?" General Buckley looked sourly at Sir Hereward. "You should have turned the matter over to the army. It's a military affair, and I don't see why the India Office believes itself competent to handle the enquiry."

An Arctic chill wafted through the room. Sir Hereward drew himself up. "It occurred to us to contact the army, but then we remembered that it was the army who'd lost track of the rifles, and perhaps its officers were not best suited to scrutinize themselves."

The chap from the army took affront at this and began to swell like a toad that had been prodded with a stick. I hoped this wouldn't dissolve into one of those interminable finger-pointing episodes of which the civil service and the military are so fond. I checked the clock on the wall. I'd give it three minutes, and then I was leaving. Unless it came to blows, of course, and then I'd hang around to watch the outcome.

Dizzy, however, was not of a mind to let the argument proceed. That would mean that Sir Hereward and the general did all the talking and if there's one thing Dizzy can't abide, it's giving up the floor and remaining mute. All politicians love the sound of their own voices, but none loves it more than the prime minister. Mind you, he'd have given those Roman orators a run for their money and it could be a pleasure to hear the man in full flow, but only if the subject interested you. I'd pay money to hear Dizzy maul the Russians anytime, but if the topic turns to the disestablishment of the Church of England then, thank you, no, I'll hie myself off to the nearest pub. With the exception of a few members of the cloth, the rest of the populace, I expect, would join me.

Dizzy cut in smoothly now. "Both the India Office and the army have a vested interest in seeing this matter resolved as quickly and efficiently as possible. That is why I have requested that Mr. French and Miss Black delve into the issue." He held up a hand in response to a squawk of protest from the general. "It would be wise to allow an objective third party to look into the matter. General Buckley, I'd like you to collect all the documents relating to the shipment of rifles and ammunition which bear Colonel Mayhew's signature, and send them to me by runner. I shall see that they are delivered to Mr. French and Miss Black. When they have discovered the culprit or culprits behind these thefts, we shall discuss their punishment with the appropriate military officers. We shall also discuss any changes to the quartermaster general's procedures that we find to be necessary as a result of this situation."

Dizzy turned to Sir Hereward. "Are you in communication with your agent in India?"

"I am, sir."

"Then you will advise him to continue his investigation in India, and you will keep me informed of his findings."

Sir Hereward hooked a finger in his collar and stretched it gently. "I should like to do that, sir, but I fear that it is impossible to carry out your instructions."

"Oh?" Dizzy looked down his nose at the civil servant. As the prime minister has a nose the size of your average bowsprit, it took rather a long time for that searching gaze to find its mark.

"The last telegram I received from my agent advised me that he was boarding a ship bound for London. He had a lead to follow here, he said, but he did not have time to explain the matter in full and did not want to commit anything to writing which others might read. I assume I will hear from him in due course."

"And you must advise me at once if you do. We can't have your agent and my agents tripping over each other."

"Indeed not."

Our meeting broke up then, with instructions from Dizzy to the general and Sir Hereward to advise no one, other than their immediate superiors, about the subject of our conversation. General Buckley huffily announced that he knew how to be as discreet as the next man, jammed his hat on his head and strode off. Sir Hereward took a rather more graceful leave of us, assuring us he'd contact Dizzy just as soon as he heard from his man, and Dizzy thanked him prettily.

Then it was our turn to leave, and Dizzy shook hands with us both.

"There's liable to be bad blood between the two offices. I don't doubt that I'll have to arbitrate matters before long. Let me know how you get along, and whether there is anything I can provide you. Now off with you both, and catch me a thief."

It was a pleasant afternoon, so we decided to forgo a cab ride and strolled in the direction of Lotus House. French walked along with his hands in his pockets. I could tell he was cogitating about something.

"I'm glad Dizzy told the general to supply us with his records. I doubt he'd have cooperated with us otherwise," I said.

French grunted.

"I wonder what Sir Hereward's agent has found that's

bringing him to England. We'll have to link up with the chap when he gets here."

"Mmm."

"You're a bit broody," I said.

"Am I?"

"Yes, you are." This elicited a faint growl. We trudged on in silence.

"And why the devil did the gang kill Mayhew?" I wasn't about to let French repress my natural investigative instincts. "Haven't they heard of the goose that laid the golden egg? How will they get their hands on the rifles now?"

That finally got his attention. He took his hands out of his pockets and smoothed the wrinkles from his coat. "That's a damned good observation."

"Yes, I know."

His lips quirked and I could see that he was biting back a smile. He glanced at me and the smile disappeared, to be replaced by a look of irritation. Now the poncy bastard was scowling at me.

"What is it?" I asked. "Piles giving you trouble? Your valet forgot to iron your cravat this morning?" I grabbed his coat sleeve and swung him round to face me. "Out with it, French. I won't stand for you sulking like a child. If you've something to say to me, then say it."

"You'll have to choose, you know."

"Choose?"

"Between that bloody Philip, and your duty."

Normally, any discussion of my "duty" would cause me to howl with derisive laughter. The only duty I recognized was the obligation I felt to pile the sovereigns as high as I could, but one look at French's face and I could tell he was deadly serious. It wouldn't do to mock. On the other hand, I do not take kindly to getting a Bible lesson from a sinner.

"And what of your duty to Lady Daphne?"

Rage kindled in his eyes. "That is a low blow, India. The circumstances are entirely different."

"Are they?"

"Certainly. I know that you're fond of that bastard, though God knows why. I know you think you owe him a favour for cutting us loose on that ship—"

"I do owe him, and so do you. We owe him our lives."

"But he's in league with a gang of murderers. He may not have known those thugs would kill poor Mayhew in such a dev-ilish fashion, but he knows now what they've done, and what they planned to do to us. You can't make excuses for the man."

"I don't have to, not to you or anyone else. Hang it, French, he is on a boat to India. If there's one thing I know about Philip, it's that he's a coward. Now that he's got the wind up, I expect he'll find plenty of excuses to linger in Calcutta. We won't see him again."

"Why do you persist in protecting that wretched man?" French's face was twisted in anger.

Sometimes I can be as thick as two bricks, but usually not when it comes to men. I've a remarkable insight when it comes to the sons of Adam, if I do say so myself. However, upon reflection, it occurred to me that my transactions with the male sex have been of a commercial nature for the past several years, and that I was severely out of practice when it came to matters of the heart. Not that I put much stock in such things, but I'm aware that some people can be overwrought when it comes to love and affection.

"Aha! This has nothing at all to do with my duty as a government agent, does it? You're jealous, French." In retrospect, I should have sounded a tad less triumphant.

I expected him to vehemently deny such a charge, but instead he looked bleakly at me and said, "I am."

That flummoxed me. I do wish French would play this game by the same rules other men do. He was supposed to hotly dispute my evaluation, and assert that I had misinterpreted his interest and all the normal sorts of bluff and bluster that accompany such a conversation. I opened my mouth to tell him so.

"And I am jealous of Lady Daphne," I said, and then I blushed. God help me, the words had just spilled out. I clapped a hand over my lips, horrified that something else equally revealing might issue forth.

French smiled wanly. "I'm glad to hear you say that. I wondered whether you cared for me at all. I was afraid I might be just another chap to you."

"You are sui generis, French." I took his arm and steered him toward Lotus House. "I will make this promise to you. If resolving the case means that we must apprehend Philip, then I will not stand in the way."

"Fair enough."

We walked along in silence for a few minutes. Then French spoke. "As for Lady Daphne . . ."

I put a finger on his lips, a daring move on the pavement of a busy London street and one that would normally have caused French to bolt for a hiding place. Today, he remained motionless, his eyes boring into mine. "If you cannot come to me with an easy conscience, I will understand," I said, poking him in the ribs. "I'll be annoyed, naturally, and probably not very nice to you for a long time, but I will understand."

I thought my little speech, which had cost me a great deal of something I value rather highly, namely my pride, would ease the poncy bastard's mind, but I'll be damned if he didn't look even more troubled than before I'd absolved him of any obligation to me. These gentlemen are a breed I know nothing about, and if they're all as irresolute as French I'm not sure I want to learn more. How is it that a chap can whoop and smile and charge into battle, but mope around like a bloody spaniel when it comes to women? Well, I'd done all I could to relieve French's mind about that blond wench of his, at great cost to myself, for I'll admit I've grown very fond of the bloke and had been looking forward to finding out if his manservant starched his unmentionables. It was down to French now, and he would have to decide what his blasted honour could bear. There was nothing more for me to say.

And I particularly did not want to say that the decision as to whether the case required Philip's capture would be mine and mine alone.

It was teatime when we returned to Lotus House, and Fergus had supplied an excellent repast that was being enjoyed *en famille* in the study by the marchioness, the whores, Vincent (in a pink silk peignoir that I recognized immediately as it came from my wardrobe), Fergus, Maggie and her pups, the other three dogs, and to my astonishment, Mrs. Drinkwater.

The marchioness, who was making herself comfortable in the chair behind my desk, spied us and waved a scone in our direction. "Come in and put on the feedbag."

"Why are you wearing my dressing gown, Vincent?" I asked.

"Och, one of the puppies had an accident on Fergus's gown and it's being washed now," said the marchioness.

"That pink gown is a favourite of mine. If one of the puppies has an accident on it, he or she will be tossed into the street."

"Settle yerself, India. I'll pay for any damage."

A couple of the tarts stopped stuffing their faces and vacated their chairs, deuced considerate of them, I thought, seeing as how I was their employer and until today they had never been invited to sit in my study. I needed to have a word with the marchioness, and soon, before I lost control of my employees.

At least Mrs. Drinkwater remembered that I paid her wages. She lumbered out of her chair and cut two slices of fruitcake, handing them to French and me. "Have a piece of this excellent cake. Fergus made it."

Now I knew how the little Corsican felt at Waterloo when the mighty Imperial Guard broke and ran. If my cook had gone over to the enemy, then the battle was lost. I should start planning my exile now.

"You look very fetching, Vincent." I tasted the cake and found it delicious, which no doubt accounted for Vincent's presence in such a getup.

He smiled serenely. I noticed that one of Maggie's pups was asleep in his lap.

The tarts chattered and the marchioness held a spirited debate with Vincent over the virtues of collies versus deerhounds. Vincent had a decided opinion about the matter, though he wouldn't have known a Scottish deerhound from a pony. Fergus declaimed the virtues of candied ginger to Mrs. Drinkwater, who hung on every word. French stretched out his legs and drank tea while he looked benignly around the room. I found myself studying the domestic scene with a sense of foreboding. If this kind of thing continued at Lotus House, I'd soon be darning socks for Vincent and cleaning up after puppies while the marchioness plotted new ways to squeeze the clients.

In my current state, was it any wonder that I was almost pleased to see Inspector Allen? I was in a devil of a mood and ready to lock horns with the world and the supercilious twit had the nerve to waltz unannounced into my study. Conversation ceased. The collies bounded to their feet and began to bark hysterically. Maggie lunged at the inspector, teeth snapping. The tarts looked up alertly.

"No need for alarm, ladies. He's not a customer," I said.

"Who the devil are you?" shouted the marchioness over the uproar.

The policeman bristled. "I'm Inspector Allen of Scotland Yard. Who the devil are you?"

The marchioness flung back her head. "I am the Dowager Marchioness of Tullibardine."

Allen had been looking a trifle flustered at the turmoil as any reasonable man would, but the presence of aristocracy positively bewildered him, particularly as said member of the aristocracy was an ancient biddy made up to look like a witch doctor.

"Fergus," I said. "Take the dogs to the kitchen. Vincent, you help him. Girls, upstairs to your rooms. Mrs. Drinkwater—"

"I'm leaving," she said. I'd wager ten pounds she was headed straight for the gin.

It took some time, but eventually the room was cleared of dogs, tarts, servants and Vincent. I debated whether to insist that the marchioness retire to her room, but I knew the old pussy would ignore me and I didn't care to display any weakness to the chap from the Yard.

I have to hand it to the inspector: He was game. He tackled the marchioness right at the kickoff. "May I enquire as to your presence here?" he asked her.

"You may not," she snapped.

If there's one thing I enjoy, it's seeing a policeman slapped in the face. It's a fault of mine, I know, but if you'd had as many run-ins with the peelers as I've had over the years, you'd be forgiven for feeling a bit of pleasure when one of them gets it in the eye.

Allen, deciding the marchioness was not to be trifled with, turned away from her loftily and swiveled his guns in my direction. "I am still waiting for you to produce an alibi for the night of Colonel Mayhew's death, Miss Black."

"Now see here," said French. "Are you accusing Miss Black of being involved in the colonel's murder?"

"Stands to reason, doesn't it? The colonel was blackmailing her. She decided to put a stop to it."

"Blackmailing her?" French jumped to his feet, his expression thunderous. I put a restraining hand on his arm.

"Calm down, French. I have a perfectly good alibi for the night of the murder, as you well know. Inspector, I shall insist that we visit the prime minister so that he can confirm that I was in his presence for most of Saturday night and a good part of Sunday morning."

"Right. Lord Beaconsfield is going to give you an alibi."

"Yes, he is."

"Blackmail?" French repeated. "Why would Mayhew blackmail India?"

I had been hoping that the inspector wouldn't trot out his

theories regarding Mayhew's disclosure of my relationship with French to the poncy bastard's friends and families.

"Your conjectures are irrelevant, Inspector. I insist that you speak to the prime minister, or I shall do so myself."

"You insist," said Allen, sneering at me. "A woman of your class is in no position to insist that an inspector from Scotland Yard do anything at all."

"Your class," the marchioness echoed, rising from her seat.

Allen looked contemptuously at me. "You're a whore."

The marchioness emitted a strangled oath. French stood stock-still, the colour draining from his face, then let out an inarticulate roar and launched himself at the inspector. It wasn't wise, but it was damned chivalrous of the fellow. I just hoped that Dizzy would view French's action in the same light. I'd have intervened but French was too quick for me. He flew at Allen, catching him in a waist-high tackle that sent the two of them crashing to the floor. The windows rattled. In the kitchen, the dogs began to yelp. The study door flew open and Fergus charged through it with Mrs. Drinkwater in hot pursuit. Fergus took one look at the two figures struggling on the floor and seized the poker from the fireplace. Vincent hobbled in, still wearing the pink silk dressing gown, and threw himself into the melee. Fergus bobbed and weaved like an aging boxer, looking for a clear shot at Allen's head. The marchioness danced around behind Fergus.

"Lachlan!" she screamed. "Stop that this instant!"

It took a moment for this to register, but then I remembered that French actually had a Christian name, and this was it.

I added my voice to the chorus. "Don't hurt the man, French."

French was not inclined to listen to anyone. He'd gained the upper hand and now sat astraddle the inspector with his hands locked around Allen's throat. Vincent was assisting his hero by hanging determinedly onto Allen's feet.

"You bloody swine," said French, and cocked his fist. I seized it from behind and hung on to it with the grip of a drowning woman.

"Don't do it," I said, panting.

"Get up off the floor this minute, Lachlan." The marchioness grabbed French's collar and shook him. "Fergus, put down that poker. Vincent, let go of the inspector's legs."

The participants obeyed, reluctantly. Allen struggled to his feet, massaging an elbow and huffing like a Welsh pit pony. A thread of blood trickled from his nose.

"You'll wish you hadn't done that," he said to French.

"If you impugn Miss Black's honour again, I'll thrash you within an inch of your life," said French. His black curls were tousled and the fight had brought a flush to his cheeks. His grey eyes looked as cold as granite. He presented a magnificent sight. My pulse quickened.

"And I'll 'elp 'im," said Vincent. His show of defiance was diminished somewhat by the torn silk negligee he wore, but deuced if he didn't sound grand.

The inspector clapped his bowler on his head and gave us all a poisonous look. "You haven't seen the last of me."

"I rather think we have, Inspector," I said. "If you come back again, I'll set the dogs on you."

"Hear, hear," said the marchioness.

Allen shook his finger at me. "You're treading on thin ice."

The marchioness drew herself up. "I know you're a crude

man, Inspector, but do keep in mind that you're addressing the Countess of Strathkinness. Fergus, see this man out, and then fetch my snuff box."

It was difficult to settle after that contretemps. I thanked French for his gallant defense of my good name and he said it was his pleasure, and then I had to thank Vincent and Fergus and the marchioness, who had, truth to tell, enjoyed the incident to an unseemly degree. The dogs finally stopped barking and were allowed back into the study, the tarts dressed for the evening's work, and Fergus contrived to teach Mrs. Drinkwater how to roast a chicken. A messenger arrived with the documents Dizzy had requested from General Buckley, and French and I made ourselves comfortable with a glass of whisky while we perused the pile of paper. Vincent's leg was sore from diving into the melee so the marchioness insisted that he recline on the sofa, swaddled in blankets while she fetched him a glass of whisky and one of Maggie's pups for company.

"Do you reckon you're in any trouble, guv?" Vincent asked, stroking the black-and-white bundle in his lap.

"Of course he isn't," said the marchioness. "That bloody fool of an inspector don't know who he's tangled with. I'm the Dowager Marchioness of Tullibardine and a cousin of the Queen's to boot. Just let that jackanapes come round here again and I'll plant my Scottish boot in his backside."

French grinned. "I expect you would. But Allen won't be back. I'll have a word with Dizzy tomorrow and have the inspector brought to heel."

"What a relief. He's a tiresome man."

I'd been meditating in the corner, only half listening to the conversation. "We need to visit Mayhew's office again and see what more we can learn about him. If he signed all the orders transferring the weapons to the Bradley Tool Company, then I assume he was in league with the ruffians who caught us on board the *Sea Lark*."

"It would appear so," said French. "Yet if he were, why did he send the bill of lading to Lotus House? And why was he killed? Maybe he'd gotten cold feet and decided to leave the gang."

"My thoughts exactly," I said, a little irked that French had articulated them before I'd gotten the chance. "Was the bill of lading some sort of insurance? A way to blackmail the others? And to what purpose? Mayhew could hardly implicate Philip and the rest without indicting himself. And please don't frown every time I mention Philip's name. How else am I to refer to him?"

French growled a few suggestions.

"You'll blister Vincent's tender ears."

Vincent laughed scornfully, as I had intended, and the mood lightened.

"We need to know more about Mayhew," I said. "I suggest we visit his office again, and see what we can learn about his background."

"You see what information you can charm out of the clerks," said French. "Vincent can talk to the soldiers on duty."

"I don't think Vincent should be up and about yet. The doctor—"

"'Ang the doc," said Vincent. "I'm goin' wif you."

French smiled. "That's the spirit. I want a look at Mayhew's service record, and to have a chat with his second in command. What was his name?"

"Captain Welch. The little chap with the pink face."

We made plans to visit the War Office the next morning, and French rose to take his leave. I escorted him to the door, leaving the marchioness and Vincent straining to hear our conversation.

"I'll say good night," French said. He hesitated, then leaned forward and brushed my cheek with his lips. It felt heavenly, and it was all I could do to restrain myself from forcing him into a headlock and upstairs into my bed. Then I remembered that I had no bed. I'd be sleeping in the study tonight. It was just as well, for I could see that the temptation in French's eyes was tempered by anxiety.

"I'm terribly sorry about my behaviour, India. I've been intolerable."

"You redeemed yourself when you collared Inspector Allen. I felt quite fluttery about the whole thing, seeing you spring into action to defend my honour. Mind you, I haven't much honour to defend."

"You've enough for me."

"I fear that prolonged exposure to me has resulted in a depreciation of your standards." I gave him a chaste kiss and saw him out the door.

# FOURTEEN

I felt a bit ragged the next morning. The sofa was not comfortable and I'd spent a sleepless night. My nerves had been further aggravated by Maggie, who'd been given a box in the corner (filled with a blanket from my bed, mind you) for her pups. Every time I'd rolled over, she'd lifted her head and growled at me. If I was going to occupy the sofa for the foreseeable future, we'd have to come to some sort of arrangement.

Vincent had stumped downstairs in a new pair of trousers run up by one of the girls, and eaten a massive breakfast. The marchioness had demanded her breakfast in bed, and I watched despairingly as Fergus heaped a tray with toast, boiled eggs, several rashers of bacon, porridge, deviled kidneys and a small beefsteak. At this rate, the coffers of Lotus House would be empty soon.

French arrived and he and Vincent and I climbed into the hansom French had left waiting at the curb. The ride to the War Office took some time as the streets were choked with omnibuses, cabs and carriages as the populace of the Big Smoke headed off to work. After a good half hour we were set down at the entrance and Vincent immediately sauntered off to prowl around the edges of the building, hoping to find a few common soldiers to share a smoke and a gossip.

French and I stopped first at the records office. The same six myopic clerks were bent over their desks, shuffling documents with alacrity. Six heads looked up at our entrance. French beckoned to the fellow who'd answered our previous enquiries.

"Good morning, Major. How may I be of service?" he asked.

French produced a folded sheet of paper from his breast pocket. "I have here a letter from the prime minister, authorizing me and Miss Black to make a full investigation of the late Colonel Mayhew's death. I should like to see the colonel's service record, please."

The clerk read through the letter slowly. He inspected the seal at the bottom of the letter and rubbed a thumb over the wafer of sealing wax. He contrived to appear casual, though I doubt he was accustomed to reviewing correspondence from the prime minister. The clerk handed the letter back to French.

"It will be just a moment, sir," he said, and scurried off to dig through a filing cabinet.

"Still flaunting that bogus letter?" I asked.

"On the contrary, this letter is real. I asked the prime minister to provide it when I saw him yesterday."

The clerk returned with a thin folder of heavy paper stock.

The flap was secured by a string looped through a metal tab attached to the folder.

"You shall have to sign for it, sir. There's a room next door where you may review it. When you're finished, please return it to me."

The room to which we were directed was windowless and completely utilitarian, containing only a scarred oak desk, two chairs and a gaslight on the wall that flickered annoyingly. French hefted the folder as we sat down.

"There's not much here."

"Good. I can think of nothing more dull than reading someone's service record."

For the next several minutes we occupied ourselves turning over the thin sheets of paper in Colonel Mayhew's file, reviewing the meticulous notes and copperplate writing of a generation of army clerks. It was riveting stuff. There were details of the colonel's postings beginning from the date he'd graduated from Sandhurst, which had been approximately concurrent with the time Noah had commenced building the ark. There were itemized descriptions of the provisions issued to the colonel during his career, including the fascinating information that he'd once been trusted with a box of quill pens with steel nibs. He'd advanced steadily, but slowly, up the ranks, and his entire career had been spent making sure that our brave lads had salt beef and cartridges when they needed them. A model of rectitude, Colonel Mayhew. He'd never put a foot wrong in his army career.

"What a tedious life the man had," I observed. "Trundling about from one drab army depot to another, all over Scotland, England and Wales. No wonder he turned to theft."

French turned over the last sheet. "I didn't expect to find

anything here, but we needed to be thorough and go through his record. Let's return this file and pay a visit to Mayhew's second in command."

Captain Welch was not pleased to see us, which was understandable given that his desk had disappeared under a mountain of paperwork, and several clerks and a few junior officers hovered anxiously in the background waiting for his signature. His pale blue eyes were red with exhaustion. His expression of exasperation turned sour when he saw us, but he composed himself and said he was very pleased to see the major and nodded briefly in my direction.

"You look very busy, Captain," French said. "I take it Colonel Mayhew's replacement has not been named yet?"

"He has been, sir. But he's not due to arrive until tomorrow."

"I've no doubt he'll find everything to his satisfaction. You seem to have things well in hand."

Captain Welch spared a small, gratified smile. "I do my duty, sir."

"That is all any of us can do. I have my own duty, and I am sorry to tell you that I shall need a few minutes of your time." French unfolded Dizzy's letter and held it out to Welch.

The captain's pink cheeks grew darker as he read. "Begging your pardon, sir, but I don't understand. I thought you said that Scotland Yard was looking into the colonel's death."

"Inspector Allen was, but the investigation has uncovered some unpleasant facts about the colonel's activities."

Welch's forehead wrinkled. "Unpleasant facts?"

French lowered his voice. "A large number of Martini-Henry rifles and a sizeable quantity of ammunition have been stolen from British armouries."

"Good God!" Welch spluttered. He looked nervously at the

chaps milling about the office and barked an order at them. "Come back in an hour's time."

I say, I'm going to have to send my tarts over to the War Office and let these military chaps instill a bit of discipline in them. I'd have given up a night's earnings to have my bints display the unquestioning compliance of the poor sods who'd been waiting for Welch and now marched out without a word of complaint.

Welch swiped a hand across his forehead, removing the beads of sweat that had accumulated there. "I confess you have me at a disadvantage, Major. I've heard nothing of these thefts. Why haven't I been notified by my superiors?"

French can be deuced tactful when he wants to be (that is to say, he can be tactful with everyone but yours truly) and he was courtesy itself as he explained how the thefts had come to light and how we had been deputed to get to the bottom of the whole sorry mess.

"When we spoke to you on the morning after the colonel's murder, you told us that you had not noticed any sort of change in the colonel's demeanour recently."

"I had not. He seemed much the same as usual to me."

"You're quite certain of that?"

Welch put a hand to his face and stroked his chin, his eyes on the wall behind us while he thought the matter over. "Well," he said, "It may not mean much, but there was something."

"Yes?"

He hesitated. "I feel ridiculous mentioning this. It was only a small thing."

"Go on."

"The colonel did seem a bit secretive about something,

almost furtive. It wasn't much, really. I just walked into the office once or twice and he put whatever he was reading into the drawer and shut it. I didn't think much of it at the time. There might have been money problems, or perhaps an issue with the family." Welch glanced obliquely at me. "The colonel, er, might well have been involved with a woman."

"I can see that you did not feel comfortable confronting him about his behaviour."

"Good Lord, no. I shouldn't have dreamed of intruding into the man's personal life. And I had no reason at all to think that his actions were related to his duties."

"Quite." French changed tack. "Did he appear to have come into money recently? Did he gamble or indulge himself with whisky or cigars?" French was careful, I noted, to exclude whores from that list of vices.

"He always seemed an upright gentleman to me, save for the incidents I just described to you." Welch mopped his brow again. "Can you tell me how the guns were stolen? We have procedures, you see, and they're rigorous. I don't understand how this could have happened."

"It appears that Colonel Mayhew complied with the procedures. He had the authority to sign any orders transferring the weapons, and that is what he did. What was irregular was the destination of the weapons. They were removed from the armouries and delivered to a private company, which was nothing more than a front for criminals."

"Captain," I said, "you told us that you handled the colonel's correspondence and draughted orders for his signature."

Welch bristled. His face flushed a rich crimson. "I hope you're not implying that I assisted the colonel in these thefts. I am appalled at the suggestion."

"My dear fellow, she is suggesting nothing of the sort." French poured a bit of oil on troubled waters. "We are merely pursuing an investigation, and it is necessary to ask some unpleasant questions."

Much as it chaps me to have to cater to the sensitivities of others, I assumed an emollient manner. "You are obviously a very busy man, Captain. I was simply trying to ascertain whether the colonel had asked you to prepare an order authorizing the delivery of weapons to this private company. You might have noticed such instructions among the dozens of orders you must see each day."

Welch drew himself up to his full height, which was not impressive. His voice was firm, however. "Certainly I would have noticed. That is such an egregious breach of policy that it would have leapt out at me."

"The colonel had the final authority to sign off on all transfers of munitions? Was his signature subject to review by a superior?" French asked.

"Indeed it would be." Welch grinned humourlessly at French. "This is the army, after all. Of course the colonel's superiors in the department could have looked at any of the correspondence from this office, but they would not have done so as a matter of routine. The department is audited annually, and any questionable issues would be resolved at that time."

"When was the last audit?"

"Nearly a year ago."

"A review would have turned up nothing," I said. "I can hardly imagine that Mayhew left a copy of these suspicious orders lying about for anyone to find."

French asked to look at the colonel's desk, and the long-suffering Captain Welch stood aside while French pawed through the contents. French established himself in the chair just vacated by the captain and took his time going through the drawers. Welch paced fitfully during this procedure, and I gazed out the window and indulged in some serious rumination. At last, French was satisfied that he'd examined every nook and cranny. I tilted my head and he shook his and I knew he hadn't found a thing of interest.

"We need a sample of the colonel's handwriting," I said. "Can you provide us one, Captain Welch?"

The beleaguered fellow rooted around until he produced a piece of paper that he deemed appropriate for us to remove from the office. It was a scrawled note from the colonel to the captain, reminding him that the garrison at Shorncliffe was running low on tinned sardines and asking if the captain would take care of the matter immediately. I thanked him prettily and we strode out into the fresh air. Vincent was waiting for us on the pavement.

"Any joy?" he asked.

I looked round for a cab. "The captain thought the colonel was furtive."

"Does that mean the colonel was worried 'bout something?"

"No, it means the colonel was acting as if he had something to hide."

"Oh." Vincent chewed his lip.

"What is it?"

"I 'ad a word wif a guard—"

"How did you manage that?"

"'E was off duty, 'avin' a smoke round back." Vincent waved a hand impatiently. "Anyway, I was tellin' you wot this bloke tole me and 'e says the colonel had worked 'imself into a lather of late. Somethin' was worryin' the colonel dreadful-like."

"That doesn't jibe with what Captain Welch had to say," French mused.

"Do we believe an officer of the army or a chap who stands in a sentry box and has a smoke with Vincent?" I asked.

"'Ere, now. There's no cause for that," said Vincent.

"I didn't mean to be impolite. I've had a lot of experience with military gents, and they're just as likely to lie as the average costermonger. My money's on the guard. Something about Welch rubbed me the wrong way."

"What?" asked French.

"He only remembered the colonel's shifty ways when you pressed him. He didn't mention that the first time we talked to him. And he also said that he draughted all the colonel's correspondence and so forth. You saw the amount of paper on the captain's desk. The colonel must have been just as busy."

"You appear to be trying to make a point and taking a deuced long time to do it."

"My point is this: Do you think the colonel signed every bit of paper that left that office? I'd wager that the captain signed a few orders himself, only he didn't sign his own name. He signed Mayhew's."

"You think Welch may be involved?"

"It might explain why Mayhew was killed. He might have stumbled onto Welch's perfidy and was trying to collect the evidence to nab the captain. That could be the reason Mayhew sent the bill of lading to Lotus House for safekeeping."

"Surely Welch wouldn't have been so careless as to leave the bill lying about for Colonel Mayhew to find."

"Probably not, but if the colonel was suspicious he might have gone through Welch's desk or his case and found the bill."

French reached up and tapped on the roof of the cab. The driver pulled to the side. French lowered the window and stuck out his head.

"Back to the War Office," he said. He settled back into his seat. "Vincent, have another word with your friend the guard and see what he can tell us about Welch."

We wound our way back through the traffic and lurched to a stop outside the War Office. I was getting heartily sick of the place by now and prayed that we wouldn't have to paw through any more dusty files today. I prefer action. I'll take a sword fight or a bit of gunplay any day of the week over reading spidery handwriting. Vincent tumbled out of the hansom and disappeared around the corner of the building.

French and I sat for several minutes while he drummed his fingers on his knee. I was about to inform him that this behaviour was highly annoying and should be stopped immediately when Vincent yanked open the door of the cab. He climbed inside with a smug expression on his face.

"I fink you're goin' to like this," he said. "My friend says Captain Welch is a nasty little bastard. 'E says 'e wouldn't piss on 'im if 'e was on fire and most everybody feels the same."

"That doesn't make him a criminal," I said.

"No," conceded Vincent. "But the guard says the captain 'as started to strut around like a rooster. 'E bought himself a gold watch that 'e flashes about, and 'e's 'avin' 'is uniforms custom-made."

"How does the guard know that?"

"'Cause 'e was on duty the day they was delivered."

"That's not unusual," I said. "Just ask French. He has a closet full of tailored uniforms."

"Yeah, but the captain ain't got a rich family. The guard reckons 'e's come into some money lately."

I was skeptical. "That's weak, Vincent."

"But it's suggestive." French leaned out and gave the driver the address of Lotus House. "And we haven't many leads to follow."

"*Any* leads," I corrected him.

"Then we'll chase Captain Welch for a while and see what we can learn about the man."

Upon our return to Lotus House, Vincent said he felt peckish and shot off to the kitchen to see if there were any sides of beef left lying about. French and I adjourned to the study for a discussion, which was not going to be a private one as the marchioness was lounging on the sofa, sipping a whisky and going through my accounts.

I whisked the ledger from her hands as I stalked past.

"That belongs to me, and I do not remember giving you permission to look at it."

"Weel, now. Someone got up on the wrong side of the bed this mornin'."

"Correction. I got up on the wrong side of the sofa. And since there's only one side of the sofa from which to rise, I expect I'll be in a foul mood until a certain someone vacates my bed and leaves me in peace. When are you returning to Scotland? Doesn't the present Marquess of Tullibardine need you there to chivvy him along? Aren't the deerhounds pining away for you?"

The marchioness ignored my questions. "Pass me my snuff box, dear."

I summoned Fergus to minister to Her Ladyship's needs.

Vincent wandered in, brushing crumbs from his coat, and went immediately to check on the litter of pups. "Oi! Their eyes are open."

The marchioness beamed proudly. "Indeed they are. They'll be up soon and scamperin' about."

"When they walk, they travel." I was going to have to be firm about that. I couldn't have a passel of pups underfoot. As it was, my first-class brothel seemed to have metamorphosed into a combination of boarding house, hospital and kennel.

It was time for a council of war among French, Vincent, me and, since she showed no signs of stirring from her seat, the marchioness.

"Let us review what we know," said French. I only stayed in my seat because I knew it would be a short recitation, as we knew very little indeed.

"We haven't much to go on," French said.

"Only the word of a guard who thinks the colonel was a deuced fine fellow, if a trifle distracted, and that Captain Welch is a bastard of the first water who's recently acquired a few coins to rub together."

"The latter is at least subject to verification." French lit a cheroot and lay back in his chair. "I will make some discreet enquiries into the fellow's background and finances. I'm reluctant to go through the usual channels at the War Office, for fear he might find out that we're checking up on him. The records office is right below his office, and it would take only one slip from one of the clerks there to alert Welch."

I was not sanguine about French's enquiries. If Welch was a wrong 'un, he'd probably have been drummed out of the service long ago. I said as much to French.

"Agreed," said French. "I doubt that I'll find anything that implicates Welch, but I may find some connections."

Vincent had been listening closely to the conversation. "Wot do you want me to do?"

"I've an important job for you, providing you're feeling well enough to do it."

"'Course I am." Vincent bounded up and dropped the puppy he'd been holding into my lap. Then he engaged in a heated round of athletic maneuvers, hurdling chairs and hopping on his injured leg. "See?"

"That grimace when you put your weight on your bad leg?" I asked. "Yes, I saw that."

Vincent shot me a dark look and then turned a pleading face to French. "I'm alright, guv. Really I am."

"I doubt the work will be that strenuous. In fact, it may involve a good deal of sitting around and waiting."

"You want me to follow this Welch chap?" Vincent practically quivered with delight.

"I do. And if you have to enlist a few of your friends to help you, I'll pay the usual rate."

I hate surveillance as it is almost as dull as listening to a parliamentary debate on agricultural policy, and I was therefore glad to hear this plan.

"India and I have spent too much time with Welch. It would be difficult for us to follow him without being spotted. I think it's best if we leave this to you, Vincent."

"And what shall I do?" I asked.

"For the moment, nothing at all. I'll get in touch with my

contacts and Vincent can follow Welch when he leaves the office tonight."

I know what you're thinking—that I should kick and scream and throw a royal tantrum at being left out of the picture. I've asserted on many occasions that women are just as, if not more, capable than men at this government agent business and to be told to stay home by French while the boys handled matters should have resulted in at least a tongue-lashing for the poncy bastard, if not outright violence to his person. But (and follow this bit closely now) my willingness to let French have a yammer with his old army buddies and some bank managers and to allow Vincent to stay up all night trailing Welch around London is direct proof of female superiority. While they were running around the filthy streets of the city I'd be tucked up at Lotus House, albeit with several unwanted guests (I include the dogs in this category), and that suited me fine. I needed to pay some attention to my business for if I was not careful I'd come back one day from playing spy and find the marchioness had pitched up in London for good, the collies had popped out more litters and the whores had eschewed their regular duties and were camped out in the study, inhaling snuff with the old bag. Consequently, I was more than happy to let the blokes do the heavy lifting for a bit. I'd weigh in with strategic insights and tactical suggestions as needed. In the meantime, I needed to wrest control of my kingdom from some liver-spotted, blue-veined hands.

It was a deuced fine plan, but after several days of living cheek by jowl with the marchioness, Fergus, four dogs and a litter of pups whose number I never did ascertain, my nerves were

stretched as tight as a Mongol's bow. I had some small suc-
cesses, notably in rescuing my ledger from the marchioness
and stowing it away in my desk under lock and key. The key I
strung on a gold chain and wore around my neck. I reckoned
that I had flummoxed the old crone until I found her using a
hairpin to probe the lock on the drawer. I banished Maggie
and the pups to the kitchen and told the marchioness that if
any dogs were seen in any part of the house frequented by customers, she'd have to collect the animal from the nearest taxi-
dermist. I had a devil of a time whipping the tarts back into
shape. They'd developed some very bad habits under the marchioness, sashaying into my study and plopping down on the
furniture for a natter. I set that to rights, but not without
some complaints from the girls. That's what comes of being
lenient with employees. Pretty soon they start to think they
have the right to lounge around drinking tea instead of lying
on their backs and before you know it, they'll have formed a
union and demanded a reduction of hours and an increase in
pay. It's shocking, the things business owners have to put up
with these days.

It did not help that French and Vincent blew in at odd
hours of the day and night to discuss Welch's latest movements, looking self-important and chattering at each other
like two parrots while they absentmindedly thanked me for
the sandwiches and brandy I handed to them. After a week
with the marchioness and the canines, the prospect of slog-
ging about the city while keeping an eye on Captain Welch
was beginning to sound attractive.

The captain was a very busy man. Vincent had been forced
to enlist a few of his friends to help keep track of Welch as he
flitted from brothel to gaming house to theatre. Or so he said;

knowing Vincent as I do I reckoned that the little heathen had just invented a few foot soldiers and was collecting a healthy sum from Her Majesty's government. In any event, every minute that Welch was off duty he was gallivanting about, playing cards and watching cockfights, dropping in at various music halls and visiting the city's best establishments.

French had shared with us the few scraps of information he'd discovered about Welch. The captain had had an undistinguished career in the army, due partly to the fact that he was not the most diligent of men in the service, and partly to the fact that he was loathed by his superiors.

"What's wrong with the chap?" I asked.

"His fellow officers think he's common." French had the grace to look a trifle sheepish. "It's hard for a fellow to fit in if he didn't go to the right school or doesn't come from a good family. Welch's father was a schoolmaster and a lay preacher. Captain Welch found those origins difficult to overcome. And his own personality didn't help matters any. He's always been considered a dull dog by his fellow officers, though they all describe his rather desperate attempts to run with the rest of the pack. Unfortunately, he's one of those unlucky chaps who gets bullied and ragged and develops a kind of servile, cringing attitude as a result. Of course that means the bullying just gets worse. The fellows in his regiment were glad to see him transferred into the quartermaster general's office."

"He didn't cringe when we met him."

"No, he did not. It appears that Captain Welch has adopted a new persona in the last few months. He's become quite the lad. When he's off duty he spends his time mingling with the fancy at prizefights and dining at the finest restaurants in the city. He's developed a fondness for champagne and women,

238

CAROL K. CARR

and he's purchased a box at the opera. His transformation is the talk of the department."

I raised an eyebrow. "That's interesting. Would this transformation have begun at the same time as the theft of the rifles?"

"It did. The captain, being the sort of friendless chap who's always the butt of every joke, couldn't resist trying to ingratiate himself with his fellow officers. He's been inviting them out to dinner and the theatre and footing the bill. I've learned where he banks and persuaded the manager there to let me see the captain's account. Large amounts of money have been deposited into it over the last few months."

"That explains where he got the dosh. No one thought to question how a captain from humble origins could afford to treat his fellow officers so well?"

"Captain Welch has frequently alluded to the generosity of a maiden aunt, recently deceased."

"That old dodge. He really isn't very bright, is he?"

"No. I think further proof of that, if we needed any, is that he's going on about his business just as though Mayhew hadn't been murdered and we hadn't been round to his office asking questions. You'd have thought all the ruckus would have sent him scurrying for cover. Everyone else has."

"You mean the three thugs who accosted us, and Philip."

"It is odd that Welch has remained behind. With Mayhew dead and the government investigating, surely the scheme can't be resurrected. Welch is a fool to stay at the department."

"Agreed. Unless he's been ordered to stay, by someone who wants to know how the investigation is proceeding."

"Dear me, India. Sometimes the subtlety of your reasoning amazes me."

"Do I detect sarcasm in your tone?"

"Only a smidgen. I think it obvious Welch has been ordered to remain at the War Office."

"The question is, by whom?"

"If we find that man, we find the villain behind the whole scheme."

Vincent had been listening to our conversation with an expression of perplexity. "Anged if I ain't lost. Was Mayhew stealin' the rifles, or is Welch the one we're after?"

"I don't know about Mayhew," said French. "Given what we've learned about Welch, I'm inclined to think that he's been forging Mayhew's signature and the colonel was innocent."

"Then why don't you 'ave Welch arrested?"

"The captain is bright enough to forge a signature, but I doubt that he put this scheme together himself. More likely he was approached by someone else, someone who has contacts in Ganipur and arranged the sale of the rifles to the rajah there. That's the man we need to find. If Welch is arrested, the organizer will just find another means to acquire the weapons."

"It seems a risk, leaving Welch at the office. If he's threatened with arrest or court martial, he might reveal the names of the others who are involved."

"He might not know their true names. And I expect that if the leader of this gang believes Welch is about to crumble and confess to his role in the thefts, then Welch will get the Mayhew treatment."

I shivered, remembering the gore in Mayhew's room. "If I were Welch I'd be quivering in my boots."

"Welch seems singularly unimaginative to me. He may not feel himself in any danger. He certainly doesn't appear to be afraid."

"Then he's a fool."

"Money is a great solace. As long as it's coming in, I doubt Welch permits himself to think that things could go wrong for him."

# FIFTEEN

Several very dull days passed, during which Vincent dropped in periodically to inform us that Welch had lost a pile of coins at cards or found a new whore and lavished her with trinkets. Neither French nor I enjoyed this forced inactivity. Nor did the presence of the marchioness add a festive note, as her presence prevented French and me from having the sort of conversation that had been lurking in the background like the proverbial elephant in the room.

The one bright spot in the whole affair was the day French stepped out for a couple of hours and returned with a wrapped parcel, which he deposited in my hands with a flourish.

"Courtesy of Her Majesty's government," he said, "but I took the liberty of selecting it."

I stripped off the paper and found a wooden chest with the

name "P. Webley & Son" engraved on a brass plaque on the lid. My heart beat faster. "I do hope this isn't a piece of jewelry in here."

French snorted, which he does from time to time, although there is nothing gentlemanly about it. "Would I dare bring you a rope of pearls? Go on, open it."

I lifted the lid and beheld my new weapon. French had had the kindness to select another .442 Bulldog revolver, but this one put my previous weapon to shame. It was nickel-plated, elaborately engraved and sported thick ivory grips. The whole thing shone like a diamond necklace against the royal blue velvet interior of the box.

"Well done, French," I said as a I checked the grip and spun the cylinder. I took aim at the Georgian candlestick on the mantel. "It's a beauty."

"Please limit your use of the weapon to villains, India." He smiled mockingly, and I knew this was a peace offering.

Despite the distraction of my new revolver, which I carried around and practiced drawing and aiming at various mutts, I noticed that Vincent was looking pale and drawn, and that his leg was giving him trouble. He had a pronounced limp now and he winced when he sat down to bread and cheese in the kitchen. French badgered him to take a respite and leave most of the work to the gang of street Arabs Vincent called his friends. The runt, being a plucky chap, refused. But one night when the rain bucketed down and there was a chill in the air, he arrived at the kitchen door soaked to the skin and shaking uncontrollably. French ordered him to bed. I expected fireworks but Vincent must have been feeling bloody awful for he acquiesced readily enough, provided he was permitted to venture out once more to arrange matters with his cohorts.

"I'll go with you," said French. "The boys will have to come to me with their reports."

Vincent coughed and nodded, and the two wrapped themselves up and vanished into the storm. I sat at the table and nursed a whisky while I waited for their return. Oh, I could have made myself useful, but the marchioness had assumed command and was barking orders at Fergus and Mrs. Drinkwater to lay a fire in Vincent's room and to prepare a nourishing broth for the boy.

"I hope the lad will be alright. Shame on ye and French for makin' him walk the streets for days on end."

"Vincent never does anything he doesn't want to do. Besides, we had little choice. Welch knows French and me and could easily have identified us."

"Ye'd have thought the prime minister of Great Britain might have more than two agents workin' for him. Why didn't ye ask for help?"

I didn't have a good answer to the question. In fact, the thought of requesting assistance from Dizzy had never occurred to me. No doubt he would have provided additional men to help shadow Welch, but French, Vincent and I were used to acting alone. I suppose we thought we could handle just about anything, having had some success at capturing Russian spies and saving the Queen and dismantling an anarchist operation.

I elected to change the topic rather than respond to the marchioness's question. It's a tactic I've learned from politicians.

"Shouldn't Vincent have a hot water bottle for his feet?"

"Aye. I'll see to it, as ye seem to have nothin' better to do than drink whisky and twiddle yer thumbs."

An hour later French and Vincent returned with Vincent wobbling into the kitchen on unsteady legs, supported by French. He summoned Fergus and together they carried Vincent up the stairs. The marchioness slammed drawers and opened cupboards until she found a ladle and filled a bowl with the broth Fergus had prepared. She took it upstairs herself.

French came down and slumped into a chair. He'd removed his outer garments, but his boots and trousers were sodden. I poured him a large glass of whisky.

"How's Vincent?"

"He has a fever. If it's no better in the morning, we'll summon the doctor. Fergus and Aunt Margaret are looking after him."

"Fergus is an efficient bloke. He'll get Vincent up on his pins in no time. And if he doesn't, the marchioness will drive Vincent mad and he'll recover just to escape her clutches."

French laughed. "She's an indomitable soul, isn't she?"

"That's one way to describe her. Did you meet Vincent's friends?"

"He introduced me to his lieutenant, a lad named Tommy. My word, he was a wretched little thing. No shoes and a shirt that was nothing more than holes held together by a few rags. He seems bright, though."

"He'll have spent his life dodging villains and do-gooders. Trailing an oblivious army captain won't be a challenge."

As I predicted, and I am rarely wrong, it was not. French set up headquarters in the kitchen, where he received a steady stream of odiferous urchins with reports of Welch's location and activities. The youngsters left clutching a few coins and French spent his time writing down copious notes, trying to discern a pattern in Welch's movements and jotting down descriptions of Welch's associates. Occasionally, French would dart off to some mysterious destination where, he informed me, he checked the descriptions of Welch's contacts against the sketches of the tsar's agents known to be working in Britain. It was just possible that if a Russian spy was operating in Ganipur, then one of the tsar's men might be keeping an eye on the weapons' transfers here in England. If the captain had any direct communication with an agent of the tsar, then we could take Welch into custody and exert some leverage, in the proper British manner, of course. These forays proved futile, however, and we were all feeling a bit down at the mouth about the state of affairs when our fortunes changed.

It was a quiet afternoon at Lotus House. The marchioness was upstairs reading the Bible to Vincent, poor little blighter, and Fergus and Mrs. Drinkwater were mucking about in the kitchen while French sat at the deal table there and drank cup after cup of strong tea. I was beginning to wonder about the marchioness's manservant and my cook. They'd been at loggerheads for weeks and now they were as cozy as two old cats. Fergus was dishing out advice on how to make a proper tart and Mrs. Drinkwater was actually listening, staring intently with a queer expression on her face as the wall-eyed cove sifted flour. I'd only ever seen her look that way at a bottle of gin. If I didn't know better, I'd swear the old lush had been struck by Cupid's arrow.

I had retired to the study for some blissful, solitary amusement of my own: relishing a glass of brandy and reviewing my account books without the marchioness leaning over my shoulder. I was pondering the question of whether it was lawful to turf out your aunt and her retinue, or merely immoral—neither situation giving me much pause, if I am truthful—when

French rushed into the study, his hair standing on end and his eyes bright with excitement.

"Get your revolver, India. We're off."

The prospect of gunplay is a wonderful tonic. I snapped out of my lethargy and retrieved my new Webley Bulldog from my desk. I popped open the cylinder and rotated it. It was fully loaded as I had left it but it never hurts to inspect one's equipment. I wouldn't have put it past the marchioness to remove all the bullets from the gun after my various threats against her collies. My precautions were unnecessary, however, and I looked forward to the opportunity to test out the revolver, preferably on the chap who had carved up Colonel Mayhew.

"Where are we going?" I asked, as I filled a pouch with extra cartridges.

"I've had word from Tommy. He followed Welch to Waterloo Station and Welch boarded a train to Redhill, in Surrey, not half an hour ago."

"Let's hope he's going to meet the man who's pulling the strings. I shall be cross if the captain is off to some local hunt."

"Whatever the purpose of his journey, we're going to follow him. It's the only aberration we've seen in his schedule."

We rushed upstairs so that French could inform Vincent of our plans. He wanted to come with us, naturally, but French dissuaded him by asking him to stay at Lotus House in the event we needed him to deliver a message to Dizzy. The marchioness demanded that we keep her informed and I lied and said that we would. I fetched a hat and a purse and deposited the Webley and my spare ammunition in it. Then we were off to Waterloo Station.

The station was a nightmare to navigate, as it always is. Fine ladies who'd come to the city for a day's shopping traipsed along the platforms, trailed by porters juggling armfuls of parcels. Shop assistants and office clerks jostled for position on the outward-bound trains, headed back to their homes in the suburbs. Middle-class families negotiated the crowd and aristocratic types lounged about with their luggage piled high, guarded by an army of servants. The clamour was deafening, as the conductors shouted and the trains came huffing into the station with their brakes squealing.

French was in a fever, worried that there would be no more trains to Surrey until tomorrow, but as luck would have it there was one leaving within the hour. French bought tickets for us in the first-class carriage, an action of which I heartily approved. If one must chase villains, one should do so in style.

It was an hour's journey to Redhill and we spent it in the company of a vicar and his wife, which meant that French and I were unable to discuss Welch, the arms thefts, Lady Daphne or any other topics of interest. We were limited to tame subjects such as the weather, the novels of Mrs. Gaskell, spaniels, the Old Testament, fossils and gardening. The vicar and his wife were enthusiastic about all of the foregoing. I need hardly say that I was not, but I summoned the fortitude to smile and look interested and to interject a few comments where appropriate. French professed a fondness for *Euhoplites* ammonites, lying bastard. Well, I assume he's lying but perhaps there really is a rose of that name, or an ancient tribe of the Hebrew race.

We exited the train at the small station at Redhill. I was greatly relieved that the vicar and his wife were traveling on to Newhaven for I fear that if they'd lived in the Redhill area a dinner invitation would have been issued and I'd have been forced to draw the Webley.

We waited until the rest of the passengers had cleared the station and then wandered around the platform, looking bewildered. After we'd performed that pantomime for a few minutes, French marched up to the ticket kiosk.

"Pardon me. My wife and I were supposed to be met here by a friend. He hasn't arrived and I wondered if you might have seen him earlier." He described Captain Welch.

The ticket chappie didn't hesitate. "Yes, sir. I've seen your friend. He arrived on the four o'clock from London and hired a carriage."

"Hired a carriage, you say?" French looked befuddled. "Now where would he be going?"

The ticket chappie shrugged. "Don't know. But you can ask Isaac over there. 'Twas his rig your friend hired."

A venerable fellow with a seamed face lounged on the ground with his back propped against the wheel of a dilapidated carriage. The bony nag between the traces cropped grass and twitched his ears at our approach. The driver knocked the dead ashes from his pipe and fumbled in his pocket for his tobacco pouch.

"Would you folks be needing a carriage?" he asked.

"Perhaps," said French. "We were to meet a friend here. I understand that he hired you." He hadn't finished his description of Welch before Isaac was nodding.

"He did."

French turned to me. "That's deuced odd. Welch said he'd wait at the station for us."

"He must have changed his mind," I said, playing my part.

"He could have sent a telegram," French fretted. "I suppose

he's gone on ahead and wants us to follow." He addressed Isaac. "Could you drive us to the captain's destination? It seems we are to meet him there, rather than here."

"Aye, I can take you to Hilltop Farm. It's out by Salfords, but I reckon you know that."

"Mmm," French murmured noncommittally.

"Quite a distance," said Isaac around his pipe. "Reckon it's three miles or more. That'll cost."

"Of course," said French.

Isaac looked us up and down, taking in French's tailored clothes and my own elegant self and then named a sum that would have made the most hardened blackmailer blush. French agreed to it without blinking, though I daresay he'd have a hard time prying the reimbursement out of those niggling clerks in Whitehall. As the sun was sinking from sight, our driver/extortionist lit the lamps on either side of the carriage before clucking at the horse and slapping his rump with the reins.

Our route took us through the countryside for a short while. As it was rapidly growing dark, I can't describe the scenery well but I suspect it had all the virtues of the countryside: the smell of manure, muddy farmyards and vicious geese. We trundled across a wooden bridge and into the small village of Salfords and approached a public house called the Duke of Wellington, from which light and laughter spilled into the night. It was a substantial establishment and I thought longingly of a stiff drink and a bite to eat, but Isaac snapped his whip and we surged past. We drove on for a quarter of an hour. The lights from distant farmhouses dotted the landscape. We were at the back of beyond by now, and I was feeling some trepidation about following Welch into this dark and remote region. London is dangerous, but nothing makes my skin prickle like quiet roads and isolated farms. At least in the city I know where danger lurks. I'm out of my element among the cabbages and cows.

Isaac hauled in the reins and the carriage slowed and turned into a graveled drive flanked by two tall stone columns.

French leaned forward. "You can set us down here. It's a fine evening for a stroll. We'll walk the rest of the way."

Isaac gave him a look I expect he usually reserved for the village idiot, and accepted his fare with a shrug. We waited until he'd turned the carriage and rattled off down the road toward Redhill.

"We've certainly made ourselves conspicuous," I said. "We've no luggage and we've just gotten out of a perfectly good carriage to stretch our legs and take the air. The story will be all over the county by morning."

"It can't be helped," said French. "I assume there's a house at the end of this drive and that Welch is in it. We could hardly allow Isaac to drop us at the front door. We need to be cautious, India. We saw what these fellows did to Mayhew and they're liable to do the same to us if they catch us wandering around."

The reminder of the carnage in Mayhew's room sent a chill through my bones. I grasped French's coattail and we set off, skirting the drive by traversing an adjoining field. The pasture was dotted with trees and thick with grass. My skirt dragged over the turf, producing a swishing sound that could be heard in the next county. Low clouds scudded over the sky, occasionally obscuring the nearly full moon that shed a bit of light over the countryside. A breeze had kicked up, smelling of rain. I do not enjoy the elements, and was considering informing French that I would wait for him at the Duke of Welling-ton when he hissed sharply and dropped to a crouch. I followed suit, craning my neck around his solid figure to locate the reason for his wariness. He touched my arm and pointed ahead of us. I dutifully peered in the direction he indicated. A pinprick of light appeared, faded to a tiny red dot, then flared again.

"A guard," French whispered. "Having a smoke. Let's avoid him."

We set off at an angle, bent over at the waist to lower our profiles against the night sky. We crept along like this for some distance until we had flanked the guard. He'd been sta-tioned on the drive, some distance from the house, but now I could see a large structure looming ahead of us. It was a two-storey house of brick, squat and ugly, with a tiled roof. A low verandah ran across the entire length of the house. From the number of windows, I estimated there were only two rooms on either side of the double front door situated at the center of the facade. Each of the rooms nearest the main door had a set of French doors facing the verandah. Curtains had been drawn at the windows, but thin lines of yellow lamplight indi-cated that the first room on the left as you entered the house was occupied. The remainder of the house was dark, and not a little foreboding. An ornamental hedge in need of clipping ran parallel to the front of the house. The gravel drive ran through an opening in the hedge and expanded into a large courtyard of chipped stone.

French put his lips to my ear. "There may be other guards. You go left and I'll go right. We'll meet on the other side, just opposite of where we are now. Have your Bulldog ready."

I counted this as a significant and positive development in

our relationship. Not so very long ago, French would have insisted that he conduct the reconnaissance alone. I was pleased to be deemed capable of creeping about in the darkness looking for criminals.

French drew his weapon, and I saw that he had replaced his Webley Boxer with a new one. The pistol was chambered for .577 cartridges, which are about the size of your average railroad spike. The bloody thing could take down an elephant. The recoil from the shot could take down the shooter. I'd shot the gun once, at a Russian spy, and damned near concussed myself.

Bending low, I scuttled to the shelter of the ornamental hedge and surveyed the grounds. With the light emanating from the windows, the figure of a sentinel would be outlined against the house, that is unless of course the chap was hunkered down somewhere out of sight. But I had to assume that any sentry would be up and patrolling the area for interlopers rather than having a kip while he waited for them, meaning us, to come to him.

I gripped the handle of my revolver and proceeded at a stealthy pace, using the hedge as a backdrop to hide my silhouette. The hedge would also hide me from the view of the guard down the drive, in the event he turned around and looked at the house. It was slow work and nerve-wracking to boot. I'd slide a few steps forward and pause, straining my eyes as I searched the inky shadows for a silent form. My shoulders and neck ached with tension. I hadn't forgotten the butcher's job our opponents had done on poor Colonel Mayhew, and I half expected a blade at my throat at any moment.

I edged around the corner and found myself at the back of the house. There was another gravel courtyard here, containing a stone drinking trough for the farm stock, and an assortment of dilapidated outbuildings. A soft whicker emanated from one of them and I tiptoed across the crushed stone to find that one building was in use as a stable. Two horses in the stalls lifted their heads when I poked mine inside, and I saw a carriage covered by a canvas tarp to keep out the dust. I slithered out and crept warily through a shed (the prior occupants of which had been, by the smell inside, chickens) and another small building that might have been a smokehouse, based on the acrid odor of old soot.

I will confess that my journey was ponderous and by the time I'd ascertained that there was no one lurking in the gloom and had sidled up to our rendezvous, French was wound as tight as a spring.

"What took you so long?" he snapped.

"I was being thorough. I hope you didn't miss anything in your rush to meet me," I snapped back.

French snorted, which I thought a feeble reply. "I didn't see anyone. Did you?

"No. It looks as if there's only the one bloke down the drive. There's a team of horses in the stable and a carriage," I reported.

"Let's see if we can find a way into the house," said French. "Only one of the rooms at the front appears occupied."

We crouched behind the stone trough for a bit, to be sure that our approach had not been noticed. Have I mentioned how much I detest waiting? I'd be very pleased with this secret agent business if only it involved shooting Russians and did not require that I hang about watching people or places, with no dinner and no means of amusement. After three hours or so (alright, it wasn't that long, but it surely felt like it), French deemed it safe to try the windows at the back of the house. All were locked. There was a door too, which likely led into the kitchen, but as it also was bolted we could not confirm our hypothesis.

"Confound it," said French, when we'd exhausted the last of our possibilities. "There's got to be a way in."

"Shall we try the front?"

French sucked in his breath. "It's too risky. What if the guard walks up the drive, or turns round and sees us?"

"Our only other option then is to wait until whoever is in there leaves the house and follow him, or them. But we could wait here for days."

French hesitated, but the idea of staking out the house held as little appeal for him as it did for me. "I had hoped to avoid this, but we'll have to break in. The noise may alert the guard or people in the house. If it does, then dash out of here and head north for a distance. Then cut back west. You'll reach the main road and you can walk to the Duke of Wellington. I'll meet you there."

"An excellent plan, French. Which way is north?"

"Bloody hell." He stabbed a finger at the fields behind the house.

"So west would lie in that direction?" I held out a hand uncertainly. "But isn't the road behind us? Wouldn't that be south? If I go north and then west, how will I cross a road that's south of us?"

"Because the damned road curves. Didn't you notice how we changed directions as we drove?"

"You mean to tell me that you did?"

"Naturally."

"Well, I'll be hanged if I know which way is north or south and I'm damned sure that if I'm being chased over the fields like a bloody fox that I won't remember which is which. I have a much simpler plan. If we are pursued, I shall just run until I'm exhausted. Then I'll cower in a ditch until dawn and head for the first farmhouse I see and beg to be taken to the nearest station. I'll meet you back at Lotus House. Agreed?"

"We're wasting time," said French. "Just do what you like. You always do, anyway."

"That's the first sensible thing you've said all night."

We crept back to the last window we had tried, which, being as far from the presumably occupied room at the front of the house as was possible, represented our best chance of entering undetected. French extracted his knife from his boot and inserted it into the frame, trying to pry open the latch. The grating of the blade against the metal fastening sounded unnaturally loud in the quiet of the countryside. My ears were pricked for any noise from within the house. French worked the blade back and forth. I heard a creaking noise, followed by a crack that to me sounded as loud as a gunshot. French and I froze.

"What happened?" I whispered.

"The frame is rotten. I've split the wood."

We waited for what seemed an eternity, but the house remained quiet and the sentinel down the drive did not come to investigate.

"I believe I can dig out enough of that frame to get to the lock," said French. He probed the wood with his blade, flicking small pieces of it away with each movement of his hand. It can't have been very noisy, for the timber was old and soft, but each time French dug the blade into the frame it sounded to my ears as if a corps of lumbermen was felling oaks.

There was a snapping sound and French grunted in satisfaction. "Just a few more minutes and I'll have this lock out."

He was as good as his word and in no time at all he had pulled the lock from the flaking wood and set it on the ground. He grasped the sash and pushed upward gently, and the window slid open—not, I would note, as silently as we would have desired, but with much rasping and shuddering. This necessitated another wait, but finally French was satisfied that we remained undetected and levered himself up and over the window ledge. He was gone for a few moments sussing out the situation, but returned soon to offer me his hand. I wished I'd had time to change into my trousers, for scrambling through a window encumbered by a full skirt is deuced difficult.

We were in the kitchen. I could see the bulk of a cooking stove against one wall and a row of cabinets against another. Crockery, pots and pans were heaped on a table in the center of the room. A small wooden table and four chairs occupied one end of the room. The air in the room was fusty, and smelled of stale food.

French put a hand on my arm and whispered. "Through the door is a dining room, and then the entrance hall. There appear to be four rooms on each side of the main hall and I assume the same number of rooms upstairs. Welch is in a room at the front of the house with another man. I could only get a glimpse in there. It appears to be used as a library. I don't think there's anyone else in the house, but I didn't have time to check the rooms upstairs. I don't see any lights up there but keep your eyes open just the same."

I tugged my Bulldog from my purse. French took my hand firmly in his and we negotiated our way out of the kitchen and into the dining room. When my eyes adjusted to the dark, I could see that the furniture was covered in sheets. This room also smelled musty, and there was an air of disuse and neglect about the place. We navigated around the furniture and reached the entry hall. French poked his head around the door frame and then pulled me closer, gesturing for me to have a look for myself. Directly in front of me I saw the side of a set of stairs leading from the ground floor to the first. The space beneath it had been sealed off and there was a small door into a cupboard. I reckoned the space would be used for storage. Turning my head toward the left, I could see a white sheet draped over a large dresser or chest. Ten feet beyond the chest lay the front door to the house. Craning my neck farther out of the dining room entrance, I could see a set of double doors between the chest and the main entrance. The doors were closed. I could tell that because a thin wafer of yellow light issued from the room French had referred to as the library. The door to this room, which stood directly opposite the set of closed doors, was cracked open a few inches. I heard muffled conversation.

French touched my hand and we left the safety of the dining room and crept into the entrance hall, edging closer to the library. I winced as a floorboard squeaked under my weight. We stopped short of the open door and huddled against the wall. There was a lively discussion taking place in that room, but the occupants were obviously sticklers for privacy for they were speaking in hushed tones. Once I heard Welch's voice raised in protest but someone shushed him peremptorily and the palaver continued. I could hear only snatches of the exchange. I heard the words "weapons" and "shipment," but the heavy oak door effectively deadened most of the sound from the room. Still, some of the tone came through and from it I gauged that Welch was the inferior in the room. It was frustrating not to be able to hear what was being said, but short of sashaying in and seizing the men at gunpoint . . .

Well, why not? I nudged French and held up the Bulldog so that he could see it in the faint light filtering through the edges of the door. I mimed opening the door and charging in with gun in hand. French frowned and shook his head.

"Why not?" I said against his ear.

"No proof," he whispered into mine.

I've no problem with securing evidence, but I do think it somewhat overrated as an effective means of solving a problem. What the devil were we doing here, if we weren't going to take Welch and his compatriots prisoners and present them to Dizzy wrapped in a bow? We might never have another chance like this. I fumed and blustered (as well as one can when one must remain silent) and French waved me off and put his eye to the crack in the door, ostentatiously ignoring me.

A chair grated on the floor and French jerked back his head. He seized my arm and we slunk away down the corridor to the dining room. French pulled the door behind us, leaving an opening just wide enough for us to peer out into the entry hall. I had to crouch under French's arm to see, but I had a good view. Yellow light flooded the hall as Welch opened the door. He was dressed in a dark suit and carrying a grey bowler.

"Then I shall hear from you soon?" He turned the hat in his hand nervously.

"You shall. In the meantime, you must keep your head." The voice was a honeyed tenor with the faintest of accents. "Those two who are nosing around have nothing on you and cannot tie you to the thefts. As long as you remain silent, you are safe."

"I'm glad you think so, but I feel damned uneasy about the matter." The captain clapped the bowler on his head.

"You shall contact me if the investigation gets any closer?" his companion asked. He stepped into the light. From my vantage point I caught a glimpse of a slender old coot, with a wrinkled face and a slight stoop. One of those Levantine types, I said to myself, for his skin had an olive tone and his eyes looked almost black in the dim light. He was a foreigner, which would account for the accent I'd detected.

Welch laughed, but there was no humour in it. "Yes, I will contact you. In fact, I'll be on your doorstep. You did say you could smuggle me out of England on a moment's notice, didn't you?"

"I can arrange all sorts of things," said the older man. "Transportation poses no problem. Rest assured, Captain Welch. I shall look after you." He clapped a hand on Welch's shoulder. "Speaking of transportation, how do you plan to return to London?"

"There's an inn down the road. I'll walk there and spend the night, then catch the first train in the morning."

"There is a train back to town tonight, leaving at nine o'clock. I shall have Dudley harness the horses and drive you to the station. You should make it with time to spare."

"That's very good of you," said Welch.

"It is my pleasure."

The two men shook hands and walked out to the verandah facing the gravel drive. I heard the older man call to the guard, Dudley, and direct him to make haste and see that the captain made the last train to the city. I heard the crunch of footsteps as Dudley walked off quickly to the rear of the house, making for the stables. The older man offered Welch a cigar and they smoked in companionable silence until the clatter of hooves and the jingle of harness heralded the arrival of Dudley in the brougham. Welch thanked his host and climbed into the carriage. French and I waited quietly while the sound of the brougham disappeared down the drive. The slender fellow entered the house and returned to the room where he'd met Welch. I heard his chair creak as he settled into it. The faint smell of cigar smoke reached my nostrils.

French pulled at my sleeve and I stood aside as he eased open the dining room door. We crept stealthily away, quiet as two Apaches looking for scalps. I didn't take an easy breath until we were well away from the building and were hunkered down in the deep shadows cast by a line of trees.

"I suppose we've improved our skills at breaking and entering, but I'll be damned if we accomplished anything else tonight." I tend to get fractious when I'm hungry, and I was starving.

"We've confirmed that Welch is involved in the thefts although we haven't a shred of evidence to prove it," French said. "Frankly, I'm not terribly worried about rounding up Welch. He's a mere puppet. The chap we want is that foreign fellow back there."

"We could have picked up both of them tonight."

"I know that you're itching to haul out that Bulldog, but as I said, we've no proof against either of them."

"Then we're no further along than when we left London. And I've missed my dinner."

"We have made progress tonight. We have a new lead to follow. We'll walk to the Duke of Wellington and I shall buy you a meal. We'll catch the first train back to London in the morning and I'll make arrangements to watch the house and our mysterious foreigner."

"Are you sure this man and Dudley are actually living in the house? It may only serve as a meeting place. Dudley could return from dropping Welch at the station and he and the old chap could be gone before dawn. As much as I'd like to eat, I think we should stay here and watch the place."

French thought it over. "You're right. We'll stay."

"The next time we dash out of London, remind me to fill a flask with whisky. It's going to be a long night."

Our revised plan required that we return to the house, so reluctantly we left the shelter of the trees and cautiously retraced our steps. We settled ourselves among some rhododendron bushes. From here we could see the drive and the front entrance to the house. It was growing chilly and a fine mist had started to fall. I cursed Colonel Mayhew, Martini-Henrys, Captain Welch, all foreigners and French. I suppose there are rules of etiquette governing how ladies are to sit upon the ground, perhaps when they are at a picnic beside a stream on a sunny day, with servants in attendance to hand out finger sandwiches and such, but I wasn't in a mind to follow any rules. I just plopped down on my bum, drew up my knees, wrapped my arms around them and rested my check on my arms. My stomach sounded like Mount Vesuvius just before it blew and I'd developed a headache.

There was a moment of excitement when Dudley returned. French and I both sat up straight, our discomfort forgotten. The guard did not stop at the house but drove around to the stables and we heard the distinct noises of harness being removed and hung up and the stall doors being shut. Dudley swung into view and crossed over to the verandah, entering the door without knocking. Obviously, the men weren't leaving tonight. That fact was confirmed a quarter hour later when the lights were extinguished.

"Gone to bed," French muttered.

"I wonder if there's any food in the house. I'm tempted to sneak in and see if there's a crust in the larder."

"If they're still inside in the morning, I'll go to the village and send a telegram to the prime minister. I'll bring you back something to eat."

"Why can't I walk to the village?"

"You're a vain woman, India. I can't imagine that you'll want to go anywhere in a stained dress and with your hair in a tangle."

He had a point. I acquiesced to his plan, though it meant he'd be wolfing down some clabber well before I got my hands on any. I added a comb to the list of items I needed to bring on our next outing.

The hours passed slowly. I tried a number of tricks to stay awake: counting to one thousand (I wouldn't recommend that as it had a pronounced soporific effect), devising schemes for ejecting the marchioness and contemplating the contents of my next meal. I gave that last one up as it was too painful and finally decided that it didn't much matter if I fell asleep as our quarry surely would be driving the brougham if they left and the sound would wake me. I was just nodding off when someone stuck the barrel of a revolver in my ear.

"Don't say a word," a voice hissed.

Next to me French's head jerked. He must have been dozing as well.

"If you've got a weapon, take it out slowly and toss it behind you."

French was turning round.

"Don't move," said the voice.

"Homer?"

"French?"

# SIXTEEN

At least this chap had a flask of whisky and a thermos of tea, and he proved very generous with both as well he should have, being, as it turned out, an old acquaintance of French's from army days. We'd retreated to the end of the drive, out of earshot of anyone who may have been in the house, and gathered in a tight huddle.

"Homer, may I present Miss India Black? India, this is Tom Homer. We served together in the Forty-second."

The clouds had obscured the moon and it was too dark to see all of Homer's face, but I could tell he was a stocky chap with a full beard, and could hear his cheerful voice.

"A pleasure to meet you, Miss Black. Now then, French, you must tell me what the devil you and this young lady are doing prowling around an old farm in the middle of the night."

"Very much the same as you, I suspect. We're on the trail of thieves who've been helping themselves to rifles and ammunition from British armouries. I've a feeling you're here on the same mission. Are you working for the India Office?"

Homer chuckled. "There's no moss on you, French. How is it that you know who I'm working for and what I'm doing here, but I had no idea that you were involved in this matter? And pardon my impertinence, miss, but what is your role is this affair?"

French summarized the events of the last few days (skating over the fact that Colonel Mayhew had deposited his envelope into the care of this madam) while Homer listened attentively. He started involuntarily and shot a glance at me when French told him I was a bona fide agent of Her Majesty's government. I didn't mind; it's sometimes difficult for me to get used to the notion that I am a spy.

"So you see," French concluded, "the prime minister asked Miss Black and me to look into the matter. Your chap in the India Office told us his man had sailed for England following a lead. I anticipated that we would run into him at some point in our investigation. Of course, I wasn't expecting the India Office's man to be you, Homer. You always said you were going to retire to the country and farm after your stint in the Forty-second."

"One day I will, but after I left the regiment I knocked around India for a bit. I've a fondness for the country and wasn't quite ready to leave it yet. I knew some fellows in the civil service and it turns out they needed someone who spoke Hindi and Urdu and who knew about intelligence work. They hired me to keep an eye on activities in the princely states."

"We've heard about Ganipur. Your superior at the India Office seems to think there's a Russian hand in the rebellion there."

"You know the government. They see Russians everywhere. But in this case, it's true. There's a fellow named Mirov who's been chumming around with the rajah of Ganipur, urging him to expel the British, which he's done, and assuring him of Russian backing. We believe Mirov has supplied the money to buy the British weapons that have been stolen."

"How did Mirov suborn Welch?" I asked.

"He didn't, not directly anyway. I believe Mirov hired a Greek, Aristotle Vasapoulis, to supply the arms. That was Vasapoulis in the farmhouse, and he's the man I've followed to England from Calcutta. I'd done some digging there and I knew that he was the registered owner of the South Indian Railway Company. When he left India, I was on his trail. I was hoping he would lead me to his contact in the army and now he's done so. I reckoned it would be a long haul once I got here but what a stroke of luck I've had tonight with this Captain Welch turning up and then running into the two of you. We've closed the pincers neatly."

"Tell me more about Vasapoulis," said French.

Homer obliged. "He's an arms dealer with a vast network of contacts. If a client wants the latest Mauser *Gewehr* 71 rifle, then Vasapoulis calls on his friends in Germany. Mauser Brothers and Company is a new enterprise and eager to find clients for their munitions. But when a client wants the Martini-Henry, Vasapoulis must find sources other than the manufacturer. The rifle is only made by the Royal Small Arms Factory in Enfield, which is owned by the government."

"And thus Vasapoulis must find someone in the military who will provide the rifles to him," I said. "That's where Welch entered the equation."

"India and I have been trying to collect evidence against

Welch but we've found nothing solid yet," said French. "But given what you know about Vasapoulis, I suppose we have reasonable grounds for military officials to detain the captain."

"That will halt the thefts, but it won't stop Vasapoulis." Homer paused for a drink of whisky. "He'll merely find another source, although I think he'll avoid recruiting at the quartermaster general's office. You know the army. There'll be a whole raft of new regulations and procedures put in place. You won't be able to get a nail without an order signed in triplicate by five generals."

"Then what of Vasapoulis? We've nothing on him, other than the fact that he met with Welch. Would Welch give evidence against him?" I asked.

"The method of Colonel Mayhew's death must have shocked the captain," said French. "If we can assure him that he'll be safe, he may give evidence against Vasapoulis."

"I wouldn't want to be Welch. Vasapoulis has survived this long because he's utterly ruthless." Homer sounded grim. "He'll find a way to get to Welch, and he'll be sure that Welch knows it."

We stood about for a minute, passing the flask among us and contemplating our next move.

As I wanted my dinner, I made the first suggestion. "We should have Welch arrested. But it should be done quietly. As soon as Vasapoulis gets wind of it, he'll leave the country and we'll miss our chance at him."

"I'd like a crack at Vasapoulis," said Homer. "I've been chasing the bloody man from Calcutta to Surrey and some of our best lads are dead because of the rifles he has supplied to the rajah. I've a score to settle with him."

"But what proof can we hope to find?" I asked.

"He's got a case with him," said Homer. "I saw it on the ship. It never leaves his side. I'd be willing to bet there are some interesting documents in there."

"If he keeps it with him at all times, how were you planning to get a look inside?"

"He's got to sleep sometime. That's why I was at the house tonight. I was planning on burglarizing the place."

"Vasapoulis would make for the nearest port if he woke up to find his case gone," said French.

"No doubt. But if I were lucky enough to find some hard evidence of the thefts, I'd immediately alert the authorities and place a watch on the coast."

"And if there is no evidence in the case?"

"There will be something of value in there, something I can use as leverage against him. I'll stay after the man until I bring him down."

"We'll do everything in our power to help you do that," said French. "I suggest that India and I return to London and have Welch taken into custody immediately. If he is willing to provide evidence against Vasapoulis then we'll arrest the man. If the captain won't speak against Vasapoulis then we'll watch the Greek until we have the opportunity to examine the contents of the case. Should we send some reinforcements for you?"

"I think not. Too many strangers in the neighborhood will attract attention. I'm used to discomfort. I'll keep watch and wait to hear from you. In the meantime, I'll look for a chance to get my hands on that case."

"Be careful, Homer. I've told you what these chaps did to Mayhew. Vasapoulis won't hesitate to kill you."

We bid adieu to Homer and watched as he crept away into

the night. By now it was getting on toward dawn and French and I faced a long hike to the station. I was hungry, tired and chilled to the bone. My clothes were damp and my hair was in knots. I was certain my skirt was ruined from sitting on the grass. To take my mind off my condition, and to pass the time, I proposed to have a friendly conversation with my companion.

"I should like to discuss our ancestry, cousin. Just how is it that we are related?"

French took a moment to light a cheroot. "I'm afraid I stretched the truth a bit when I told Bunny Alcock that we were cousins. There are no blood ties between us. We share a great-aunt in the marchioness, but I'm descended from her husband's side of family. My grandmother was a sister of the Marquess of Tullibardine, the marchioness's husband."

"He's dead, I suppose, as the marchioness carries the title of Dowager."

"He died some years ago. They had a son, David, who assumed the title of Marquess. I don't think Aunt Margaret thinks much of the poor chap. He's a bookish fellow who can't shoot, can't ride and can't abide dogs."

"He must have taken after the marchioness's husband."

"He did. I don't think she cared much for him either."

"Have you been to Strathkinness?" I asked.

"Strathkinness? Oh, your family seat. Yes, I have been once. I went there as a small boy."

"I suppose there's a great house?"

"Um, yes, I think it was quite distinguished." French puffed on his cheroot and added, "In its day."

"The marchioness says it needs a new roof."

"I shouldn't be surprised," said French. "Tell me, do you think you'll ever be able to think of the marchioness as family? I've noticed that you don't call her 'Aunt.'"

"This is all so sudden. One minute I'm the owner of a brothel, the next a spy and now I'm the Countess of Strathkinness. It makes my head hurt just to think of it. And I don't know if I'll ever reconcile myself to being kin to the marchioness, although she's certainly acting like an annoying relative, popping into Lotus House and usurping my position. I've been wracking my brain trying to think of a way to get her to leave London. Any ideas?"

"If I know Aunt Margaret, she'll leave when she's ready and not a moment before. And there's Maggie to consider. I don't think your houseguest will be going until those pups are ready to travel."

"Vincent seems quite taken with those creatures."

"I've noticed that. I have a feeling that one of those puppies may be staying behind when the marchioness leaves."

"What? With Vincent? How's he going to take care of an animal? Half the time he sleeps on the street and the only time he eats a meal is when he cadges one from me."

"He might leave the dog with a sympathetic friend."

I stopped in the road and grabbed French by the sleeve. "Oh, no. You tell Vincent that I refuse to keep a puppy at Lotus House."

"The little fellows are awfully cute."

"I run a business. I can't have a dog underfoot, humping the customers' legs and leaving bones about the parlour."

"Then I suppose Vincent will have to seek companionship elsewhere. It's a shame, really. There's one little pup in particular that he dotes on."

I could see I was going to have to nip this plan in the bud, just as soon as I returned to Lotus House.

We had passed the Duke of Wellington by then and still had a mile to travel before we reached the station.

"French, I want to talk with you about something. Please try not to explode when you hear what I have to say."

"This is about Lady Daphne, isn't it?" The poor fellow sounded resigned.

"It is. I want to be absolutely clear about my position regarding your engagement." I'd given quite a lot of thought to this and I think you'll be jolly well pleased to find that I intended to take the high road, at least for the moment. Well, there really wasn't an alternate route, to be honest, what with French insisting on playing the gentleman and being torn between his duty (marriage to a dull wench) and his base desires (represented by yours truly, in case you were wondering). I'd been riding the chap pretty hard, encouraging him to indulge both his honour and his lust, but I could see that French was mighty uncomfortable at the notion. I found that hard to fathom, frankly, but then my morals have an elasticity that French's do not. In truth, it's one of the things I find most endearing about him, if a little frustrating.

"I realize you feel honour bound to go through with the marriage."

French said nothing but drew deeply on his cigar and expelled a stream of smoke.

"I've made it clear to you that neither your engagement nor your impending marriage is an obstacle to me, but I know that you feel differently. I propose that in the future we merely regard each other as friends and associates."

Now I had no intention of giving up on the poncy bastard.

You may think less of me (though I don't care if you do) when you hear that I consider French to be a particularly well-defended fortress which could be worn down by an unremitting siege. Even the most priggish of chaps is bound to succumb to my charms if exposed to them constantly, and I intended to bombard French until his walls crumbled. In the meantime, I had the added advantage of appearing to sacrifice my personal feelings so that French wouldn't have to violate his bloody principles. I felt rather pleased with myself for thinking of this stratagem, though it would be difficult to chase villains with French when I wanted nothing more than to disarrange the bedclothes with him. This would call for a great deal of patience on my part, and I have frequently made the point that I possess very little of that characteristic. I would have to exert all my will to keep my hands off the man, but the game should be worth the candle.

French had stopped in the middle of the road. "I can't tell you how relieved I am to hear that, India. I had been thinking the same thing."

Bloody hell. I hadn't seen that coming. I thought he would protest for form's sake, capitulate reluctantly to my plan and spend the next few months fighting his lust for me until in a moment of weakness he gave in. I felt as if I'd received a blow to the solar plexus, but I'd be damned if I would let French know that his words had affected me so.

"We're agreed then." I said it nonchalantly, although I nearly choked on the words.

"Good. We'll be friends." French sounded casual, but I thought I detected a hint of remorse in his tone.

"And associates," I said. "We've got a job to do now, and I suspect Dizzy will come up with a few more for us."

"Right," said French, who resumed walking. I trudged after him, pondering just how it was that I had misjudged things so badly. I've a superior strategic mind and I rarely make mistakes, but I'd made a real dog's breakfast out of this situation.

We bought tickets at the Redhill station and caught the first train to London. French and I sat in silence for most of the journey, making a few desultory and awkward comments just to prove that we were indeed chums.

I did not expect to be cheered by my return to Lotus House. Normally, I would have relished a return to my haven, where clean clothes, a hot bath and copious amounts of whisky were on offer. Instead we had to contend with an interrogation by the marchioness and another by Vincent, while fat puppies waddled about underfoot. At least Fergus was there, carrying in a breakfast tray laden with eggs, bacon and porridge. I ate like a coal miner and was finally permitted to trudge upstairs for a bath and a change of clothes.

Fergus had brushed French's clothes and poured a bath for him in the servants' quarters. His nibs was enjoying a steaming cup of coffee when I entered the study.

"Welch lives in Fulham. I've a cab waiting outside to take us there."

"Are we going alone? I'd have thought a few soldiers or policemen might be useful."

French produced a pair of handcuffs from his pocket. "I believe we can handle him. I'd rather not make a scene, in the event Vasapoulis is keeping an eye on Welch. We'll show up at the captain's door as if we're paying a call and spirit him out the back."

"I'm fightin' fit," said Vincent from the sofa. "I'd better come along."

French raised an eyebrow at the marchioness.

"I dinna see why the young rascal shouldna go. He's liable to rip that wound open again if he's too lively, but I admire spirit in a boy. Take him along and get him out of my hair." The marchioness and Vincent shared a conspiratorial glance. Dear God, that's all I needed, those two in league against the rest of the world.

Apparently, Captain Welch was the type to fritter away his ill-gotten gains on gambling and whores rather than invest in real estate. He lived in lodgings that could charitably be described as modest and more accurately as crumbling.

"Blimey," said Vincent. "Wot the 'ell was 'e doin' livin' 'ere?"

"Perhaps he preferred to spend his money on dice and dogs, rather than superior digs," I said.

"Vincent, find a convenient location and keep an eye on the neighborhood," French directed. "If you see anyone who looks as if he's watching Welch, come inside and tell us. If the area is clear, then meet us at the back of the house in ten minutes."

Vincent scuttled off to check the lay of the land and I stood aside to let French rap on the door.

The landlady, Mrs. Bostwick, was a large, cheerful woman with a dingy apron. She was surprised to see us, but enormously pleased by our visit.

"Well, well. This is the first time the captain has had visitors. I always tell him he should have his friends round. It's no trouble to make a meal for them, I say to him, and the price would be reasonable. All I need is a day's notice, I tell him, and I can serve a meal fit for a king. But he keeps himself to himself, as you know, and usually dines out. The poor man works too hard is what it is. He's out till all hours of the night. He'll break his health if he's not careful, I tell him. I'm glad you've come by to see the captain. Just the other day, I said to him, I said . . ."

With difficulty, French stopped the spate of words. "We'll not trouble you, ma'am. We're in a bit of hurry, you see. Would you be kind enough to show us to Captain Welch's room?"

"I'd be delighted to, but unfortunately you won't find him in today."

"Ah," said French, feigning absentmindedness. "He must be at the office."

"I couldn't say. All I know is that he left here yesterday afternoon and I haven't seen him since."

"Did he say when he was planning to return?"

"I thought he'd be back today. He said he had business out of town but would be back on the first train this morning. I expect he went directly to the office. As I said, that man works all the time."

"Would it be too much trouble for you to knock on the captain's door, just to be certain that he's not here?" I asked.

Mrs. Bostwick looked puzzled, but she trotted out dutifully.

"Why the devil did you ask her to look?" French hissed. "If Welch is dead, we'll have another hysterical landlady on our hands."

I regret to say I hadn't thought of that because I'd been so intent on finding Welch. To my great relief, Mrs. Bostwick returned to the room shaking her head. "He's not here, Major."

French looked relieved as well. "Thank you. We'll look for him at his office."

Out on the pavement, French whistled and we waited until Vincent had materialized from an alley across the street.

"Nobody about, guv," he reported. "Where's Welch?"

"I don't know," said French.

"Vasapoulis had Dudley drive the captain to the station last night, but perhaps he didn't make the last train," I said. "He might have spent the night in Redhill. But if that's the case then he certainly would have caught the first train this morning. Yet we didn't see him at the station."

French hailed a cab and we clambered aboard. "To the War Office," French commanded the driver.

"He might have taken a later train," French mused. "There was a local leaving at midmorning. If he took that train he should be back in the city by now. Perhaps he did go directly to the office."

Vincent and I waited in the hansom while French darted into the War Office building. He returned moments later and climbed into the cab, his face grim. "Welch failed to appear for work this morning."

"Do you think that Vasapoulis . . ." I said, then stopped before I could verbalize the sinister suggestion.

"I fear he may have decided that Welch was a weak link who needed to be eliminated."

"Or Welch might have come to the same conclusion and left London before Vasapoulis could kill him," I said.

"I hope you're right, but I can't help remembering that the last time we saw Welch he was in the company of Dudley." French hadn't shaved since yesterday and now he scraped a thumb thoughtfully across the bristles on his chin. "Vincent, I want you to go back to Welch's lodgings and see if he turns up there. If he does, send a message to Lotus House."

"What do you propose to do?" I asked.

"We should return to Hilltop Farm. Since Welch has disappeared, our only hope of pinning the thefts on Vasapoulis is to help Homer get a look inside that case."

"If Dudley dispatched Welch last night then he and Vasapoulis may already be on a ship out of England," I observed gloomily.

"Perhaps. We shall just have to hope they are still at the farm."

"You know, Vasapoulis is not a British citizen," I said. "What's to prevent us from taking him into custody and filing a trumped-up charge against him?"

"That would be a perversion of the justice system, which in my view is one of the great glories of the British system of government."

"Don't be sanctimonious, French. What's a little perversion of justice if we can snag an arms dealer? And he's a murderer to boot. I should think you'd like him locked away."

"As desirable as the ends are, I don't think they justify the means."

"Well, if you want to play it straight, then we'll have to lay hands on that case of his and hope that it contains something other than the morning paper and a packet of sandwiches."

Before leaving for Surrey, I insisted that we return to Lotus House for provisions. Fergus and Mrs. Drinkwater were dragooned into rustling up some comestibles. I did not plan on forgoing my dinner for the second night running. I added a flask each of rum and brandy, extra ammunition for the Bulldog, a pencil and paper, some pound coins and a waxed cotton jacket in the event it rained. Then I donned the trousers and jacket I'd worn the night of our ill-fated foray onto the *Sea Lark*. If there was going to be action, I did not intend to be cursing my skirts while I pursued our quarry. French checked his Boxer and tucked it into a holster at the small of his back.

He drew his knife from his boot and ran a thumb along the edge. From inside his jacket he drew a short wooden truncheon. I hadn't known he carried a billy club. I'd have to get one of those. I opened the Bulldog's cylinder and confirmed it was fully loaded, then tucked my silver dagger into my boot. If French had a knife, then I needed a knife. I rather liked the piratical air it lent to my costume.

The marchioness looked me over approvingly. "Damned useful things, trousers. I've often considered wearin' 'em meself. Very convenient for muckin' about in the garden and walkin' the hounds."

"I plan to have a pair made in tartan when I get to Scotland. There is a family tartan, isn't there?"

The marchioness cackled. "Aye, and it's a beauty. But we say trews, not trousers, north of the border."

"I suppose I shall have to bow to respectability and cover these with a skirt." I sent Mrs. Drinkwater to fetch one for me.

While we waited, French issued instructions to the marchioness. "Aunt Margaret, if Vincent returns with news or sends a message to you, send a telegram to Mr. Scott at the Duke of Wellington in Salfords."

"Ye'll be masqueradin' as Mr. Scott?"

"I will."

"And who will ye be, I wonder?" The marchioness fixed her beady eyes on me. Confound the woman, I almost blushed at her words.

"If we follow our usual pattern, French will be swanning it up at the pub while I'm parked under a bush in a rainstorm, keeping watch on the villain."

The marchioness hooted. "Off with ye, then, and don't come back without that Greek's head on a platter."

"You're a bloodthirsty old cat. You've spent too much time reading the Old Testament."

"Heads on platters can be mighty useful. Has a salutary effect on the other thieves and traitors."

I couldn't argue with that.

# SEVENTEEN

Our search for Welch and provisioning at Lotus House had eaten up a good part of the day and it was midafternoon before we were back on a train to Redhill. We were both feeling a bit disheartened for fear that we'd let Welch slip through our fingers, or that Dudley might have murdered the captain under our noses.

"What shall we do when we arrive?" I asked.

"We'll call in at the Duke of Wellington to be sure that Vincent hasn't tried to reach us. Then we'll go back to Hilltop Farm to find Homer and see if he had any luck in getting into the house and searching Vasapoulis's case."

"If he had, wouldn't we have heard from him?"

"Perhaps. But it's several miles from the farm to the nearest telegraph, which is at the station, and I doubt he'd trust anyone to send a message for him. He'd want to keep Vasapoulis in sight. I anticipate that he'll be waiting for us somewhere in the vicinity of the house."

As the train slid into the station, French leaned forward to peer intently out the window.

"Damn and blast, India. Something's happened."

The platform was abuzz with activity of the official sort. Two blue-coated constables with bewildered expressions watched as bowler-hatted men with notebooks in hand debated strenuously. The press had arrived in the person of an alert little chap in a garish tweed suit, brandishing his own notebook. A half-dozen spectators had gathered to watch the show.

"You don't suppose it's Homer . . ." I left my question unfinished.

French's jaw was clenched. "I hope not. When we get off the train, I'll talk to the man in charge and see what I can learn."

"Your curiosity may arouse his interest."

"I've a story to tell him. Just follow my lead."

"I will," I said. "*This* time."

We disembarked and French tucked my hand into the crook of his elbow. He steered us in the direction of a harried-looking chap with a pock-marked face, a Roman nose and grey eyes that narrowed sharply when we appeared in his field of vision.

"Pardon me," said French, doffing his hat. "I'm Major French and this is my wife, India. We have come down from London for a quiet country outing, but your presence at the station, needless to say, has alarmed us. Has something occurred in the neighborhood? We had planned to walk to the Duke of Wellington and enjoy the countryside for a few days." He gestured toward the basket we carried containing food and drink and my other necessaries.

At French's introduction, the fellow had touched the brim of his hat and nodded to us. "Very pleased to meet you, sir, ma'am. I'm Inspector Cole. As you've ascertained, we've had a situation develop here and I do believe it would be best if you reconsidered your plans for the day."

"What a shame," said French. "Can you tell us what has happened?"

The inspector glanced at me, and I could see he was eager to spare my feelings.

I squeezed French's arm. "I'll wait by the ticket office, dear. From the inspector's face, I can see that his information may be too indelicate for a lady to hear." God, it chapped me to say that, but I reckoned French would get more out of the inspector if I weren't around to inhibit the conversation. I dutifully retreated and spent the next few minutes gazing around the station with the petulant expression of a vacuous wench who's just had her holiday ruined.

French and the inspector held a brief discussion, with French listening more than speaking but occasionally asking a question. When they'd finished, French thanked the law officer and came to join me.

"What's happened?" I demanded when French was within speaking distance.

"A man's body was discovered this morning in a field not far from the station. From the description, it would appear to be Welch."

"The poor fool. He was in over his head. Did the inspector say how he died?"

"Strangled, with his own tie."

"At least they didn't slash him to ribbons."

"Unlike Mayhew, they did not need information from Welch. Only silence."

"We need to find Homer."

"Granted. The inspector does not think it wise for us to dally here. He urged me to take seats on the next train back to London. I informed him that we should be perfectly safe if we travel to the Duke of Wellington as we'll be there long before dark."

"Does the inspector know that it's Welch who's been murdered?"

"No, and I did not inform him of that fact."

"Do you plan to?"

"Not yet. It would be deuced hard to explain how I know the victim without going into some detail about the matter. And I want to talk to Homer first. We shall certainly have to tell the prime minister and devise a plan, but until we know what Homer has found, it would be premature for us to share information with the local constabulary."

"Who found the body? And when?"

"A farmer, who went out to check his crop and found a man's body shoved under a pile of leaves in a covert. That was around four hours ago. The inspector has just arrived and has barely had time to start his investigation."

"Bloody hell," I said. "You know the ticketmaster and Isaac the carriage driver will remember us from yesterday, enquiring about Welch. We left a trail a mile wide."

"Yes, we did. And the inspector is going to be on it, but not for a while yet. He's a garrulous chap, the inspector, and he was pleased to inform me that he is waiting for the ticketmaster who was on duty yesterday to be located and questioned.

The inspector has also been told that if the captain was looking for transportation he would have hired old Isaac, who is
presently delivering a load of provisions to a local village and
won't be back for several hours."

"We'd better cut out of here before the ticketmaster or Isaac
returns and describes us to Inspector Cole."

"I told the man that the Duke of Wellington was our destination. We'll head in that direction, and get off the main road
at the first opportunity."

We sauntered out of the station and down the road in the
direction of Salfords. When we came to the nearest copse of
trees we glanced around surreptitiously but the station still
bustled with activity as the inspector and his fellow policemen planned their campaign. No one was looking in our
direction. We plunged into the thicket and dropped to the
ground. I fumbled with my skirt.

"What the devil are you doing?" asked French.

"Removing my skirt. Fleeing from the law will be much
easier in trousers."

"When you're ready, let's move. I won't feel comfortable
until we're miles from that station."

When I hear the word "miles" I automatically associate the
distance with a hansom cab or a carriage. I can assure you, I
am not one of those hearty types who thinks a hike of several
furlongs is a reasonable way to spend an afternoon. Nevertheless, that is how we occupied the rest of that afternoon. You
could not describe our physical exertion as even a vigorous
walk. It was more like an army training exercise: dashing
from cover to cover, crawling beneath fence rails, leaping
stone boundaries, creeping on our bellies through open fields
of rye and wheat. Boys are said to enjoy this sort of thing and

I expect Vincent would have found it great fun, but within a quarter hour all the flesh had been scraped from my elbows and knees. My hairpins had come loose and my hands were as filthy as any street urchin's. I seriously considered surrendering myself to Inspector Cole and his minions, on the off chance that the nearest gaol would offer at least a jug of water and some soap.

French forced a grueling pace, his long strides eating up the ground. I had to trot along to stay up with him. I am not used to trotting. It is undignified, not to mention debilitating. By the time the sun had fallen to the horizon and French deemed it safe enough for us to rest, I was jolly well wrung out. If I'd been a horse, the glue factory would have been in my immediate future. I believe I emitted a quiet moan when I collapsed to the ground, for French suppressed a smile and fished out the flask of rum from our basket.

"That was hard going. Can you carry on after a rest?"

"Don't worry about me." I chugged rum and coughed. "I can walk all the way to London if it's necessary. Will it be necessary?"

"No. We're not far from the farm." French munched on a roll from the basket and scanned the sky. "It will be dark soon, and we'll be able to approach the house."

"We may find Inspector Cole and his men waiting for us. If he's talked to either the ticketmaster or Isaac, then he'll know that we were here last night."

"I'm not concerned about us. We can easily prove our innocence. But if Cole appears at Hilltop Farm, Vasapoulis will either fight or flee. Neither he nor Dudley will be apprehended easily. I doubt the inspector has ever encountered anyone as ruthless as those two. I doubt that he or his constables are armed. They may walk right into a death trap. Perhaps I should have warned the fellow."

"Cole may prove to be made of sterner stuff than you think. For all we know, the inspector may have Vasapoulis in custody already."

"If he does, the Greek won't be there long," said French. "The man's an international arms dealer. He slips across borders like we cross the street. He'll have powerful connections. And I doubt that he'll use his real name when he announces himself to Inspector Cole. Vasapoulis will be hiding behind a web of identities. In fact, Vasapoulis probably isn't his real name either. In any event, Inspector Cole is playing out of his league. Vasapoulis will be free almost as soon as he's gaoled. *If* he's gaoled."

"If that's the situation, then we will need to be there when Vasapoulis is granted bail and walks out a free man. It may be time to call in more of Dizzy's agents to help us shadow him."

A second, more tempting thought struck me. "If Cole arrests Vasapoulis, then we'll have the perfect opportunity to look in that case of his. Either he'll leave it behind at the house or he'll take it with him to gaol. If he does the latter, then we merely have to inform Cole of our identity and have a good look through the contents."

"First, we must find Homer and see if he's gained any evidence against Vasapoulis. Then we'll plan for all contingencies."

It was dark now, and the lights from the farmhouses glowed warm and inviting in the distance. A full moon had risen and a soft silver light blanketed the countryside. There was hardly a breath of wind, and noises carried far in the still night air. I heard the sound of a cart on a nearby lane, the tuneless whistling of the driver and the weary footsteps of the nag.

"Are you ready, India?"

We gathered our things and cautiously made for the farmhouse, taking a circuitous route that led across pasture and field. Once a humpbacked bull raised his head as we skirted past and a calf shied away from us, his hooves thundering across the ground. I'll tell you, I'd rather be accosted by a gang of cutthroats than thread my way through a field of cattle. Oh, they look nice enough, with those sad brown eyes and those docile expressions, but they're ruddy great beasts who could knock you down with one swish of a tail, and they seem rather territorial to boot. That bull was far too interested in our passage for my liking. By the time we'd cleared the pasture my heart was racing like a locomotive.

We found shelter behind a hedge and French softly whistled a series of notes. A moment later his signal was answered by a muted trill. Homer joined us, emerging so quietly from the darkness that I nearly fainted when his stocky frame dropped to the ground next to me.

"What news?" he asked.

I handed him bread and meat and offered the flask of rum while French briefed him in low tones. At the news of Welch's death, Homer gave a start.

"Good God. These fellows are callous."

"All the more reason for us to proceed carefully. Were you able to get into the house?"

Homer sighed. "I was halfway through that window you'd so thoughtfully left open when I heard a noise from the other side of the building. I shot out of there and it's a good thing

I did, for that Dudley fellow came out of the house and patrolled the area. He did it twice more before dawn. I hid in the rhododendrons and watched."

"Didn't Dudley notice the broken window frame?" I asked in alarm.

"No. I closed the window and jammed the lock back in the frame as best I could. Then I smeared a bit of dirt around the casing. It won't fool anyone under close inspection, but from a distance you wouldn't notice anything amiss. And Dudley didn't bother to inspect the windows, though he did try the back door to see that it was locked."

"You've been here all day?" French asked.

"Most of it. I walked down to the Duke of Wellington for a bite to eat around midday, and to see if I could pick up any gossip. I learned that Vasapoulis and Dudley have been here for a little over a month. They call themselves Señor Gomez and Mister Blake, and they claim to be businessmen who are here for a short holiday. They never seem to leave the house, but in the time they've been here, there's been a steady stream of men coming to see them."

"I suppose Vasapoulis is posing as a Spaniard to explain his complexion and accent," observed French.

"I should imagine. Anyway, Vasapoulis and Dudley have steered clear of the locals. When the two of them require food or drink, the grocer from Salfords or the landlord at the Duke of Wellington drives out to the house with provisions. And that is all I could learn over a pint."

"Have the police been to the house today?" French whispered.

"I don't think so. They might have come while I was at the pub, but Vasapoulis and Dudley are still in the house and I

don't think they would be there if the police had come sniffing around."

"Then the inspector hasn't talked to the ticketmaster or
Isaac yet."

"Who?"

"The man who drove Welch, and us, to the farm last night.
As soon as Isaac or the ticketmaster tells Cole about that, he'll
be on the doorstep. I'm afraid we haven't covered our tracks
very well, Homer."

"It makes no difference. Now that those men have disposed
of Welch, I should think they'll be leaving. In fact, I'm surprised they haven't gone already. It was damned risky, leaving
Welch's body so close to the house."

"The inspector said it was well concealed. Our friends
might have thought they'd have more time to get away."

"All this palaver is getting us nowhere," I said. "Any minute
Cole will show up with a couple of plump constables. I doubt
they'll pose a challenge to Vasapoulis and Dudley. If we don't
want a trio of dead policemen, we've got to do something.
There's two of them and three of us. Are you armed, Homer?"

"Always."

"Then into the house we go. French and I will enter through
the window as we did last night. You give us ten minutes and
then kick in the front door."

I sat back, pleased with my plan. It was simple and direct
and if an arms dealer and his henchman died in the firefight,
who would care? I said as much, to be greeted with a chuckle
from Homer and the familiar horrified silence from his nibs
that comes whenever an idea is floated that doesn't comport
with his Etonian ideals. But it was imperative that we tackle
Vasapoulis and Dudley before the police arrived and so French

reluctantly agreed to the plan, though he spent several precious minutes tamping down my enthusiasm for gunplay and affirming the value of taking Vasapoulis alive so as to extract useful information. I let him finish his sermon uninterrupted. It was a great strain on me, but as time was wasting I refrained from squandering more of it by arguing with French. In the end I vowed to do my best to capture Vasapoulis rather than kill him and that seemed to satisfy the poncy bastard.

"I'd feel better about this if we had any idea where the men were sleeping," French fretted.

"I've only seen lights in two rooms," said Homer. "I think that Vasapoulis sleeps in the room at the front of the house, the one where he met with Welch. I believe Dudley sleeps in a room at the northwest corner of the house. I've noticed a light there the two nights I've been watching."

"So there are French doors from the verandah into the room where Vasapoulis sleeps?" I asked. "Then don't bother with the front door, Homer. Smash in the French doors. You'll gain a few seconds and Vasapoulis will have less time to arm himself."

"Quite right," agreed Homer.

"As India and I are entering the rear of the house, we'll head for Dudley's room. Can you take Vasapoulis on your own?" French asked.

"Of course." Homer sounded offended.

"I should have stopped by the prime minister's office when we were in London," said French. "It would be useful to have more men."

"Well, you didn't and that's that," I said. "The odds are in our favour. We have the numerical advantage and we have the element of surprise."

"I shouldn't count on surprise. These chaps live in a dangerous world and they're always on the alert."

As if to demonstrate the truth of his assertion, we heard the front door of the house open and a figure appeared.

"Dudley," whispered Homer and the three of us dove to the ground. "He'll have a look round the grounds and then go back inside."

"This is a perfect opportunity," I whispered. "If we can eliminate him, we'll have a clear path to Vasapoulis. He'll just assume that it is Dudley returning to the house when we enter, and we'll catch the Greek off guard."

"Excellent idea," said French. "What's Dudley's route, Homer?"

"He'll walk down the drive fifty feet or so, then check that the stable is secure and complete a circuit around the house until he's at the front door again."

Indeed, Dudley had already set off down the drive.

"I'll take him now." French eased his truncheon from his coat pocket. "The trees will provide cover and he won't hear me coming through the pasture. If I wait until he returns to the house, he'll hear my footsteps on the gravel."

"I'll come with you," said Homer.

"It will be easier for one of us to get close to him than for two of us to try to hide our approach. I won't be a minute."

French slipped away into the dark and Homer occupied himself by slipping off his belt and flexing it gently, careful not to make a sound as he did so. "Have you anything else we can use to tie him? And we'll need a gag."

"You can keep your belt. French has a set of handcuffs and

I've a scarf. That should work admirably." I used the knife from my boot to cut off a portion of the scarf sufficient to fit inside Dudley's mouth, then sliced the remainder into long strips that I wove together to hold the gag in place. Our preparations complete, we had nothing to do but wait.

Now I have every confidence in French, except when I don't. I know he's a soldier and has seen some action (not that he'd been the one to inform me of that, but I'd winkle the story out of him soon), and of course he's one of Dizzy's most trusted agents, so he must be competent at sneaking up on fellows and bashing them on the head. I'd have felt much better if I'd been allowed to go along, primarily because I suspect French would use the minimum force necessary to render Dudley unconscious while I would have ensured that Vasapoulis's henchman didn't wake up until next week, if at all. French likes to portray me as a savage, but one man's savage is another man's realist.

I was about to suggest to Homer that perhaps we should meander over and see how the ambush was developing when French loomed up out of the shadows with the inert figure of Dudley over his shoulder. He lowered the fellow carefully at our feet, straightened one of Dudley's arms, which had been pinned beneath his body (I told you French was too bloody solicitous) and sat down with a grunt. Homer and I busied ourselves trussing Dudley like a Christmas goose.

French massaged his fist. "That fellow has a head like a blacksmith's forge."

"Did he give you any trouble?" asked Homer.

"Not a bit. I was on him before he knew it. He heard my footsteps just before I reached him and started to turn round, but I clipped him behind the ear and he toppled over and that was that."

I could hear the satisfaction in French's voice. Felling Dudley was small recompense for the beating French had received at the hands of Vasapoulis's gang, but it must have felt fine to strike at least one blow in retaliation. I was looking forward to some of the same.

When Dudley was bound and we'd all had a swallow of brandy to fortify us for the assault on the house, we checked our weapons and made sure our extra cartridges were at hand. We'd held a quick debate while we prepared and decided that since Vasapoulis was now alone in the house, Homer would bash in the French doors of the room where we thought the Greek was sleeping, as planned, but now French would join him in this activity and I would cut off Vasapoulis's retreat by guarding the back of the house. Frankly, I did not regard this as a suitable plan as it left me far from the action but as much as it pains me to admit this, I have neither the strength nor the experience to plant a boot on a door and break it open. I slithered off to circle behind the house. I proceeded cautiously, keeping an eye open for armed scoundrels, until I came to the stone drinking trough and crouched down behind it. From here I had a clear view of the rear entry to the house, and I'd have the drop on Vasapoulis if he managed to evade French and Homer and tried to escape.

I had just settled into position when I heard the ruckus begin. The sound of boots thudding against wood broke the silence as Homer and French struck at precisely the same moment. Glass shattered as the French door from the verandah gave way, and I heard the lock crack and wood splinter. The house seemed to quiver from the attack.

"Hands up!" Homer shouted. A revolver boomed and someone yelled. Footsteps thundered through the house and suddenly there was the crackle of sustained gunfire. Unless Vasapoulis had a Gatling gun in there, he was not alone. I raced for the back door, Bulldog in hand. I may not be able to open a door with a flying leap, but I could blast open the lock with my pistol.

This plan, however, proved unnecessary. I was twenty feet from the door when it sprang open and two men rushed out. I flung up the Bulldog, cocking the hammer as I did so. It was too dark to see clearly and these two could be Homer and French exiting a firefight they hadn't anticipated, but it was better to have my weapon at the ready while we sorted that out.

"Halt!" I cried. I sounded dashed calm under the circumstances.

One of the men skidded to a stop, shocked into compliance. The other swung deliberately in my direction and raised his hand. I assumed he had a weapon in it and I hit the ground, rolling frantically through the gravel in the vain hope of finding shelter somewhere in this exposed courtyard. The fellow pulled the trigger and the gun in his hand barked. The gravel where I'd been standing a moment before exploded and I ducked my head to shield my face. I yelped as a quantity of gravel pellets slammed into my body. It hurt like blazes, as if I'd been stung by a dozen wasps or hit by a load of buckshot. By God, if that chap had damaged my goods, I'd make him pay. I propped myself up on my elbows and took aim. In the moonlight I could see his pale face turning this way and that as he searched for me. He'd been blinded by his own muzzle blast and his night vision had not returned. I suffered from no such impairment. I squeezed the trigger.

I hit him well. His body jerked backward from the force of the bullet and his arms flailed. The revolver in his hand went

flying, and then he collapsed. I turned my gun in the direction of the second fellow, but now my vision was obscured by
the flash from my Bulldog's muzzle and I couldn't locate the
man. I blinked and scrambled to my knees. The chap I'd shot
was keening softly, clutching his stomach. Of the other, there
was no sign. I held the Bulldog at chest level and swept the
courtyard. Either the second man had gone back inside the
house or he'd hared off into the night. I sincerely hoped he'd
chosen the latter course. Otherwise he might be inside waiting for me or, even worse, about to take a potshot at me from
one of the windows. I dropped to a crouch and scuttled to the
side of the house, where I leaned against the brick and took
stock of my situation. My wounds were slight and not especially painful, though I could feel blood trickling down my
legs where the gravel had struck me. But I was still on my feet
and I needed to get inside the house. From the front rooms I
could hear an occasional gunshot and ragged shouts. I had
no idea what I'd find when I got there, but I had to reach
French. And Homer, of course.

I wasn't about to enter the building without a bit of reconnaissance, though. I leaned well back out of sight and thrust
one hand into the open doorway, waving it ostentatiously.
Nothing happened. I took a deep breath and blew it out, then
swung the Bulldog up and darted through the doorway, tuck-
ing my shoulder as I went through the opening and hitting
the floor in a roll that brought me to my feet inside the room.
An excellent maneuver and damned well executed, if I may say
so myself.

The moment I regained my feet I brought up the Bulldog
and lunged sideways. I hit the wall and hunkered down, my
shoulders tensed, waiting for a blast of lead. Again, nothing.

Either the second villain was a cool fellow and was laying a trap for me or he had run like a rabbit to join his friends in the house or through the fields away from the skirmish. Since he'd scampered off without offering even token resistance and left his compatriot bleeding to death in the courtyard, I reckoned he'd concluded that discretion was the better part of valour and was now headed into the distance at speed.

Nevertheless, I moved forward cautiously, peering quickly around door frames and then drawing back to avoid offering an easy target. It took some time to navigate through the dark house and I did it with my heart in my throat. The gunshots had subsided now and the house was eerily quiet. What the devil was happening? Where was French?

I reached the dining room that opened onto the entry hall and paused here to collect myself. I remembered that if I walked into the hall I'd be facing the side of the set of stairs that ran from the ground floor to the first, and that if I turned to the left I would see the dresser in the hall and beyond it, to the right, the room Vasapoulis occupied. There was also, I recalled, a room directly across from Vasapoulis's. It had been closed off behind a set of double doors when French and I had slipped into the house, so I had no idea what purpose it served.

I was chewing my lip and wondering what in blazes I was going to do when I heard snatches of a whispered conversation. I inched forward with the Bulldog at the ready and ventured a peek into the hall. I drew back in alarm. A hulking figure was stooped down behind the great chest in the hall, not ten feet from me. I could clearly see his body outlined against the white sheet that covered the chest. That certainly wasn't French, and though Homer was stocky, this lout looked like a gorilla compared to him.

I heard stealthy footsteps from overhead and risked another quick glance. The light was dim, but I could just make out a figure crouched at the top of the stairs. I couldn't tell if the second figure was Vasapoulis, but it didn't matter. A scheme was forming in my head. I was busy calculating distances and trajectories and which of the men out there should get the first bullet when a throaty voice with a distinct Mediterranean accent called out.

"Major French? I assume you are across the hall from me, in the parlour. You are outnumbered, my friend. It would be best for you if you surrendered now. Otherwise you will try my patience and that is not wise, as Colonel Mayhew learned."

The voice had not come from the top of the stairs, but from the room where French and I had seen Vasapoulis and Welch meeting. That meant there were at least three men in the house I would have to eliminate or capture. The order of those options was not unintentional. If you have been assaulted in your own home and intended to be shark bait, you tend not to worry about such details. I did however have to recalibrate my plans, and while I was contemplating whether to go for the cove behind the dresser and then spin round and take out the chap upstairs or vice versa, I heard glass break and wood splinter as the window in the parlour exploded. French's .577 Boxer roared, followed by a barrage of shots. I confess my mind took a split-second holiday while I tried to absorb this new information. Had French and Homer elected to break out the window and make a run for it (in which case my own position had just become more precarious)? Or had the bloke who'd scampered off outside (and the friend I'd shot) been ordered by Vasapoulis to circle around to the front of the house and attack French and Homer in the parlour?

Well, he who hesitates is prone to get a bullet through the head and besides that, the fellow behind the dresser had stepped out from behind its shelter and was advancing down the hallway as Vasapoulis emerged from his lair with a revolver in his hand. There was no more time to think, so I stepped out into the hallway, leveled my Bulldog and pulled the trigger. Now if you're the effeminate type who thinks the lions should lie down with the lambs, I must inform you that such action is merely a prelude to the lions dining heartily. Consequently, I did not hesitate to shoot the chap in the back on the theory that had he the opportunity, he'd have done the same to me. He went sprawling, the gun flying from his hand and skittering across the floor to Vasapoulis's feet.

The Greek hesitated a moment, and I thought it best to deal with the chap upstairs before bagging my first international arms dealer. I whipped round and detected a dark shadow crouched behind the balusters of the staircase. I knew my shot would have to be quick; my back was to Vasapoulis and any moment I reckoned he'd snap out of his stupor and unload on me. I fired and then fired again. The first shot shredded a baluster, and the second whistled past the head of the crouching man. I heard his exclamation of surprise. Then he collapsed backward, out of my line of sight. From the parlour I could hear a fusillade of gunshots. It sounded like the Battle of Inkerman in there.

I whirled round to find Vasapoulis drawing a bead on me. I dove into the dining room as a bullet whined past my ear and buried itself in the door frame. I scrambled back to the doorway and peeked round, my head just a foot off the floor. Vasapoulis was wheeling in a half circle, pointing his gun alternately in my direction and then into the parlour. I took aim and squeezed the trigger and my bullet caught Vasapoulis in the thigh. He spun round and crashed to the floor, uttering a guttural cry as he fell. I'd used every bullet in the revolver. I extracted the empty casings and fumbled in my pocket for my extra cartridges. I reloaded with trembling fingers.

There was one more exchange of fire from the parlour, then a single shot.

"Got him!" I heard Homer shout.

"French?" I called.

"India? Where are you?" My knees almost buckled with relief at the sound of the poncy bastard's voice.

"In the dining room. There are two men down in the hall, including Vasapoulis."

"Dead?"

"One is, I think. I've only wounded Vasapoulis, though."

"Homer and I are coming out. Cover us."

"French, there's another man, up on the first floor. I shot at him, but I'm not sure I hit him."

"Alright. We'll watch for him. You keep an eye on Vasapoulis until we can be sure he's unarmed."

My gaze was fixed on the Greek, but I heard the creak of the wooden doors to the parlour as they swung open and a moment later French and Homer crept into view. French advanced on Vasapoulis, his Boxer in his hand, while Homer covered the hall. It did occur to me that if the chap on the floor was playing dead and suddenly reared up, Homer and I might end up shooting each other, but there was nothing to be done about it but hope that I had shot the chap thoroughly. I heard a scuffling noise as French kicked Vasapoulis's gun out of reach and jerked him upright by his collar.

"Bastard," said French. "You're lucky my associate didn't kill you."

"Like this one," said Homer, bending over my first victim. "He's dead."

I charged out of the room and trained my Bulldog on the stairs. "There's another one up there. I'm going after him."

"India, wait!" French shouted, but my blood was up and I was going to get that last chap. I'd spotted him, so I had first dibs.

Dimly, I heard French calling to Homer to guard Vasapoulis. I knew it. His nibs was about to horn in on my capture. I lunged up the stairs with my Bulldog in hand. Now I'm not a complete idiot. I did have the foresight to stoop down and poke my head around the corner. The hall was clear in both directions.

French rushed up behind me, panting heavily.

"You go right," I told him. "I'll go left."

"I suppose that means you know the man went left."

"I've no idea which way he went. He may have jumped out a window by now."

"I suppose there's no point in telling you to be careful."

"I suppose you're right. Bloody hell, French, if not for me, you and Homer would still be pinned down in that parlour."

"I only suggest that you be careful so that I can enjoy more of these debates in the future. I wouldn't dream of impugning your ability to deal death and destruction to our enemies."

"To the right, French."

"Yes, ma'am."

I crept slowly down the hallway, alert to every movement and sound. A plank squeaked under my foot and I shuffled hastily to one side, but the sound did not draw fire. I came to the first room on my right. The door stood open and I could see that this was a bedroom. The furniture was recognizable under the drapery of white sheets. I ducked in for a quick look, my heart hammering, but the room was quiet as a tomb. Not, in retrospect, a well-chosen comparison.

The door across the hall was closed. I knelt down against the wall and warily tried the knob. Locked. Was the villain in there? I must remember to have French show me the trick of kicking open a door sometime. At the moment, I did not trust myself to pull this off. I tiptoed past the door. I'd clear the remainder of the unlocked rooms and then fetch French to act as strongman.

The second door on the right was open, and it too appeared to be a bedroom. This one had been occupied, however, for the covers had been flung off the bed. I inched through the door, the Bulldog at the ready. I swept the room with my revolver, staring into the dark shadows at the corners of the room, kneeling down to look under the bed, cautiously opening the wardrobe and darting back out of the way to give myself a clear shot. But the room was empty and silent.

I felt as weak as a kitten suddenly. I suppose in all the excitement I'd forgotten that I'd had very little sleep for two nights, not to mention that hiking over the country is damned tiring and that popping a couple of thugs is hard going. The bed looked tempting. All I wanted to do was collapse on it and let French and Homer clean up the mess. I steeled myself to finish my work, though, shaking my head in an attempt to clear the cobwebs before I set off again.

One last room to clear before I summoned French to deal with the locked room down the hall. The door into this room was closed so I knelt with my back against the wall and reached up for the knob. I rotated it slowly and felt it turn. I pushed the door gently with two fingers and gripped the Bulldog firmly. No sound emanated from the room. Down the hall I could hear French opening and closing doors. I could feel the drumbeat of my pulse in my throat. I stood up and squeezed through the door, aiming right, then left. It was dark as pitch in there, for the room was bare. No ghostly shapes of sheet-covered furniture shone in the moonlight. The room smelled of dust and dry wood. There was only one place I hadn't searched. I risked a quick look behind the door. And came face-to-face with the barrel of a revolver.

# EIGHTEEN

"I was hoping you'd come for me, India. Now hand over your gun." I did so reluctantly. Philip bent down gently and placed it on the floor, all the while covering me with his own revolver.

"What the devil are you doing here, Philip? You're supposed to be on your way to India."

"Some of the boys and I got off in Lisbon. Our services were needed here."

"You wouldn't shoot me, would you, Philip?"

The fellow took a deuced long time to answer. When he did, he didn't sound entirely reassuring. "Let's not put that proposition to the test. It would be best if you cooperated with me. I don't plan to be captured, India. I don't enjoy gaol. The food is terrible and some of the inmates could do with a bath."

I didn't really think Philip would murder me, but then I'd once been sure that he wouldn't use me to steal the Rajah's Ruby. That scenario had played out in my favour, but I wasn't certain this one would.

"What are you going to do?"

"I'm sure you've twigged that you're my hostage now. We'll just walk out together."

"And then?"

"What happens next depends on your friends downstairs."

I couldn't vouch for Homer but I felt sure that French would not do anything that would result in my being harmed. Unless he thought I'd surrendered myself to Philip to ensure my old lover's escape. Oh, dear. I cast back over the past weeks. Had I been convincing when I'd assured French I had no feelings for Philip? God, I hoped I had, or things might get sticky.

"India?" French's voice, coming from the hallway.

"Are you ready?" Philip grasped my right arm using his left hand. His right hand held his revolver, which he pointed at my head. "Open the door and step into the hall."

I did as instructed. As I stepped into the corridor I saw French stalking slowly toward us. The big Boxer came up and locked on me, then realizing it was me, French let it fall.

"No luck?" he asked.

"Only the bad sort," said Philip. He shoved me into the hall and followed on my heels. Then he clamped his arm tightly around my neck and pulled me to him so that our bodies presented a single silhouette. French's arm jerked up and once again I found myself on the business end of his Boxer.

"Put it down," said Philip.

"You're not going to shoot her," French said. "You had your chance to kill her on the *Sea Lark* and you couldn't do it."

"I was leaving the country. Since she posed no threat to me then I could play the gentleman and arrange for her escape. But the stakes are rather higher for me now. I don't want to shoot her. God knows I'm fond of the wench. But I'll do what I must to leave here a free man. Put down your weapon."

You may have thought that I would say something idiotic like, "Shoot him, French!" but I chose not to for fear that French might actually fire the gun, and for fear that if he did he might miss his target and end up putting a bullet squarely between my eyes. Better to let this play out and see what developed.

French let the Boxer fall from his hand. The heavy revolver sounded like a cannon as it crashed to the floor.

"And now?" asked French.

"Tell your compatriot down there that we will be coming down the stairs and he should place his weapon on the floor. If he doesn't comply, then I'll shoot you."

I could almost feel the anger rising off French. He leaned over the banister. "Homer, India and I have been taken hostage. We're coming down. The chap up here has a gun pointed at India and he's threatened to shoot us both. Put your gun on the floor."

"Dammit, French. I can't do that. Do you know how long I've been pursuing this bloody Greek?"

"I'm sorry, Homer. Please do as I ask."

I heard a clunking noise as Homer placed his pistol on the floor of the entry hall.

"Step away from the gun, Homer," called Philip. He waved his own weapon at French. "You lead the way. India and I will be right behind you."

French walked slowly down the stairs. I stumbled along

behind him, it being difficult to navigate a series of steps when a bloke's got you in a chokehold. I could feel Philip's breath on my cheek, hot and ragged. He was scared, poor chap, and that scared me. I hoped French and Homer wouldn't mount a rescue operation once we reached the entry hall, for it was very likely Philip's nerve would give way and French and I might end up in a touching farewell scene, if I lived long enough to participate.

We reached the bottom of the steps after an agonizing descent.

"Barrett," said Vasapoulis hoarsely. "I've been shot in the leg, but I can still travel. Shoot them all. Then fetch my case from the library and harness the horses. Hurry, man!"

"I'm afraid I can't do that."

"What? Why not?"

"Sorry, old boy, but you'll only slow me down."

"You won't live long enough to regret that decision," said Vasapoulis. "I've men all over the world. Your life is mine."

I recalled the fate of Colonel Mayhew. I couldn't help but feel that Philip had made a tactical error. Gaol couldn't be any worse than being hunted across the globe by Vasapoulis's henchmen.

"Oh, I can't live like that." Philip's tone disturbed me. It was febrile and high-pitched and he sounded nothing at all like the suave fellow I knew. He dragged me closer to Vasapoulis and we looked down into that dark face, now twisted with pain. But there was no fear in the Greek's eyes, only contempt.

"You and Welch were two of a kind," said Vasapoulis through gritted teeth. "Two weak links. I should have killed you earlier."

"You'll never have the chance now," said Philip. His body

shook and I could feel the moist heat rolling off him. He aimed the revolver at Vasapoulis's head.

"Don't do it, Phillip. You can testify against him. The authorities will protect you," I said.

A bark of laughter from Vasapoulis ended in a snarl. "I own the authorities. Your life is forfeit, Barrett."

I sighed. Really, Vasapoulis was doing nothing to aid his cause, taunting and provoking Philip like that. The Greek surely knew what kind of man he was dealing with; Philip was a coward. But the prospect of being cut to ribbons did not entice. Under those circumstances, my former lover did what most men would do. He steadied his wavering hand and shot Vasapoulis in the face.

The noise deafened me, but the audacity of his act must have stunned Philip for he loosened his grip on my neck. French, dedicated agent that he was, decided that Philip was likely to be distracted, having just murdered the Greek, and launched himself at my captor. But Philip still had the presence of mind to raise his revolver and I tore loose from his arm, wrenching my neck but freeing myself for action. I shoved Philip's arm skyward and there was a second great explosion as he pulled the trigger again. Then Philip stepped aside and shoved me at French and the poncy bastard crashed into me and knocked me arse over teakettle. I heard Homer shout and French grunt as the door to the house burst open and Philip pelted out of it. There was a mad scramble in the hall as Homer searched for his weapon and French scrabbled on the floor for the dead Greek's gun, but by the time the two men had secured revolvers and followed Philip out into the night it was too late. The gutless poltroon had vanished into thin air. Homer and French spent a half hour crashing through bushes and checking the outbuildings but the search was in vain. Philip would be bolting over the hills, no doubt headed to the nearest bolt-hole he'd created for himself. I had no doubt he'd snatch the first opportunity to board a ship out of England.

As for us, we'd done well. The prime minister would be pleased that the smuggling ring had been broken up, and no one would mourn the loss of the thugs lying dead in the farm-house. I knew French would disagree, but I had no qualms about Philip's escape. I had no doubt that Vasapoulis was merely a cog in a machine, and that when it became known that Philip had shot the Greek like a rabid dog, someone from Vasapoulis's organization would be on his trail. It would be a long time before Philip could rest his head at night without fear of being yanked out of bed and cut down. I cannot say the prospect pleased me. But for him, French, Vincent and I might be floating in the English Channel now. I felt we all owed him a bit of gratitude for that. However, I did not take kindly to being held hostage, nor did I approve of Philip's attempt to shoot French. I wasn't sorry to see Philip go. He needed a change of scenery, for England would be too hot for him for years to come.

I found a box of matches and a candle on the chest and lit the wick. The scene in the hallway was macabre, what with Vasapoulis and his henchman lying on the floor in separate pools of blood. I scurried upstairs and retrieved my Bulldog and French's Boxer. I'd have been damned displeased if I had lost French's gift. Then I went to the library. I rounded up all the loose papers and documents lying about and stuffed them into Vasapoulis's case and carried it into the hall.

Homer and French returned, winded and irritated at Philip's escape.

"Bastard," said French.

"He is that. But he'll be running for the rest of his life once the rest of Vasapoulis's gang hears about this. They'll be out for revenge. Philip will have to lie low for a long time. We won't be troubled with him anymore."

French came to stand beside me and rested an arm around my shoulder, pulling me close. "*We?*"

"Yes, we."

# NINETEEN

I've never had the vapours before, but I came damned close during the exercise of loading humans, canines and luggage into the three hansoms and the wagon we'd hired to take us to King's Cross station so that we might catch the train to Perth. The marchioness demanded that Vincent, Maggie and some of the pups accompany her in one cab, while French and I were to occupy another and Fergus and the remaining dogs were to ride in the third. I did my best to impose order on the process, but after having my directions countermanded at various times by French, Fergus, the marchioness and Vincent, and completely ignored by Maggie and the other collies, I finally admitted defeat and retreated to the pavement. I was joined there by approximately half the London population come to watch the free circus. When the final stray pup had been rounded up and the last chest lashed into place on the precariously tottering pile of luggage on the wagon, I deigned to join the traveling party. Mrs. Drinkwater and the bints came out to see us off, ululating like a group of Egyptian women at a funeral. I've always forbidden any embraces or displays of affection, so the tarts restricted themselves to wringing my hand and expressing their intentions to abide by the rules, which, I need hardly mention, I didn't believe for one minute. Then the treacherous wenches fell on the marchioness, weeping copiously and demanding she return soon and bring the puppies and generally behaving as if their dear old granny was leaving town. The marchioness had a tear in her eye and looked as sad as if one of her favourite dogs had been run over by the mail coach. It was a damned good thing I was getting her out of here or I'd have had a palace coup on my hands.

We were standing in a knot on the pavement trying to extract ourselves from the clutches of my employees when a comely young fellow with mild blue eyes walked up briskly and doffed his hat to me.

"Miss Black?"

I recognized the amiable face under the cloud of blond curls. "Mr. Brown, how nice to see you again."

French detached himself from the spectacle and wandered over. "Hello, Brown."

"Hello, French."

It was no surprise the two knew each other as they both worked for the prime minister. I'd made Brown's acquaintance a few weeks ago, when Dizzy had dispatched him to Lotus House to plant some information among the anarchists.

"What brings you here?" asked French.

"I've a packet from the prime minister for you." Brown handed it to French and I looked over his shoulder as he opened it. He pulled out a handful of papers and thumbed through them. He glanced up at Brown.

"What is this?"

"They are tickets, sir, for Reverend Edward Campbell and his wife, Rachel, and for their ward, Vincent Smith. You'll be sailing tonight on the Castle Mail Packet Company's steamship, the *Dunrobin Castle,* bound for Durban, in South Africa."

"I can see that they are tickets, Brown. I meant, what is this about?"

"In a word, sir? Zulus."